THE LONG JOURNEY

SONG OF THREE BANNERS

Book 1

Aidan Tautin

PROLOGUE

For many a year, the ancient island of Yrfel has been sought after by the three great races of the world: the elves of the west, the humans of the east, and the Drangarian Vikings of the north.

The first people to ever inhabit Yrfel were the elves, sailing to the island long ago, making their home in the southwestern corner of the island. Then came the humans, inhabiting the mountain range on the east side of Yrfel. Lastly came the Vikings, occupying the snowy Frostlands in the north part of the island.

The first war of three banners started in the year two hundred seventy-four, and so began the age of Yrfel. A clear winner of the island had never arisen, and the first war ended in the year two hundred ninety-nine. The second war began just a year later. Each race was led by three new leaders, all of them quite young, all of them thrown into a situation they didn't completely understand.

There are three prominent races in this world, led by three prominent houses. To the west, in the land of the Ancestral Grove, hundreds of years ago, the House Keawynn took charge. They were the richest and were very smart people, gathering large followers with their logical choices. All elves were smart people. It just so happened that the Keawynns were the cream of the crop.

Far to the east, the Steel Isle resided. The humans made their living off blacksmithing and fighting. Many power grabs took place in the early days, dozens of families vying for power, and the Eastmoores were the ones who were the eventual victors, and King Brandon Eastmoore installed a dynasty that lasted for hundreds of years.

Then in the far north lies the snowy, barren land of Drangar, inhabited by the savage Vikings. Long ago, the Vikings fought many a war among each other, then their god Thalmur punished them with a yearlong blizzard. A man who was called "the giant" united the Vikings of Drangar, and the blizzard ceased. For this, he earned the surname Frostbane, and Clan Frostbane has been the head of Drangar ever since.

HIGH YRFEL

Nathan Eastmoore was a young eighteen-year-old boy with jet-black hair and bright blue eyes. He was a fantastic sword fighter with the heart of a lion, but he had no true battle or leading experience.

Nathan sat in his quarters, looked out his window, and watched the rain fall. Watching the rain made him think about everything going on. He was a young boy, commanding an army and making decisions about things he didn't quite understand.

He walked out the door and walked down the hall out into the throne room, seeing his personal advisers, guards clad in steel armor, and mages in white-and-blue robes.

The humans decided to make their home in Yrfel inside a mountain range, making walls to connect the mountains with the castle of High Yrfel on a hill and the town down below on the ground.

Nathan sat on the throne, and one of his advisers approached him.

"High King," he said with a slight bow.

Nathan replied with a nod, "About your plans with Ravenhall."

The adviser's name was Robb Brightfield and one of Nathan's personal friends.

"Yes, gather everyone in the war room," Nathan said.

Rob bowed and left out the big double wooden doors at the front of the throne room.

Nathan stood up, walked back down the hallway, and opened the door to the war room. He walked over and took a seat at the head of the table, which had a map of Yrfel on it. Nathan sat alone in silence, staring at the little wooden castle figure that represented Ravenhall, the Viking stronghold in the Frostlands. He thought that going to battle would win him some respect. He could show his army that he could lead like his father could even though he had never fought in any battle.

Finally, the door opened. The first to enter was Archmage Tymirial Lamarius, leader of the mages of the Steel Isle. He wore a fine white and blue cloak, made of fine silks, and it had gold trimmings throughout. He held his staff, which was engraved with runes and had a large blue crystal at the top. Tymirial removed his blue hood, dramatically revealing his long silver hair, and he scratched at his long silver beard. He was a father figure for Nathan after his actual father died, but his and Nathan's relationship went way back to Nathan's childhood.

He was followed by Aedric, one of the commanders of the army, a person Nathan quite disliked only because of his name. There were two Aedric Eastmoores' who were both remarkable people, but Nathan felt slighted that he had the name that two of his family members did. But Aedric had been commander a long time. He even knew Nathan's father. Then in came Robb and a few more of Nathan's advisers, who were deemed necessary to the meeting, although not by Nathan himself.

"I am sure you all know that over the past few days, I have been planning an attack on Ravenhall," Nathan said. "Our scouts have informed me of a route to get there, where we will be unnoticed for the most part." Nathan pointed to where he was talking about. "I want us to attack in two waves, the first wave led by myself, then the second led by Aedric," Nathan finished.

"A fine plan, Commander. How many men do we have?" Tymirial asked.

"Roughly one hundred fifty thousand fighting men," he replied.

"How many are at Ravenhall?" Nathan asked.

"My scouts have told me the same amount or less," Aedric replied.

"Commander, ready the men, and find some-one to gather enough provisions for the journey and have horses fed and rested," Nathan said.

"At once, High King," Aedric replied.

He then left the room.

"Anything else you would like to add, High King?" Tymirial asked, raising an eyebrow.

"What wildlife will we encounter on the journey there?" Nathan said.

"When we get to the Frostlands, most likely giants, wolves, and other beasts, I'm sure," he said.

"With that, make the necessary preparations. This meeting is adjourned," Nathan said.

Everyone left, all except Tymirial.

"I'm surprised. You seemed so confident when talking to all these important people," Tymirial said.

"Did you doubt me?" Nathan said, smiling.

"Perhaps, you have quite big shoes to fill," Tymirial said. "Indeed I do. Hopefully, I do right by him." Tymirial simply smiled. "If you can become half the swordsman your father was, you will be just fine."

RAVENHALL

Vigrod Frostbane, a young twenty-year-old Drangarian Viking, a legacy of the Frostbane clan, was nearly seven feet tall, with long brown hair, icy blue skin, and a peculiar crescent moon–shaped birthmark behind his ear.

Vigrod led his Viking army from the stronghold of Ravenhall. Ravenhall was a large place with a main courtyard where everyone gathers and, on the walls, sat all the doors leading to the places the Vikings used, the blacksmith, stable, and great hall, which was its own building, but it was a part of the walls. A floor above that was all the living spaces for all the people of importance and a war room. Off to the left was a section designated for all the warriors to stay.

Vigrod and his childhood friend Brodir Bothvar, who was about the same age as Vigrod, stood atop the ramparts of Ravenhall, looking out on the frozen wastes of the Frostlands.

The Frostlands were quite empty. A large forest sat at the northernmost part of Yrfel. A few villages were scattered throughout the Frostlands and lived in by refugees from Drangar. But at the border of the Frostlands, three mountains were purely made of ice due to the frost giant's death millions of years ago. The body of the frost giant caused the northern part of Yrfel to be covered in snow and the people who lived there to have icy skin.

"Do we have enough food to pass out?" Vigrod asked. "We have enough for about a month. I'm not sure where we should get more from. The surrounding villages are starting to run dry," Brodir replied.

"I have an idea. I'll write a message to Lord Kolvar asking him for a meeting. The elves probably have enough food for the next five years," Vigrod said.

"It is worth a try. I doubt he will help. They are too proud to help us out," Brodir said.

"It is our only option," Vigrod said.

He gave Brodir a pat on the back as he walked off into his quarters.

Vigrod wrote the message and walked out to the rookery.

"Good day, Einar," Vigrod said.

Einar was the man who took care of all the messenger birds. Messengers were large black birds capable of flying through storms and strong winds, but their purpose was, of course, to deliver messages.

"Highlord, to what do I owe the pleasure?" he asked.

"I need a message sent to the Elder Branch. How fast can they get it there?" Vigrod asked as one of the messengers flew down and landed on Vigrod's shoulder.

"They can get it there in at the very latest in a week, but if the weather permits, it can take four to five days," he replied.

"Very good." Vigrod handed the message to Einar, grabbed the bird off his shoulder, and let it fly up to where it was perched before. "I will leave you to it," Vigrod said.

"As you wish, Highlord."

Vigrod walked down the steps and requested for the gate to be opened. He went outside Ravenhall and walked around to the back. Vigrod approached his father's mausoleum. Just last year, his father was murdered by the leader of the shrouded, an organization of assassins. But everyone, including Vigrod, believed his father was killed by an eastern assassin, and Nathan believed that his father was killed by a Viking.

Vigrod opened the stone door to see the altar where his father's body was placed. The walls had many designs on them, showing various moments of Rhangar's life. Vigrod scanned over them as he always did. He looked at the design of his father holding him up as a child. He looked at the battles and achievements. Vigrod took a torch from off the wall and lit all the candles and said two prayers, one of mourning and one to wish a great feast in Thalmur's halls for Rhagnar. Vigrod blew out the candles, walked out the door, and shut it as he left.

He walked back into the great hall to be welcomed by his soldiers, most of which were friends with him. Vigrod wasn't in a particularly great mood, but the offer of drinking until the night's end quickly raised his spirits.

hopefully make a fair deal that
makes both of us happy. I expect
a quick reply.

Vigrod Frostbane

"Well, I am willing to give up a little bit of food,
but I need something in return, something of value,"
Kolvar said, scratching his chin. "Perhaps a few prisoners, but I can't think of a number," Kolvar added.

"I would ask for at least a few hundred, but you
may be able to push for more in exchange for more
you give him," Thaedra said.

"Hmm, I'm not sure. A few hundred really won't
affect the total state of their army, but those prisoners
do give me some leverage over Vigrod," Kolvar said.

Kolvar walked back out to the balcony, staring
out to the north, thinking about what he could do.

"Send a message to Ravenhall and request for
the Highlord's presence, but I would not like Nathan
to find out about this little meeting," he said.

Thaedra and Kolvar walked out of the room
and started to walk down the ramp down the Elder
Branch. About an hour later, they reached the bottom, and Thaedra walked off to the right toward the
Rookery, and Kolvar took a left to the throne room.

The Elder Branch throne room entrance was a
large opening at the bottom of the tree, and it led
into the large hollowed-out throne room. At the back
sat the throne carved out of the tree itself. One large

chandelier hung from the ceiling, which was very high up from the ground.

Kolvar walked up to his throne and sat down to his left stood his grandfather, Aerimir Keawynn. He was about three hundred years old, and elves' maximum life expectancy was around five hundred years. Aerimir taught Kolvar's grandfather and father about how to rule and how to do it correctly.

"Ahh, Kolvar, welcome," Aerimir said.

He was wearing a dark robe with golden linen. Kolvar noticed that first when he looked at Aerimir.

"Aerimir, good to see you," Kolvar replied.

Thaedra walked into the room. "Lord Kolvar, the message has been sent," he said while walking toward him.

Kolvar leaned forward. "Very good, Thaedra," he said. "Very good."

A PLEA FOR HELP

Vigrod was in the stables preparing his horse for the journey ahead. He had received Lord Kolvar's message yesterday. Vigrod was glad he was getting a chance.

Brodir walked by as Vigrod was getting ready to leave.

"Bring us back something good," Brodir said, laughing.

"I will try my best, but if this does not work, I have another idea," Vigrod said.

"What's that?" Brodir asked.

"Oh, please, Brodir. We're Vikings. You know what the alternative is," Vigrod answered.

"The journey there and back will take about four weeks on horseback, so try to keep them alive while I'm gone," Vigrod said seriously.

"We might need to go hunting, but that won't keep them sustained forever," Brodir said.

Vigrod climbed on the back of his horse and put a little bit of food in one of the pouches on the sides of the saddle. He said his goodbye and trotted off toward the gate.

"Open the gate!" Vigrod yelled up to the gatekeeper.

The gate opened, and off he went. He turned right and headed toward the large tree in the distance.

It took Vigrod one day to get out of the Frostlands, following the main road, which the Vikings called the Raven Road, which eventually gave way to the Rose Road. He passed through a village on the way out. They gave him a proper welcome and gave his horse food and water along with himself. Vigrod enjoyed his time outside the Frostlands. It was a nice warm day. It was the eleventh of July, in the fifth year of summer. The lakes and rivers were shining. The land was beautiful, but Vigrod still preferred the snow. Something about it made him feel comfortable.

Vigrod was entering the Greenlands, the elf lands. He approached a large wall made of bleak gray stone, about fifty-feet high, stretching miles long to the other side of Yrfel. He stared in awe as he slowly rode under the large entrance. He noticed different drawings and designs throughout the walls, which he could not understand.

It was about midday when Vigrod reached the gates of the city of the Elder Branch. He thought his home back in Drangar was impressive, but he thought this made it look like a small village in the Frostlands.

He approached the gate when the guards up on the ramparts stopped him. A few pulled out bows and aimed at him.

"Highlord Vigrod Frostbane, you are expected," the guard said. Vigrod could tell the guard was a woman based on the sound of her voice.

"Open the gates!" she yelled loudly.

The gates rumbled, and Vigrod rode in and was met by two more guards.

"Please get off your horse and give me your weapons, then I will escort you to Lord Kolvar," the guard said.

Vigrod reluctantly handed over his axe and climbed down from his horse. The guard nodded toward his partner, and the other guard took his horse. The guard talking to Vigrod told him to follow, and they headed toward the great tree.

They approached the Elder Branch, and Vigrod stared in awe. He had seen mountains, but he had never seen trees the size of mountains. They entered the throne room, and Vigrod saw who he thought was Kolvar sitting on a fancy wooden throne.

"Highlord!" Lord Kolvar yelled from across the room.

Kolvar stood up and approached Vigrod. Vigrod extended a hand to Kolvar. Kolvar reached out to shake his hand when one of the guards grabbed hold of Vigrod. Vigrod used all his strength to break free, and he faced the guard who grabbed him, and Kolvar quickly stepped between them.

"Enough!" Kolvar yelled. "It was a gesture of kindness. I doubt Vigrod will beat me to death in front of everyone now."

Kolvar then again extended a hand toward Vigrod, and they got to shake hands that time. Vigrod looked back at the guard who grabbed him and said something in the Drangarian language.

Kolvar walked back to the throne and sat down. "Now to discuss what you are here for," Kolvar said.

"Yes, my people need food. I don't see why you would not be able to save us," Vigrod said.

"Oh no, I am ready to give you all a year's worth of food, but I need something in return," Kolvar said.

"What is that something?" Vigrod asked.

"I will give your people food in exchange for some of your fighting men," Kolvar said.

Vigrod was stunned. He didn't think he would have to give up some of his people in exchange for their survival.

"How many would you request?" Vigrod asked.

"I want at least a few thousand," Kolvar said.

Vigrod had a stupid look on his face. "A few thousand? How many thousand?" Vigrod said dumbfounded.

"Give me one thousand, and I will give one year's worth. Give me two thousand, and I'll give you two years' worth and so forth," Kolvar replied.

Vigrod thought about it. He did not want his people in chains, but to him, the good of his whole army was more important than a small fraction of it.

"I am willing to accept your offer, but I want your word that they shall not be harmed, and they will be put in a safe place," Vigrod said while pointing at Kolvar.

"You have my word, Highlord," Kolvar replied.

Vigrod then extended an arm toward Kolvar. He then shook Kolvar's forearm, and the deal was made.

"Take the Highlord to his place of residence. Good day, Highlord," Kolvar said, nodding.

"Glad we could make this work, Lord Kolvar," he added.

Vigrod was then escorted through the large elven city. The city was a marvel to behold. The Elder Branch was colorful and extravagant, but where Vigrod came from, it was all gray and simple. Near the walls of the city, Vigrod was introduced to a smaller house, by Elven standards anyway. Vigrod thought this was much more than what he needed.

The guards left, and Vigrod went inside. The inside of the house was fully decorated. There was food and drink already prepared for him. Vigrod liked the elven lifestyle. Vigrod stoked the fire and enjoyed his dinner. He drank fine wine.

Vigrod was woken up the next morning by three guards. They escorted him to the throne room, where Kolvar was waiting for him.

"Have you thought about it?" Kolvar asked.

"Yes, I am willing to give up two thousand men, but I want to see what I am getting beforehand," Vigrod said.

"Very well, come on."

Kolvar and a few guards walked to the back end of the city, where a large farm was, with fresh grain and livestock.

"This is what you are getting," Kolvar said. "Very well. Where and when shall the exchange take place?" Vigrod asked.

"I had a feeling you would ask." Kolvar made a hand motion, and someone came forward. An elf came forward, holding a calendar, and had quill and parchment in a bag hanging from his side. "August, on the first, we will meet on the road," Kolvar said.

"Very good. I appreciate the hospitality, Lord Kolvar, but I would like to leave now," Vigrod said.

"As you wish, Highlord. It was good to finally meet you."

They shook hands one final time, and Kolvar called for someone to get Vigrod's horse.

Vigrod got on his horse and quickly left the city after getting some provisions for the return journey. In his head, he thought about how he saved his people, but at what cost.

THE MARCH TO RAVENHALL

Nathan led his army at the front, riding front and center, with Tymirial and Robb at his side.

It had been about two weeks since they made the preparations to start their march to Ravenhall, and they had been traveling for about a week, and there were still three weeks left of travel.

The army was a day or so away from crossing into the Frostlands, and they had made only a few stops along their journey. Night fell, and a camp was set up, tents were pitched, and horses were tended to.

Nathan had his own large tent in the center of the camp. It was a huge tent made for the best possible experience. Nathan thought it made the journey much more bearable.

A day later, they crossed into the barren Frostlands. The harsh winds pushed them back and made the journey a lot tougher. The horses started to struggle, and they resisted and wanted to stay still. Along with their siege equipment, it slowed them down a tremendous amount.

High King Nathan sat in his tent alone. Soon, he would fight his first battle. Nathan had been training with a sword all his eighteen years of life, but Nathan knew that nothing could prepare someone for a real battle. Soon, all his advisers, mages, commanders, and lieutenants entered Nathan's tent to prepare a plan for the battle.

"Does anyone hear that noise?" one of the advisers said, and there was a noise, like someone taking very loud and large steps from a short distance.

"I do," King Nathan responded. "Guard!" he yelled.

A guard peered in the tent. "Yes, my King?"

"We heard quite a loud noise a little bit of a ways away from our tent. I'd like you to investigate."

"At once, my King."

The guard grabbed a torch, walked behind the tent, and gazed into the dark forest just a few yards away. The guard did hear a loud noise, and it sounded like it was getting closer.

The guard stuck the torch in the snow, unsheathed his sword, and looked around. Suddenly, something walked in between the two trees in front of the guard.

He looked up and saw a gargantuan giant standing directly in front of him.

"Giant!" he screamed.

The giant grabbed the guard and flung him up in the air. The giant started toward the camp, and a few more came out of the forest.

"My king, I believe it is time to leave," one of the mages said. "That it is indeed."

King Nathan stood up, grabbed his swords, and followed everyone out of his tent. But as he left, he saw all his men with their swords, then he looked up and saw six more giants walking into their camp.

Men ran and screamed. Most of them were dead because the giants got them. Some shot arrows, some used swords, and some used magic. The giants swept through thousands of men and seemed unstoppable. Giants were the strongest creatures in the Frostlands, and the humans brought one giant down after the archers shot around three hundred arrows. Hours passed, and the men fought back the giants, but a few giants retreated, which sparked a thought in King Nathan that they could come back.

"Robb, how many men did we lose?"

"Four thousand."

"And they scared off some of our horses and stole some of the food supply," he added.

"Perhaps they just wanted to gather up our food or scare us off," Tymirial said.

"Well, they accomplished both. Gather everything up. We leave immediately!" Nathan yelled out.

After about thirty minutes of travel just trying to get away from the forest, they got to set up camp, and Nathan fell into an uncomfortable sleep.

After a few more days of travel, they were passing through a small town. Nathan desired to have a look around. He ordered the army to keep watch so no one left the town.

Nathan, Tymirial, and Robb went to the center of the town. To Nathan's surprise, they received no dirty looks, only a few waves and a few greetings. They entered the town hall to see many people working, feasting, and drinking. Nathan looked to the back to see a man sitting down at a table with a few others on either side.

"Good day. What brings you to our town? You don't look like you are from these parts," the man said.

By the looks of him, he was the town's leader. He wore fine clothes and carried no weapon.

"Just passing through, but I wonder, shouldn't you all be at Ravenhall?" Nathan asked.

Nathan noticed that no one here saved himself. Tymirial and Robb carried a weapon.

"Oh no, we are refugees from Drangar. We came here seeking a new life," he said. "Now is there anything we can offer you?"

"We were camping out and attacked by giants. Can you supply us with some food?" Nathan asked.

"I can feed you for the time being, but I cannot give out any for the coming days. We are running out as it is," he replied.

Nathan had never met a Viking before. He thought they were all outlandish brutes, but he found out it was quite the opposite.

"I must warn you, there are quite a large amount of people in our company," Nathan said with a slight smile.

"Nonsense. We have enough left for a few months. Surely, there aren't that many," the town's leader replied.

The four of them walked outside, and the town's leader's jaw dropped. "You came here to attack Ravenhall, didn't you?" he said.

"I can surround the whole town. We are only passing through, but if our presence is discovered by Vigrod, someone will have to pay for that," Nathan said.

"I see," he said. "We will be gone in a few moments. We were just passing through," Nathan replied.

Nathan walked back and got on his horse, and off they went.

The days came and went. The weather was bearable. No more giants had attacked them, and Ravenhall was in sight.

"I haven't been up here around this time of year," Tymirial said.

"We've been traveling since the middle of July. August has probably just started," Nathan said.

"That it has, but we still have two years left of summer," Tymirial replied.

The concept of time and years was first discovered by the elves. They figured out that seasons last around seven years, and they used months to measure it. For example, today is August 1 of the fifth summer.

"Only a week left to go, I'd say," Tymirial said.

"Very good. I doubt this battle will last too long," Nathan said.

By the time the last week of travel had ended, they were near Ravenhall. They were within a hundred yards when Nathan stopped around and turned around.

"Alright, men! This is the moment we have been traveling all this way for. I know I can count on each and every one of you to fight to your last breath and help us win this battle!" Nathan yelled. The soldiers cheered back. "Now first wave with me!"

Nathan led seventy-five thousand people closer to the gates of Ravenhall.

"Vigrod Frostbane! Come out and face me!" Nathan yelled.

From a distance, Nathan noticed a man come into view.

"I am Brodir Bothvar, trusted adviser of Highlord Vigrod. What is the meaning of this!" he yelled back.

"We have come to take what is ours!" Nathan screamed, and the soldiers yelled as well.

Nathan noticed something, a group of people carrying a wagon of what looked like food.

"Aedric, come," Nathan said.

The two of them rode over to the group of people. Nathan then saw Vigrod accompanied by two elves, with what was a wagon of food behind them.

"What is the meaning of this?" Nathan asked. "Just the results of a friendly exchange, High King," Vigrod replied.

"I take it you are Vigrod Frostbane," Nathan said.

"I am, and why have you come?" Vigrod leaned his head over. "With an army at your back," he added.

"We are at war, are we not? Now come with us. You are being taken prisoner," Nathan said.

"Very well, but at least let the Elves deliver the food. My people are starving," Vigrod said.

"Fine," Nathan replied.

Vigrod told the Elves to go deliver the food, and the elves made their way into Ravenhall.

"Now you are coming with us," Nathan said.

Brodir then chimed in, "No, he is not!"

6

THE BATTLE OF
RAVENHALL

The gates opened and outpoured thousands upon thousands of Vikings. Nathan and Aedric quickly rode back to the first wave of their attack force. The bitter cold of the Frostlands affected the humans slightly, but their heavy armor warmed them a bit.

Nathan drew his sword.

"For Yrfel!" he yelled.

They charged in unison. The world seemed to slow down. Nathan could feel the adrenaline. He had never taken a life before. He had never experienced a real fight before. He was nervous. But he didn't let the nerves overcome him.

They came closer and closer. Nathan could hear nothing but the sound of his breathing and his heart beating. When he realized where he was, Nathan nearly got an axe to his head. Nathan swung his sword at every Viking he saw. He killed a few of them, blood covered his sword, and some shot up and got him in the face.

Nathan didn't even recognize himself. He saw himself as a ruthless nameless beast. All he knew was killing. All he did was kill. He hated every minute of it.

Vigrod was running on foot after his horse had been killed. He swung his axe around, trying to find Brodir or someone he knew. Vigrod buried his axe deep into one of the human's heads. He then let out a loud scream. While Vigrod was holding back his enemies, he noticed a few Viking heads turn toward him and try to make their way to him.

After Vigrod had killed multiple easterners, a few hundred Vikings had come over to aid him. To Vigrod's surprise, Brodir came out of the crowd. The Vikings then created a perimeter around the two.

"Brodir," Vigrod said, going over to hug him, "good thing I found you," he added.

"Likewise," Brodir said.

"We need to mobilize the army. We are unorganized and unprepared," Vigrod said.

"Come on, Vigrod. We are Vikings. When are we ever any of those things!" Brodir said, laughing.

"I suppose you are right," Vigrod said. "Out of the way!" Vigrod yelled to some of his men in front of him. Vigrod then ran out into the fray with his axe raised high.

Nathan was regrouped with his men; they were pushing back against the Vikings. He still was sitting on his horse, and he was getting tired, swinging his sword back and forth, also riding his horse. He was focused on one Viking when, suddenly, his horse got on his back legs, and it started falling back.

Nathan tried to hang on to the reigns, but it didn't help. He was thrown from the top, and he landed on top of the Viking that was behind him. Nathan quickly got up and plunged his sword deep into the Viking's heart. He stood up and looked around him. The bodies started to pile up on both sides. Nathan couldn't tell if they were winning or losing.

Nathan then ran back to his dead horse, reached into the saddle pouch, and pulled out a torch. He looked for a match while peeking over his soldier every second. Nathan lit up the torch and threw it high up in the air. He nearly threw his arm out of place. He then looked up, and he saw the horses charging, their savior.

Vigrod killed multiple people, and he was close to Brodir. Vigrod looked out in the distance to see thousands of horses charging into the fray.

Vigrod made a conscious decision. "Go back! Back to Ravenhall!" Vigrod yelled out to his men.

He noticed his army start to make their way to the front gate.

"Form a line!" he yelled.

The line was in the middle of forming when the reinforcements came in. The cavalry claimed some of the straggling Vikings, but they gave Vigrod and the main force enough time to regroup.

Vigrod looked up to the ramparts for the gate-keeper. "Release the war beast!" Vigrod yelled up.

The Vikings held back their attackers while they waited for the gates to open.

The gates finally opened Vigrod yelled for his soldiers to move out of the way. A great bear the size of a giant, a dire bear was its proper name, covered in armor, ran out of the gates and onto the battlefield. The bear slaughtered everything in its path. The arrows of the archers didn't slow it down. The magic of the mages didn't either.

Nathan ran for his life; he didn't know where to go.

"Fall back!" he yelled.

As they ran, the dire bear chased after them. Nathan looked left and right. He saw no Vikings in view, just the dire bear chasing after his men. Nathan looked at the dire bear, and suddenly, a huge beam of lightning hit it in the head. Nathan took a closer look to see Tymirial with his staff pointed at the bear, hitting it with lightning.

Mages like Tymirial use their staffs to make magic and such. Their power is drawn from a place called the well, a realm of Caelestis, god of magic.

Tymirial was assisted by the few other mages in Nathan's army. They gave the rest of the army time to get away. All the mages focused on the dire bear, using the lightning to slow it down. They put all their energy into this, using all the power their staffs held to kill the beast. As the beam of lightning grew, the bear grew wearier when at last, a great flash of light appeared, and when the light went away, the bear was dead, burnt to a crisp.

Both sides watched in awe as the mages stood there over the bear's burned corpse. Nathan watched from a distance as the Viking army was now back inside Ravenhall. Now the attack would be much more difficult.

"What do we do now?" Nathan said, breathing heavily.

"Now we use the siege equipment and end this battle," Aedric said.

The mages walked back up to them. "Now that is taken care of, the battle should go much better," Tymirial said.

"Form up, all of you!" he yelled to the army.

He was a high enough rank where he had that authority.

"Prepare the siege weapons!" Nathan yelled.

"Archers, stay behind the main force," he added.

They were in formation, men holding the battering ram at the front, archers behind them, infantry to protect the archers, and behind those infantries were men carrying ladders. Nathan stayed up with the main force. He thought he should be there when they broke into the stronghold. They reached the main gate. They yelled out and hit the gate once. Nathan looked up to see Vikings on the ramparts, holding bows and arrows and rocks.

"Watch the ramparts!" he yelled out, holding a shield above his head.

"Bring up the ladders!" Nathan yelled back to where the rest of his men were.

They kept hitting the gate. Men kept climbing up the ladders. Most of them didn't make it. Some got through, but they didn't last too long. Vigrod was holding in Ravenhall's courtyard with the parts of his army that weren't on the ramparts.

"Man, the gate!" he yelled.

Multiple Vikings ran to the gates, including Vigrod. About two dozen Vikings sat on the gate, trying to hold back the battering ram. Vigrod said things to try to motivate them, but little by little, the gate broke down. Vigrod looked up to see his soldiers start to fall off the ramparts as more eastern soldiers were breaching their lines. Vigrod didn't know what to do. He had no solution. All he could do was try to motivate his people to fight hard and fight till their last breath.

The door finally broke in, and the men holding the door backed up and were met by thousands of eastern soldiers. Vigrod tried to hold his own, and he got caught a few times on the arm, and he ran back.

The soldiers on the ramparts were nearly finished. Vigrod ran up the steps to get up there.

Vigrod threw soldiers off the sides. He plunged his axe deep into his enemies' hearts. Vigrod was running out of energy, but he kept pushing on. Someone swung a sword at Vigrod. Vigrod took a step back. By the looks of him, he was a man of importance. He wore different armor and had some gold trim in his armor. Vigrod fired back, and the man parried and swung back. Vigrod realized that his opponent wasn't like the rest of the people he killed today.

Vigrod swung his axe and then quickly jumped on to his opponent. The man struggled, and he tried to push Vigrod off the side, but he got Vigrod off him. Vigrod tried to swing at the man, but he kicked Vigrod in the stomach and sent Vigrod back. Vigrod tried to kick him back, but he moved back and tried to catch Vigrod with his sword. Vigrod then, with one hand, grabbed the man while he was off balance. He lifted him by his neck and threw him down to the courtyard below.

Vigrod had a second to rest. His men were on either side of him. He looked out to the battlefield at the dead bodies and the blood-stained snow. He looked down to see more eastern soldiers pouring into his stronghold. Vigrod was running out of options. Their time was short. He knew he had to find Nathan, or someone of real importance, to try to cause a surrender. Vigrod saw a clump of eastern soldiers running into the courtyard. He then came up with an idea on the spot.

"With me now, with me!" he yelled.

Vigrod then jumped off the top of the ramparts onto the backs of the eastern soldiers below. There were enough down there to catch him. Vigrod pulled out a dagger from his belt and stabbed the soldier he was on top of.

One by one, his soldiers jumped down on to the pile. Vigrod felt his spirit lift. His men were truly loyal to him. He was determined to fight harder, to gift his loyal soldiers the satisfaction of a victory.

Vigrod tried to get out of the pile and find Nathan. He rolled out of the pile and quickly stood up. He stood close to the wall, looking out for Nathan. Vigrod spotted him. Nathan was on the complete other side of the courtyard, standing next to the mage who killed his war beast. A few soldiers flocked over to Vigrod. Together, they swept through the courtyard, they got closer and closer to Nathan.

Once Vigrod saw Nathan, he used every ounce of energy he had left to sprint over to Nathan. Vigrod was quite fast for being almost seven-foot. Vigrod then leaped up in the air, arms out toward Nathan. He grabbed Nathan, brought him up, and put the dagger to his throat.

"Drop your weapons!" Vigrod yelled out as loud as he could. All the heads turned. "Drop your weapons now, or your king dies!" he yelled.

All the men in steel armor slowly put their weapons down.

"All of you will leave now, or he dies. If you do not do as I say, he dies. Any of you try something, he dies," Vigrod said.

Slowly but surely, they cleared out of Ravenhall. Vigrod held Nathan until everyone was out of the fortress. Vigrod now had all the leverage in the world. He could demand anything from them.

"Now I will let your king go, but only if I receive a few prisoners and someone of importance," Vigrod said to them.

A man stepped forward. "How many of us?" he asked.

"Who are you?" Vigrod asked.

"I am Robb Brightfield, adviser to High King Nathan."

"I see, but our dungeon can fit up to five thousand, so I will have that many, or Nathan will stay with us," Vigrod said.

"No, you will not have them," Nathan said, trying to get out of Vigrod's grasp, but Vigrod was too strong for him.

"It is fine, High King," Robb said. He then looked back.

"Who among you will stand for your king?" he added.

Multiple men then stepped forward. Robb led the pack.

"Where is Brodir?" Vigrod said. "Where is Brodir!" Vigrod yelled back toward Ravenhall.

A few seconds later, Brodir walked out to Vigrod. Vigrod was glad he was alive; he didn't see him the whole battle inside Ravenhall.

"What is it, Highlord?" Brodir said breathlessly.

"Please take these men to the dungeons. Have a few other men help you see to it," Vigrod said.

Brodir then led their new prisoners back into the courtyard.

Vigrod then let Nathan go. "Now you will take your armies and march back home, or every one of those prisoners will die," Vigrod said.

"I will get them back, somehow," Nathan said.

Vigrod said nothing and walked back inside Ravenhall.

Vigrod walked up to the ramparts and watched as Nathan and his army walked away through the field of battle and out into the distance. As the sun fully set and the moon had risen, the prisoners were locked up in the dungeon, and Vigrod saw in the great hall, relaxing and enjoying a mug of ale. Brodir then walked in. He was sluggish walking in. Brodir slowly sat down next to Vigrod.

"I'm surprised we made it out of there alive. We lost nearly twenty thousand men," Brodir said.

"I agree. Tomorrow morning, we burn their bodies. Have a feast for them," Vigrod replied.

Brodir nodded in agreement. "This war is far from over," Brodir said.

Vigrod then peered over at the fire. "I know. It is what happens next that scares me."

THE FOREST OF ASHBEARD

E ver since Yrfel's creation, the forest of Ashbeard
had always been there. A dark forest with
winding paths and tall trees, it had always
been a place of mystery. People had been known to
go missing there. Legend had it that Lokfur Keawynn
went there and had never returned. His body was
never found, and many have gone looking for him.

Ashbeard was rumored to be an Ent, a tree man
made of burnt flesh and bark, and its beard was covered in ash. He had his protectors, the Ashwalkers,
just like him. They were Ents, tall burned tree people.

Two elves were tasked to go into the forest to
inspect anything out of the ordinary or find some of
the missing citizens.

"Do you really think we should do this?"
scouted Almon said.

"We're here on Lord Kolvar's orders. It doesn't matter if we want to do it or not," scouted Alinar told him.

They walked into the forest, and as they walked deeper into the forest, the light of the way they walked in started to fade.

"We're not going to make it out of here," Almon said frantically. The trees towered over the elves. There was barely any light. "You know people say if you die here the trees take you," Almon said.

"What do you mean take?" Alinar asked.

"They take your body somewhere... What was that?"

They looked around unsheathing their swords they looked and looked, but all they saw was a little rodent just scurrying around.

"Thank the gods," Alinir said.

They sheathed their swords and kept on moving. "You know people say that a spell was put on this forest," Almon said.

"People say a lot of things, Almon. Most of the things are false."

They walked through the forest and came across a man, wandering in the forest.

"You there!" Almon yelled.

The elf instantly turned and ran toward the two scouts.

"Hello, sirs. I seem to be lost. Can you tell me the way to get out of here?" the elf asked.

"Yes, I can. You just follow that path."

"Which path?" he asked.

"What?"

Almon looked back and saw multiple paths, three to be exact. Almon turned back to the citizen and shrugged.

"I thought there was only one path," Almon said.

"Why don't you just walk with us?" Alinir told him.

They walked for quite a long time until the group came across a hill in an open field. The citizen walked up on to the hill. He looked up at the sky, and suddenly, the ground opened under him, and he fell into this dark hole screaming. He fell and fell and fell, then the scream faded.

"What the hell was that?" Alinir screamed.

The scouts walked up to the hill and gazed at it. "Do you believe me now!" Almon yelled.

"Yes, I do. We should probably head back now."

"I'm going to climb one of the trees so we know where to go," Alinir said.

Alinar walked over to one of the trees and started climbing the tree and got above the leaves. "We need to head north then we'll find our way back."

"Run!"

"What Almon?"

"Ashwalkers!"

Ashwalkers were the guardians of the forest, and they all were loyal to Ashbeard, giant walking trees that were burnt, like Ashbeard himself. That's why the people called them Ashwalkers in tales of the forest.

Almon ran for his life while Alinir stayed in the tree he was in. Elves are the most athletic beings in this world, so Alinar jumped from branch to branch.

"Almon, climb!"

Almon ran to the nearest tree he could find and started climbing. They jumped for what seemed like days jumping from branch to branch, and the Ashwalkers tried to grab them from the trees, but the elves were too fast.

"I see a light!" Almon yelled.

They went a little bit farther and jumped into the light. They were on the outskirts of elven city. Then they turned and watched as the Ashwalkers walked back into the forest. The scouts started walking back after a long terrifying adventure.

When they reached the city, they immediately went to the throne room to inform Lord Kolvar of what they saw on their mission. They entered the throne room and bowed to Lord Kolvar.

"My lord we have news from the forest," Almon said.

"What is this news?" he asked.

"The forest is cursed, and the Ashwalkers are real," Alinar told him.

"What do you mean, cursed?" Lord Kolvar asked.

"The forest has a spell upon it. We saw a person, and he fell down a large hole that opened under him, then the hole closed up," Almon said.

"What do you think we should do about this, Thaedra?" Lord Kolvar asked his adviser.

"My lord, I don't think we can do anything about it," his adviser said.

Almon looked at the elf lord and waited for him to say something or dismiss them. "You two are dismissed. We will take your information and try to figure out this curse on that forest. Once the war is done, of course."

They bowed and left. The two scouts traveled back to their barracks. Troops always liked to share stories of perilous adventures that they had survived. Almon walked in, with Alinar following him. They walked in and sat down next to some of their fellow brothers-in-arms.

"So how was it?" said Arlen, another one of the elven scouts.

"It was horrible. I don't know how we survived," Almon exclaimed.

"That forest is cursed," Alinir added.

"Oh, please," Arlen said.

Almon looked at Alinar, then looked back at Arlen. "I swear it was real, wasn't it, Alinar?"

"Yes, it was. You can ask Lord Kolvar."

Arlen shook his head in disbelief.

Their loud voices echoed throughout the bar-racks and throughout the city, and people were confused about the loud noises coming from the barracks. People would say to each other, *Why are they talking about Ashwalkers?* Loud voices of soldiers echoed throughout the night, and most people had trouble sleeping.

THE SIEGE OF THE STEEL TOWER

Vigrod and a few others on his council sat in their war room. A few days had passed since the battle. Now Vigrod wanted some revenge.

"Now after what just happened a few days ago, I want to get them back. The steel tower would be the best place to get," Vigrod said.

"I agree. They surely don't have that many men held up there. It will be easy for us," Brodir said.

"We only have about eighty thousand warriors left. We can station a few thousand at the tower, and we will go from there," Vigrod said.

"How far away is the tower from here?" he added.

"It stands in the center of the Frostlands, more toward the border. It would take about four days," said one of the council members.

"I want the army prepared within two days," Vigrod said.

He then stood up and walked out of the room.

In the two days that followed, the soldiers were well-fed and rested, ready for the journey ahead of them. Vigrod walked out of his quarters and down the stairs, then walked to the front of his army. Vigrod called for the gate to be opened, and off they went.

The Viking army didn't stop too often, and no animals bothered them along the road. It cut their journey down to three days.

The steel tower was a large tower made of a white stone and was guarded by four-thousand eastern soldiers.

"Surround the tower," Vigrod said as his soldiers spread out.

Vigrod, Brodir, and a few other men went to the tower.

A few men came out from the tower to meet with them.

"Surrender now, so this can end without bloodshed," Vigrod said.

"I will not give up this tower," the man said.

His name was Rowan, a lieutenant of Nathan's army.

"Why not? Are you too proud to give it up?" Vigrod said.

"I am. You will have to kill us all if you want to take it," Rowan said.

He then spat on the ground. "Have it your way," Vigrod said, and they walked off.

When they regrouped with the army, they had surrounded the tower.

"Watch the archers up top!" Vigrod yelled. He grabbed his axe from his back. "Charge!"

A thousand or so soldiers met them in the field. The rest were held up in the tower. Vigrod and his army quickly swept through the soldiers that met them outside while the archers at the top of the tower shot down on them. A few Vikings were kicking in the large double doors.

Once they broke down the door, a bunch of eastern soldiers charged out to get them. They provided a little bit of struggle for the Viking attackers. But as the Vikings pushed on through the tower, the eastern numbers diminished. They ran up the stairs to the top of the tower where all the archers were, and all the Vikings made quick work of them.

After about an hour, all the bodies were cleared out of the tower and into the open field. The Vikings only lost about three-hundred men. Vigrod met all his soldiers outside.

"A great victory was won here today! Today, we showed those eastern bastards we are not afraid!" Vigrod yelled.

His soldiers cheered back, raising their weapons in the air. Vigrod ordered all the banners of House

Eastmoore to be taken down and replaced with banners of Clan Frostbane.

Vigrod sat in the former lieutenant's office, sitting in his chair and staring at the fire. Vigrod heard a knock at the door, and then Brodir entered the room.

"A good victory today," Brodir said.

"Quite right. Tell the men we stay here tonight," Vigrod replied.

"Of course, Highlord," Brodir said, then exited the room.

Vigrod felt a feeling of joy after what happened a few days ago. He was glad he was able to give his people an easy battle, something that didn't take more of a toll on them. He stared deep into the fire, thinking about everything that had just happened, and all he could do was smile.

THE DEEPRUN MINE

About a week after the battle, Nathan's army had been working extremely hard in their mine, trying to reforge weapons and armor.

Nathan had been going every day. It was about an hour's walk away from High Yrfel, and he was accompanied by Tymirial and his group of mages.

Once they arrived, they were welcomed by guards at the entrance of the tunnel into the mine. The group walked down the tunnel and entered the main part of the mine. Most of the mountain had been completely hollowed out. Some was due to the actual miners. Some had to do with things that already lived there.

A miner approached Nathan. "High King, good to see you," he said, shaking Nathan's hand. "Sedric, good to see you. How much more steel have you and your men produced?" Nathan asked.

"We have steel in abundance ready to head to the forges, but we are having a tough time transporting it," Sedric said.

"Is it because you don't have enough men to get it, or is it from an outside force?" Nathan said.

"The cave recluses have been tough on us. We lose more men by the day, but they leave the steel for whatever reason," Sedric said.

"I see. I can supply with more men, but Tymirial and his mages will have to deal with the spiders," Nathan said.

Sedric nodded and Tymirial stepped forward.

"You can hear them all scurrying around," Tymirial said, scratching his beard. Cave recluses were large gray spiders, the size of a house. People say that they came from the titan cave recluse that still live in the mountains of Yrfel.

"Look! A cave recluse egg!" one of the miners yelled out from a distance.

"We should burn it," another one said.

An argument started, then Tymirial stopped it when he walked over.

"Everyone, out of the mine!" Tymirial yelled.

"Mages to me," he added.

As everyone started to clear out of the mine, the mages stood over the egg.

Tymirial raised his staff in the air and shot fire toward the egg; the other mages followed suit. The spiders descended from the ceiling of the cave. The mages used fire to easily kill the spiders even though they were quite large beasts. They hated fire.

"We will have to spread out, either kill the beasts or get them to move," Tymirial said.

They spent the rest of the day killing spiders and burning their bodies.

Tymirial went off on his own, exploring some of the caves of the mountain, using his staff to light the way. He went down deeper and deeper, burning spiders as he went. Tymirial came to a dead end, but he looked at the wall, and there were plenty of cracks in it. He hit the wall using his staff, and a small explosion broke the wall down. The broken stone fell into a deep dark hole.

He used his staff to light up the whole entire area, and a whole new area was discovered. The hole stretched for miles, and in it sat a cave recluse the size of mountains.

"The titan spider. It appears to be sleeping," Tymirial said.

He looked around, and thousands of spiders crawled around. Tymirial turned his light down and quickly walked back to the main part of the mine, where all the other mages were waiting for him.

"I now know why the cave recluses dwell here," Tymirial said.

"Why's that?" one of the mages asked.

"That is because the mother of them all dwells in the depths of the mountain," Tymirial said.

"Well, in that case, this place needs to be closed off after the steel is moved, of course," one of the mages said.

The mages walked out, and everyone was there. "The steel needs to be moved, and this place needs to be shut down immediately after," Tymirial said.

"And why would that be?" Nathan asked.

"If you trust my judgment, then you will do as I ask," Tymirial said.

"If you say so, get the steel, now! I will send for more men to help you all!" Nathan yelled out.

As the day came to an end, the steel was moved and the mine was closed, and Tymirial hoped that their arachnid problems would come to an end.

THE HALL OF THE LORDS

A little under a month had passed since the siege of the steel tower, but the day was September eight, of the fifth summer.

Today was quite an important day in Yrfel's history. In the year two hundred ninety, after the first war ended, the three lords of the island, Rhagnar, Lokfur, and Robert, built a meeting place to commemorate that the war had ended peacefully. So every eighth of September, all future lords of the island must have a meeting.

The Hall of the Lords wasn't a huge structure by any means, but it was one structure with turrets at each corner and one large double door leading into the hall itself.

Nathan arrived with Tymirial and his mages. They would require no army for this. By the time they got there, Kolvar was already there, with a few elves protecting him.

"Lord Kolvar, good to see you," Nathan said.

"High King," Kolvar replied, taking a slight bow from the top of his horse.

As the two were conversing, that is when Vigrod arrived. Kolvar had greeted Vigrod, and the three of them went inside.

Nathan had never been inside the hall before. He looked around at all the marble stones used for the walls and floor. He looked up at the glass roof. Nathan walked over to the table at the center of the room. He pulled out his seat, which was made of stone from High Yrfel, and had a few blue banners around it. Behind Nathan stood a statue of his father; it wasn't a humungous statue, but it was big enough to fit inside the hall.

There were also statues of Rhagnar Frostbane and Lokfur Keawynn. Vigrod placed a hand on his father's statue while Kolvar stared at his father's. Nathan didn't know why Kolvar was doing that, but he thought it was just some elf superstition.

Vigrod and Kolvar took their seats.

"Good to see you all here," Kolvar said.

Nathan and Vigrod both nodded as they both didn't really want to speak to each other.

"Well, a few days ago, my guards spotted a person wearing all black and red," Kolvar said.

"I didn't send any scouts out there. You can ask any of the men I brought," Vigrod replied.

"Well, we think that it is the gray humans," Kolvar said.

Nathan and Vigrod had dumb looks on their faces.

The gray humans were humans that were cursed by Xydrax, the god of darkness. For years, they fought with the humans on the Steel Isle, who oppressed them and shamed them, but after a while, they ran, sailing away to an island in the south, where they hid for a few thousand years. That was known as the first gray human rebellion.

Years and years later, in year zero, the gray humans came back, trying to sweep across the world, starting from the Steel Isle and going around. They almost succeeded, but the fight ended in the ancestral grove when the three races banded together against their common foe.

"Nonsense, they haven't been seen in three-hundred years," Vigrod said.

"Then could it be the Shrouded?" Kolvar replied.

"I doubt it. The Shrouded supposedly wear all black, not black and red," Nathan chimed in.

"Have your men found the suspected gray human?" Vigrod asked.

"No, they've been searching for the past few days since we discovered them. I hope to get results by the time I return," Kolvar said.

"Are my men being treated well?" Nathan asked, looking at Vigrod.

"They are. They are being fed regularly, but I don't really know what goes on down there," Vigrod said.

"I also heard that you sieged my tower last month," Nathan said.

"I did, I wanted to take something from you, so I did," Vigrod answered.

"Next time I see you, I'll make sure to kill you this time," Nathan said, pointing a finger at Vigrod.

Vigrod quickly stood up, and Nathan did the same.

"I would rip you in two if they weren't here watching us," Vigrod said, pointing back at the statue of his father.

Kolvar sighed. "Oh my, can you two just relax for the short time we are in here?"

"No, I refuse to share the same table as him," Vigrod said.

"Well, you are going to have to manage, Highlord," Kolvar replied.

*****

On a hill, a fair distance away from the Hall of the Lords stood Commander Aegis, the new leader of the Shrouded.

"So why are we here again, Commander?" asked Arthur Riverglade, the second-in-command to Aegis.

"Just to observe. This is quite an important event," he replied.

Commander Aegis had brought along four other scouts. Aegis wanted to observe a historical moment and to protect High King Nathan, if need be.

"The plan is to bring Nathan in, right?" Arthur asked.

"Yes, when we return home, we will move forward with the plan," Aegis said.

CHAPTER

11

SHROUDED RECRUITMENT

The Shrouded were the secret organization dedicated to serving their gods, the god of darkness and the god of light, chaos, and harmony, shrouded and bright.

The new recruits all gathered in the courtyard where Commander Aegis was waiting for them. He watched as the four new recruits walked into the courtyard at the top of the mountain and then stopped, turned, then looked at him.

"Listen up, recruits," Commander Aegis said. "You have been recruited to the Shrouded. An officer will take you around the base, and you will be assigned to a group." The recruits looked at him and waited for the commander to say something else or dismiss them. "Once you have proved your worth, you will take our oath."

Two officers walked forward, and the recruits split up and started heading down the stairs deeper into the mountain. Godwin and Darwyn were in the alchemy room, looking inside, seeing many vials and potions.

"Obviously, this is our alchemy room. Here, medicines and potions are made," the officer told them.

The officer took them through the rest of the Shrouded base, the armory, kitchens, map room, scout tower, and blacksmith.

"You have all been taken through our base. You now will be assigned to a group," Commander Aegis said.

One of the officers walked up to the podium and gave him a paper. The commander looked at it.

"Godwin, you are going to the scouts, Darwyn, to the alchemists, Jackson, to the cooks, and Ayldric to the blacksmiths."

The recruits were all taken to their new stations, and they all got to work, cooking, scouting, blacksmithing, and making potions.

Darwyn was at his station making potions, minding his own business. The alchemist trainer walked over to him.

"Are you Darwyn?" he asked.

"Yes, Officer," he replied.

The officer took him over to a corner to speak with him in private. "You were the man who blew up one of our towers on the Steel Isle," he said.

Darwyn turned his head frantically. Darwyn looked down. "I am, I...I...I'm sorry."

"You are forgiven once you join the Shrouded your past lives mean nothing, but we need more handheld fire, and I thought you should do the job."

The Shrouded's alchemy branch was one of the most important. The medicines and their weaponized potions came in handy. Darwyn, trained in the ancient arts of making potions, also had some prior experience. He sat for hours each day studying and making portions, not leaving. He was prepared to devote his life to the Shrouded.

The other recruits also trained immensely, scouting, cooking, and blacksmithing. Being a member of the Shrouded was not easy, they would have to prove themselves, or they would leave. Mealtime came around, and the four new recruits met up in the dining hall.

"How has all your training been?" asked Darwyn.

They walked over to grab a bowl of rabbit stew.

Jackson made a long sigh. "The cooking officer is a piece of work," he said angrily.

"Is that because you're a bad cook?" Ayldric laughed.

Jackson shoved him while he was still laughing.

"How about you, Godwin?" Darwyn asked as they sat down.

"Tedious, but it's important to the Shrouded," he replied.

The group talked and ate a little while longer, then someone approached them.

"These are the new recruits," someone said.

The group turned around and saw a tall man gazing at them.

"Who are you?" asked Ayldric.

"Arthur Riverglade, I'm Aegis's second-in-command," the group acknowledged him, then turned back to their stew. Then Arthur grabbed Ayldric by the neck, he held him in a strong grip, and Ayldric tried to resist.

"I said, I'm Aegis's second-in-command!" he yelled. "And you'll refer to me as sir, or there will be consequences." Arthur looked at even waiting for him to say something.

"Yes, sir," Ayldric said.

Arthur violently threw Ayldric back into where he was sitting, then he walked away while a few men followed him.

"You alright?" Godwin asked.

"Yes, I'll be fine," Ayldric replied.

They walked out of the dining hall, trying to avoid any attention. They made it back to their bunks, then the door was opened, and Commander Aegis walked in by himself.

The recruits stood up and addressed the commander. "Recruits, I heard there was a problem in the mess hall today," the commander said.

They nodded.

Aegis sighed. "I understand that it was Arthur who caused the trouble. I just came to apologize for his behavior. At such a high position, he shouldn't be acting like that."

"Commander, you shouldn't have to apologize for him," Darwyn said.

"You know he is of great use to us, but he disgraces himself with his actions he said." With those final words, he left, and the group relaxed for a while, then went back to training, then finally went to sleep.

Two weeks had passed since the recruits had entered the courtyard and had been sent to work and started on the path of the Shrouded.

The recruits had walked out to the courtyard and stood in a single-file line like they had done weeks prior. Commander Aegis stood, waiting for them.

"Recruits, you have had your time to train, and your officers have told me good things about this group. Now it is time to take your vows."

Commander Aegis took them down a tunnel where they would take their vows. They walked down a long dark tunnel with torches lighting the way.

Finally, they entered a room with two statues. One was Xydrax, god of darkness, and one of Aella, goddess of light.

"Kneel in front of your gods," Commander Aegis said, and that was what they did. And in unison, they started to say the Shrouded oath.

Through light, we find peace. Through dark, we find chaos. Through days and nights, we come closer to the goals of our gods, for they are the creators, the architects, the craftsmen of this world. And we are their servants.

"Arise brothers of the Shrouded," Aegis said. "Serve your gods."

And the new brothers of the Shrouded left to serve the gods of light and dark, chaos and peace, shrouded and bright.

Late that night, Aegis came to Godwin in their bunks.

"Now, Godwin, come with me," he said.

They made their way through the empty court-yard while the wind blew, and the stars were above them. When they made it to Aegis's office, three other scouts were already inside.

"I'm sending you four on an important mission. I want you four to infiltrate High Yrfel and bring the high king back here," Aegis said.

"On second thought, I will be joining you."

"Now grab your climbing gear," Aegis said, and they were out the door.

They walked down the passageway through the mountain and down into the valley below. The Shrouded's base was on the edge of Yrfel, hidden away from the easterners. About an hour or so later, they approached the walls. This was no problem for them. They quickly scaled the walls and took care of any patrolling guards.

Getting to the village inside the walls, the five of them climbed up on top of a house and ran on the roof tops until they reached the bottom of the hill, where the castle of High Yrfel sat at the top.

Aegis led the way, using his climbing spikes to scale the large hill, the other four followed behind him. The climb wasn't too much for the five of them. After all, it wasn't a mountain. They were climbing. There was a little space behind the castle for them to stand.

"We will split into two groups, two of you go around that side. The other three will go around this side," Aegis said, whispering.

As commanded, they split into two groups, Aegis and Godwin, and the other three. Once they made their way around, Aegis peaked his head out to see two guards standing at the doorway.

Aegis saw on the other side, one of his men doing the same, Aegis made a hand motion, signaling for them to get the guards. Quickly, they ran up to the guards and slit their throats and then rolled their bodies down the hill.

"Now we wait for the next pair of guards. Surely, the same two don't stay out all night," Aegis whispered.

They all waited on one side of the door, and as expected, the door opened a few minutes later. When the guards walked out, two of the five scouts made quick work of the two guards, and they slowly walked inside. Once they closed the door behind them, they stood alone in the throne room.

"Now we need to find the high king," Aegis said.

"But how will we know where it is?" Godwin asked.

"We will have to go room by room," Aegis replied.

Aegis led them down a hallway behind the throne. They checked each room going door by door, but they came across no one's living space.

"Do you hear that?" Aegis said.

He then shushed them, went over to the wall, and stood there and around the corner to the left came two guards, and Aegis dealt with them, and their bodies dropped, making a loud noise.

"Hurry up. Someone heard that," Aegis said.

They went fast, going from room to room. They were at the end of the hall, and they opened the door. There, High King Nathan was sleeping.

Aegis looked back, and he saw four guards coming down a hallway to their right.

"Hurry and grab him," Aegis said.

"What are you five doing!" yelled one of the guards.

Godwin and two other scouts walked into the room. The two scouts went up to Nathan. They counted down, and at the same time, one bound up Nathan's hand, and the other put a sack over his head.

When they exited the room, they saw four dead guards on the floor.

"We need to leave quickly before more guards arrive," Aegis said.

One of the scouts threw Nathan over his shoulder, and Nathan tried to resist. When they got to the throne room, Aegis grabbed Nathan off the scout's shoulder, removed the sack off his head, and he put a dagger up to Nathan's throat.

"If you value your life, you will listen to me," Aegis said.

"Fine," Nathan said.

They opened the large double doors and went around the back of High Yrfel.

"Get on my back," Aegis said to Nathan.

He did as he was told, and they started to make their way down the hill. They reached the bottom of the hill, and then Nathan got off Aegis's back.

"I'm going to unbind your hands but try anything, and you will die where you stand," Aegis said.

They started to go through the empty village of High Yrfel, hoping that they wouldn't run into anyone. The group strolled through the town and didn't see anyone. Once they got out of the village, over the walls, and on to the road back to the Shrouded base, they heard not a sound.

They entered the Shrouded base, and they went up to the courtyard at the top of the mountain. Nathan looked up at the sky, wondering where the actual top of the mountain went.

"Who are you?" Nathan asked.

"I am Commander Aegis of the Shrouded," he said.

"Why have you brought me here?" Nathan said,

"I have brought you here to offer you a deal," Aegis replied.

"I offer you our services. Everything the Shrouded has to offer. Also, the truth about your father's murder," Aegis said.

"What do you want in return?" Nathan asked.

"I want a monthly shipment of supplies, food, and weapons, and this partnership to be kept a secret from everyone outside High Yrfel," Aegis replied.

"Deal," Nathan said.

The two shook hands. "Now tell me about my father's murder."

"You have been told that he was murdered by a Viking, yes?" Aegis said.

Nathan nodded.

"Well, the truth is that he was murdered by a man named Deathshade, our previous leader, before we killed him," Aegis said.

"Why? Did you allow that to happen?" Nathan said.

"He wanted to rule Yrfel, so he killed your father and Rhagnar Frostbane. I advised against it, but he was a madman. But we took him out, and I was elected the new leader," he added.

"I am starting to rethink my decision," Nathan said.

"Don't blame us for past mistakes," Aegis said.

"I suppose you are right, but I would like to go home now," Nathan said.

"At once, you three, please escort the high king back to his home," Aegis said.

A CALL TO ARMS

Vigrod sat down in the war room, surrounded by his elders, his commanders, and Brodir.

"Because of recent events, we are now the weakest army in Yrfel. I have come up with the idea to call the men and women of Frosthaven and from Bloodhall and from the Black Nest," Vigrod said. Back on Drangar, there were three clans of importance, the Frostbanes, the Bloodwolves, and the Darkwings.

"Can the messengers get across the frozen sea?" Vigrod said.

"We have birds' bread for such adventures," one of the elders replied.

"Good, I need to write the messages. Does someone have what I need?" Vigrod said.

An elder stood up and walked over to a shelf in the corner of the room and brought what Vigrod needed over to him.

Vigrod wrote three messages, asking for their support in their fight on Yrfel. "How long will these take to deliver?" Vigrod asked.

"If we send three separate messages, it will take less time. I'd say about a month to get them back," the elder responded.

"So be it. We will have to hold out until then," Vigrod said.

In the month that followed, nothing happened to the Vikings. The steel tower was retaken by Nathan and his army. The elves and humans had a few quarrels over more land. But Vigrod sat in Ravenhall idle, waiting for his responses, and about a month had passed. The day was October 11, of the fifth summer.

Vigrod was in his quarters, sharpening his axe, when Brodir walked in. "Highlord, the messages have arrived," he said.

They walked down to the war room, where the three messages were on the table. Vigrod picked up the first one. It was sealed up with a red raven seal, the seal of Clan Frostbane. He read through. In short, Frosthaven would send fifty thousand troops, keeping some behind to defend their home.

"Frosthaven will send us fifty thousand," Vigrod said happily.

He picked up the next scroll. It had the seal of a red wolf on gray wax, the seal of Clan Bloodwolf. Vigrod read the message. "Bloodhall will send fifteen thousand," Vigrod said.

"I'm just surprised they sent us anything at all," Brodir replied.

Vigrod picked up the last one, the seal of a black wing on black wax, the seal of Clan Darkwing."

"Clan Darkwing offers ten thousand," Vigrod said.

"Any mention of when they will arrive?" Brodir asked.

"They will be here two weeks from now, according to each message," Vigrod said.

"Very good, but I do advise that you tell the army. They do not like sitting in Ravenhall and going out hunting every day," Brodir said.

"I suppose you're right, gather the men if you please," Vigrod said.

Vigrod walked out of the war room and walked up the stairs to the ramparts. He watched as his soldiers filed in. Some had to stay in the barracks area.

"Men and women of Drangar!" Vigrod said. "I know that we have sat still as this war has waged on but no longer. I have called upon the people of Frosthaven, Bloodhall, and the Dark Nest," he added.

Vigrod heard his soldiers chatting. It did not sound negative to Vigrod, so he took that as a good sign.

"When they arrive is when we strike. The only thing I ask from you is patience, but trust me when I say it is worth it," Vigrod said.

Sighs came from the crowd, Vigrod tried to convince them that waiting was worth it, but he didn't think he was doing a very good job.

13

THE SCOUTS JOURNEY

The commander of the elven militia, Rion, was in the barracks talking to the scouts who would travel to the Frostlands.

"Almon, Alinar, Arlen, Lord Kolvar, and I have decided that you will go to the Frostlands and report anything you find."

Almon was surprised. "Us, Commander?" he replied.

"Yes, you three. You shall leave at sunrise."

Commander Rion left their barracks and returned to his duties.

"I'm surprised he chose us," Alinar said.

"Well, we did survive the forest of Ashbeard," Almon replied.

"We leave at sunrise. I suggest we get some rest," Arlen chimed in.

Sunrise came, and the three scouts woke immediately to their lieutenant, telling them to get up and complete their mission. They put on their leather armor and grabbed equipment that could help them on their journey. The gates opened, and out the scouts went, starting a weeklong walk to the Frostlands.

As they walked out of the borders of the Greenlands and out into what land is unowned, they tried to keep out of sight of anything, other soldiers, Shrouded, even the birds.

"We need to get there quickly. A few more hours walking, then we'll camp out," Arlen said.

The others nodded. The walk wasn't too perilous except for the wolves, and other creatures of the ancient isle. The scouts came to a river. As they approached the river, the group saw something farther down the river.

The thing started to crouch down, moving in all different ways.

"What is that?" Almon asked.

"I don't know. Should I get a closer look?" Alinar replied.

Arlen signaled for them to crouch behind one of the rocks. "Alinar, go investigate," Arlen told him.

Alinar stayed crouched and kept quiet and tried to sneak up behind the creature.

He got closer and closer, and the creature still stayed in a weird position. Alinar got behind the creature, and it heard him. It turned around. It screamed.

"I'm taking a piss. What are you bothering me for you?"

It was a man, a Viking man. Alinar stared at him. The man was obviously a peasant, torn, dirty clothes, and a certain smell.

"Wait a minute. You're an elf!"

The Viking started to run. It wasn't very fast, but still, he ran. Alinar chased after him. Almon and Arlen came to assist in the pursuit.

The three elves caught up to the Viking and held him down.

"What do we do with him?" Almon asked.

Arlen didn't say anything. Neither did Alinar.

"We have to kill him," Arlen said.

When he said that, the man didn't say anything. Almon pulled out his knife and put it to the man's throat. Almon grasped his knife tightly, and he gazed at the man, who stared directly back at him, not moving, just calmly breathing.

"Almon, do it," Arlen said.

Almon paused, and then he cut the man's throat. Suddenly, the sky began to darken, and birds flew up from the trees that were a few feet behind them. The birds scattered, and after the birds were out of sight, the sky began to lighten again.

"What was that!" Alinar screamed.

"I'm not sure, but we had best keep moving now," Arlen told them.

"Did we have to kill that man?" Almon asked.

"Yes, he could have told someone of our mission," Arlen told him.

"But…," Arlen made a long pause.

"Almon, we had to kill him. Even though he was a poor man, he is still loyal to Vigrod," Almon looked at him, then nodded.

They camped out by the river, where most unnatural events happened that day. Night came, and they heard the birds and the beasts in the night.

"We leave at first light, so get some sleep," Arlen told the group.

The first light came, and Arlen was awake first, and he awoke the other elves.

"How long until we reach the Frostlands?" Alinar asked.

"I can see the Icy Mountain. I say a day more if we keep a quick pace," Arlen said.

The day went by the elves kept a quick pace, and they reached the border of the Frostlands, and they started to make their way to the coast.

"We need to get to the edge of the island, then we can record anything out of the ordinary tomorrow," Almon said.

They finally reached the coast and started along the way to the edge of Yrfel. They made it to the edge of Yrfel as the sunset. Ravenhall was a fair distance away.

"We should camp here," Alinar said. "I don't know if we can, if we sleep, we could be found,"

Arlen responded. "It's very unlikely, but it could happen," he added.

"We'll have to build a fire," Alinar said.

"That is an unwise decision," Arlen replied. "We die if they spot us, or we die because we froze to death," Alinar told him.

Arlen nodded. They built a small fire, and the last one to fall asleep put out the fire.

Dawn came, and the group woke to the waves crashing on the island. They watched and waited the frozen wasteland. Much time passed, but as they turned to look at where Drangar was, they saw something moving in the distance.

"What's that?" Almon asked.

They watched and waited for the thing to move closer.

"That's a ship," Alinar said.

"Whose ship?"

Alinar got closer to the edge of the island. "Drangarian," he said.

"What could they be bringing to Yrfel?" Arlen said.

"Anything, soldiers, resources, maybe both," Almon said.

"We should make for the docks," Arlen said.

The others looked at him. "Every Viking's skin is made of ice. We don't look like them. We'd be spotted instantly!" Almon yelled.

"We can get a little closer," Alinar said.

They moved down the side of the island, trying not to get spotted but getting close enough to really see what was happening.

They looked at the frozen harbor that stretched for quite a long distance. None of the elves could determine its length. They all watched as more and more ships docked in the harbor, and they crept a bit closer and watched as more Vikings got off the boats and unloaded supplies.

"Those are reinforcements," Almon said.

"I agree. I think we have seen enough," Arlen replied.

"Come on," he added, motioning for them to follow.

They made their way back to the edge of Yrfel, back to where their camp was, a good distance away from Ravenhall.

"That is all we needed to see, I believe," Almon said.

"Quite right. Now let's make our way home. I hate being in this place," Alinar replied.

They packed their things and were quickly on their way back to Kolvar and their nice, warm green country.

14

SHIPS ON THE
FROZEN HARBOR

Vigrod was on the harbor, helping everyone get their supplies out of their ships and onto the docks.

A man approached Vigrod from behind.

"Highlord," the man said.

His voice was deep. Vigrod turned around to have a look at the man. He was slightly shorter than Vigrod. He was dressed in red and gray with a short brown beard. He wore fur and two blades around his waist. He had red face paint on, with his green eyes and brown hair.

"Who are you?" Vigrod asked. "I am Ulfir, the next Wolf lord of Bloodhall."

"But I would prefer you refer to me as Wolf Lord," he added.

Vigrod looked at the Wolf Lord's mouth and noticed his teeth were blood-stained.

"As you say, Wolf Lord," Vigrod said.

The two shook hands, and then two more people came up to them. One was old and blind, in a wheelchair, wearing black and purple, being pushed around by a man, wearing the same black and purple robes.

"Is this him?" the old man asked.

"Yes, Dark Bird. This is him," the young man answered.

"Young Vigrod, I am the Dark Bird, leader of the Dark Wing clan," the old man said.

Vigrod walked over to him. He knelt so they were at eye level even though Vigrod knew he couldn't see him.

"It is good to meet you. My mother and father told me much about you when I was young," Vigrod said.

"I'm sure they did. I've been around for quite a long time, but we are here to aid you and take whatever you will give to us," the Dark Bird said.

"Very good. I will escort you to Ravenhall, and then I would like to discuss my plan of attack with you all," Vigrod said.

They walked onto the snow, and suddenly, the Wolf Lord, Dark Bird, and his assistant all jolted as their skin started to freeze.

Vigrod walked up to them. "I'm sure you will all get used to it, but the cold climate doesn't affect you as much," he said.

Brodir approached the group, and he introduced himself to all the Wolf Lord and Dark Bird. The five of them walked to Ravenhall. Vigrod called over the elders who were standing in the courtyard.

The group entered the war room. They took their seats while Vigrod stood.

"Now that you are here, I would like to formally welcome you to Yrfel," Vigrod said.

The Wolf Lord and Dark Bird gave their thanks.

"Because of your reinforcements, we now have around one hundred fifty-five thousand soldiers, and while we waited for you all, our enemies have weakened each other for us," Vigrod said.

"My plan is to attack High Yrfel, here."

He pointed to show the Wolf Lord and his assistant. "I also realized that Kolvar will not budge unless we make them, so we draw out the eastern forces and push them to the Greenlands, forcing Kolvar's hand."

"Now I'm guessing Kolvar is this elf lord, you mentioned?" the Wolf Lord said.

"He is. Kolvar is much smarter than Nathan and myself. He will most likely have something up his sleeve," Vigrod replied.

"So your plan is to draw out an entire army from their fortress, get them to a certain point, and then you think another army will come out and fight also?" the Wolf Lord said.

"It is," Vigrod replied.

"It's a bold plan, a stupid plan really, but what is in it for my clan?" the Wolf Lord asked.

"If it is successful, then I promise the eastern side of Yrfel, and for you, Dark Bird, I will give your clan the western side," Vigrod said, "and I promise you, the environment here is much better than that on Drangar."

"If you want my people to follow you, you must prove to me why you are a worthy leader. I will not march my people into unknown territory, led by a Frostbane no less," the Wolf Lord said.

Brodir coughed to get everyone's attention. "Trust me when I say it, Wolf Lord, Vigrod Frostbane is the worthiest leader you will come across. He defended Ravenhall against a greater army than ours. He led an attack on an eastern tower. He led us without a mother or father to guide him. Need I say more, Wolf Lord?" Brodir said.

"You make a very good point, and, Vigrod, I am sorry to hear about your father. Even though he was a Frostbane, he deserves respect all the same," the Wolf Lord said.

He put a fist on his heart to show that he meant it. "I appreciate your condolences, Wolf Lord," Vigrod said.

The Wolf Lord sighed. "When will we attack?" he asked.

"When we are ready, are you also in on this plan, Dark Bird?" Vigrod said.

"We are. We follow your lead, Highlord Frostbane," he said.

"Brodir, send a message to Nathan. Tell him Drangar is coming," Vigrod said.

Brodir smirked. "At once, Highlord," he said, then walked out of the room.

Vigrod called the meeting adjourned and walked out and up the stairs onto the ramparts. He looked out onto Yrfel. The mountains and High Yrfel stood to his left, and the Elder Branch and the Greenlands out to his right.

"It will all be mine," Vigrod said to himself. "I'll be the greatest Viking who ever lived, Vigrod, king of Yrfel."

15

A GIFT FROM THE PAST

Kolvar sat on the throne in the Elder Branch. Aerimir walked through the entrance and approached Kolvar.

"My lord," Aerimir said, bowing.

"Aerimir," he replied.

"May I speak with you? In private," Aerimir asked.

"Very well. Thaedra, if anyone comes looking for me, send them away and tell them I will return soon," Kolvar said.

"As you wish, my lord," Thaedra said.

The two of them walked out to the forest of Ashbeard. "How private would you like this conversation to be, Aerimir?" Kolvar said, laughing.

"Come on. We need to go a bit further," Aerimir said.

Kolvar stopped. "Why would we need to go inside that cursed forest?" Kolvar said.

"I've walked this forest hundreds of times, Lord Kolvar. Come now," Aerimir said, and they started their way into the deep dark forest.

"What was it that you wanted to talk about?" Kolvar asked,

"I brought you out here to make sure no one heard us. I want to talk about your father, my lord," Aerimir said.

Kolvar had a dissatisfied look on his face. He had no desire to talk about his father and being in the place where he disappeared in.

"What about my father?" Kolvar said. "Before your father disappeared, he gave me this letter. He told me to give it to you when the time was right and when you realize the responsibilities of being a leader," Aerimir said, pulling out a note from the inside of his robe.

The seal was unbroken. Kolvar hesitated. He had no idea what his father had written down. Maybe he left him something. Maybe he just wanted to say something. Kolvar slowly opened the message, and he began to read.

Kolvar,

If you see this message, it means that I have gone away to where I cannot say. I am worried, son, because I know the truth. I know that they are after me.

The Shrouded are after me. I have figured out their deception. They killed Rhagnar and James, and they are after me.

They also mentioned James's son, but regardless, I went away.

I have left a gift for you in the Elder Branch. Ask your grandfather to give it to you.

I love you, son,
Lokfur Keawynn

Kolvar shed a tear. He wiped it off his face and looked up to the sky.

"Well, what did it say?" Aerimir asked.

"Have a look for yourself," Kolvar said, handing Aerimir the letter.

"I see. I wonder where he's gone off too," Aerimir said.

"I guess that means he is still alive!" Kolvar said happily.

Kolvar was interrupted by a loud stomping sound. He turned to see a sixteen-foot-tall tree man staring right at him.

Kolvar let out a scream. He ran back behind a tree. Meanwhile, Aerimir stood there, doing nothing.

"Aerimir, what are you doing!" Kolvar yelled.

"It's fine. I am good friends with all the Ashwalkers," Aerimir replied.

"You are kidding," Kolvar said, coming out into the open.

"Aerimirrrrrrrr," it said, its voice was deep and difficult to understand. "What brings you to our foresttttttttt?"

"I brought my great-grandson out here, Kolvar Keawynn, son of Lokfur Keawynn, lord of the Elder Branch," Aerimir said.

"Ah, a son of Lokfur. He is a good friend of oursssssss," it said.

"Of ours?" Kolvar said.

As he said that, seven more Ashwalkers came into view.

"Is he truly Lokfur's son, Aerimirrrrr?" one of the Ashwalkers asked.

"He is," Aerimir replied.

"If he is, then we pledge our allegiance to him-mmmm," it said.

"What?" Kolvar asked.

"A friend of Lokfur is a friend of oursssssss," it answered.

The Ashwalker then reached up and grabbed something off its shoulder. It held something in its hand. He brought it down to Kolvar and revealed a horn in its hand. Kolvar grabbed it and examined it. It had many different designs on it. Kolvar didn't understand any of it. He then put it on his belt.

"Use that horn to call us to your aidddd," the Ashwalker said.

All the Ashwalkers then turned and stomped away, walking into the forest beyond and out of Kolvar and Aerimir's view.

"What was that?" Kolvar said.

"I guess they are yours now. Anyways, come now. I will give you the gift your father mentioned," Aerimir replied.

They walked back into the Elder Branch's city and traveled to Aerimir's house in the residence section of the city.

The two of them walked inside, and Aerimir told Kolvar to stay in the living room while he grabbed what was promised. He entered the room a minute or so later with a large box. He set it on the table and opened it with a key.

Aerimir revealed it, and Kolvar's jaw dropped.

"That is the bow of Eldrin!" he said excitedly.

"That it is, Kolvar. It was my father's, and he received it from my great-grandfather. Now I give it to you," Aerimir said.

"But it is passed down once the wielder dies, correct?" Kolvar said.

"It is, but my fighting days are done, I think, so it is time I gave it to you," Aerimir replied.

"But you will ruin the tradition," Kolvar said.

"Oh please, what is my father going to do? Rise from the grave and kill me?" Aerimir said with a loud laugh.

Kolvar laughed too. He supposed his great grandfather had a point.

Aerimir handed Kolvar the old family heirloom. Kolvar held it in awe, running his hand along the bowstring and looking at the gold engraved throughout it.

"This is...is...I don't know how to describe it, but I would like to know more about it," Kolvar said.

"I can't tell you much about it. My father never talked about it," Aerimir replied.

"Well, I suppose I shall be going now," Kolvar said.

"If you say, my lord," Aerimir said, bowing to Kolvar and showing him the door.

Kolvar stood on the balcony on the top of the Elder Branch, looking out to the sea and the empty sky. He wondered what would happen next. They were at war, and nothing really transpired. Kolvar had a sneaking feeling that something was coming. He just didn't know when.

16

THE MESSAGE RECEIVED

Nathan sat on the throne in High Yrfel. It had been a boring day, and Nathan sat and stared at the ceiling and talked with Tymirial.

The doors opened, and one of Nathan's new advisers came walking in, holding a message.

"A message for you, High King, and it has Raven's seal," he said. "The northerners sent us a message?" Nathan said.

He grabbed the message from the adviser's hand. He broke the seal and read the message.

"Drangar is coming," Nathan said aloud.

"That's the message?" Tymirial asked.

"It is," Nathan said. He turned to his adviser. "Gather the council," Nathan added.

They gathered in the war room. "Drangar has sent us a threat. Now I have no idea where they are.

They could be anywhere at Ravenhall or just outside," Nathan said.

"What do you suggest we do, Aedric?" Nathan asked.

"I suggest that we double the number of archers on the walls and have guards patrol the old mountain paths," he replied.

"A good plan, if you would get the men prepared," Nathan said.

"At once, High King," Aedric said, bowing then leaving the room.

Later that day, Nathan was out on the walls with his men. He stared out at the barren plains and bleak gray sky. The walls connected each mountain on the edge of the range, and they made tunnels through the mountains to truly connect the wall.

The wind blew, and Nathan saw something out of the corner of his eye. It appeared to be a flock of messenger birds, and Nathan noticed that they all had a red ribbon tied around one of their legs.

"So Drangar is coming."

Nathan walked back into High Yrfel and looked for his adviser. "I want a message sent out to Lord Kolvar. Tell him to meet me at the Hall of the Lords," he said.

His adviser bowed, then walked off to the rookery.

It had been about two and a half weeks since Nathan sent his message. Kolvar had luckily agreed to meet Nathan there, and Nathan instantly set out to get there.

They had been on the road for a few days. The hall wasn't too far from High Yrfel, and the size of the group wasn't too large. Once they got to the hall, it wasn't to Nathan's surprise that they already found Kolvar there waiting for them.

Nathan trotted over to Kolvar.

"Lord Kolvar," Nathan said, making a slight bow from the top of his horse.

"High King," Kolvar replied.

The two of them walked inside the hall and sat down.

"So why is it you have requested me out here?" Kolvar asked.

"A few weeks ago, I received a message from Vigrod, and the letter only had three words. Drangar is coming," Nathan said.

"This is important to me, why?" Kolvar said.

"Vigrod wouldn't threaten me in such a way unless he had gotten something. I believe he has called reinforcements from Drangar. And he is coming for us both," Nathan replied.

"Do you have the message with you?" Kolvar asked.

Nathan nodded. He went back outside to get the message from Tymirial. Nathan showed Kolvar the message.

"Well, the threat is real, but he is most likely coming for you first," Kolvar said.

"I agree, but I propose that we band together and take out the Vikings, and we each get half of Yrfel," Nathan said.

"Hmm, allow me to think about it," Kolvar said.

"We have a common enemy in Vigrod. Our two peoples can live in peace," Nathan replied.

Kolvar was deep in thought. He was considering doing it, but he thought about the aftermath. What else would happen to Kolvar and his people? *What kind of person is Nathan really, and will he keep his word?* Kolvar thought to himself.

"No, I won't do it," Kolvar said. "Besides, if Vigrod is coming for me, I will be ready," he added.

Kolvar had no interest in hearing what else Nathan had to say and walked out of the room.

BATTLE PREPARATION

Vigrod, Brodir, the Wolf Lord, and the Dark Bird all strolled around the courtyard. Vigrod motivated his troops. They made axes and swords, they made siege weapons, and they cared for their horses.

The four of them walked outside to see soldiers sparring and being trained. Vigrod, Brodir, and the Wolf Lord walked up to the ramparts while the Dark Bird stayed outside with his men.

"A one hundred and fifty-five thousand warriors prepared to take all that is ahead of us," Vigrod said. "Are you sure these elves will actually do what you think they will?" the Wolf Lord said.

"If we force them, then yes," Vigrod replied.

The three of them remained quiet for a bit, then Vigrod broke the silence, "So how is it back on Drangar?" Vigrod asked.

The Wolf Lord sighed. "It's tough. The smaller clans are raiding each other, and food is starting to become scarce, but we aren't there just yet," the Wolf Lord said.

"We need to take Yrfel for them," Vigrod said.

The Wolf Lord replied with a nod.

"We are nearly ready to attack by the look of things," Brodir said.

It had been about two weeks since all the troops arrived, and they were in the middle of November.

"Yes, we are, I'd say another day of preparation, and we will be ready to go," Vigrod said.

One of the elders caught Vigrod's attention and approached him. "Highlord, a message for you," he said.

"It's from one of the villages to the eastern side of the Frostlands," Vigrod replied.

Vigrod opened the message and read. "It says that humans are staying there and are threatening to kill them if they try to leave."

"I will not tolerate this disrespect. Gather a thousand men. We leave immediately," Vigrod said.

They used horses to ride out there quickly, and the town was only a few hours away from Ravenhall.

The sun set, and they were right outside the town.

"Kill every last one of them!" Vigrod yelled, and they charged into the town.

The humans gathered their forces outside and tried to hold their ground, but the Vikings swept through them. Groups of Vikings went inside buildings, pulled the humans from their beds, and drove axes through their skulls.

Vigrod, Brodir, and a few other Vikings went to the inn at the center of town, and they opened the doors and were greeted by a dozen or so humans staring at them. The humans stood up and drew their swords. Vigrod ran in and killed the first human, and the rest followed behind him. The humans couldn't stand the wrath of Vigrod and his men. Blood was spilled over the tables and on the floors.

Vigrod pushed the last human to the ground and put his axe to the man's throat.

"Why have you come here!" Vigrod yelled.

"We were sent here on Nathan's orders to watch and wait for your army to leave," the man said, struggling.

"You are going to stay with us," Vigrod said.

He asked his men to keep an eye on their captive, and then Vigrod saw, out of the corner of his eye, the innkeeper come out of hiding from behind his bar.

"Have you got them all?" he asked.

"I believe so, my friend," Vigrod said, still staring at the human, not taking his eyes off him.

"Thank you, Highlord. Please stay the night, drink, and eat in my house, please," the innkeeper said.

"We would be honored," Vigrod said.

They threw the human bodies outside the town and buried the few Viking bodies, and then they all gathered in the inn.

Vigrod walked to the bar and then politely asked the innkeeper to move out of the way. Vigrod got on top of the bar table and looked at all his soldiers who were snugly fit inside the large inn.

"Men and women of Drangar!" he yelled. "A great victory was claimed here tonight! Now we eat and drink under the roof of our gracious innkeeper. Tomorrow is the day you have all been waiting for. We march for High Yrfel!" Vigrod said.

All his soldiers cheered in excitement. Vigrod was also very excited because he was one step closer to becoming the king of all Yrfel.

18

THE SHROUDED'S PLAN

Nathan was woken by his adviser at Nathan's request the night before. He got dressed in his fancy cloths, and he donned his fur cloak and went to see Commander Aegis for the night before. When they talked, he asked Nathan to come in the morning.

He entered through the tunnel at the foot of the mountain and came into the courtyard, where he saw many members turn toward him and salute. Nathan walked into the commander's quarters, where inside, he was waiting for him.

"My king," the commander said.

"Hello, Commander," Nathan replied.

"I have asked for your presence this morning to tell you of our plan to defend High Yrfel."

"Very good. Tell me," Nathan said.

Aegis signaled for his king to sit, and then he began to speak, "We've been working our alchemist's day and night to make more handheld fire," he said.

"Our plan is to use the old mountain paths to flank around and surprise Drangar launching all handheld fire," Aegis said.

"I like your plan. Is it possible to have some of my men defend you while you traverse the paths?" Nathan asked.

"If they can be quiet, remember, this is supposed to be a surprise attack," Aegis said.

"Very well," Nathan said.

They sat in silence for a moment. Then Aegis finally broke the silence.

"What if we let them into our city? We draw them in, and we can use the mountain paths to ambush them,"

Nathan liked this plan. He agreed to it.

"But what of the citizens?" Nathan asked.

"We could have them evacuate the city," Aegis said.

"But where will they go?" Nathan asked him.

"They will just have to go to the far edge of the mountain range, guarded by a few men," Aegis said. "A good plan. I doubt they will search the far reaches of the mountains," Nathan replied.

Nathan left, going through the courtyard, and backed out to the secret tunnel where he came from and then walked back to High Yrfel.

Tymirial greeted him upon his return, and he greeted him back, then Nathan then requested the rest of his council.

"I have spoken with Aegis, and we plan to lure them inside the city and use the old mountain paths to ambush them," Nathan said.

"I will get my men up there whenever you request," Aedric said.

Nathan nodded back.

Nathan called the meeting and walked off with Tymirial down to the mage's tower in the village of High Yrfel.

"I haven't been here in quite a while," Nathan said.

Upon entering, Nathan was greeted by a large circular bookcase, and all the books had a small blue aura around them. In the center of the room sat one large book on a pedestal, emitting blue and purple from its pages. Directly above that was a large chandelier, and on the upper levels of the tower is where all the mages' quarters were.

"Why is the book glowing like that?" Nathan asked.

"It is where we draw our power from, our source, a direct connection to the well, the realm of magic," Tymirial answered.

"I don't understand, so a god lives in this realm you speak of, and grants you power?" Nathan said.

"Yes, he gave the first of the mages this very book, and we channeled this power through our staffs," Tymirial answered.

"Have you ever been there? The well," Nathan asked.

"No, but eventually, when I die, my soul will live on there, and it will become a source for mages to draw power from," Tymirial said.

Nathan had a look of confusion on his face. Magic and magical realms were just things he couldn't really comprehend.

Nathan and Tymirial made their way to the ramparts, and they were welcomed by all the archers lined along the walls.

"Where do you think my father is?" Nathan said somberly.

"In Aella's realm, I'm sure. Based on what I have heard, it is quite nice there," Tymirial said.

Nathan found comfort in that, but when the battle came, he hoped he would not be seeing his father when it was all said and done.

NATURE'S PREPARATION

Kolvar was out at the archery range, shooting Eldrin's bow, accompanied by Aerimir. Kolvar knocked an arrow, drew it back, and then focused on the target. The world seemed to slow down, the birds chirped slowly, and the trees waved back and forth slowly. Kolvar let the arrow go, and the arrow picked up so much speed it started to whistle. It hit the bull's-eye with a loud thump, and half the arrow was inside the target.

"Amazing. Some enchantment or something had to have been put upon it," Kolvar said. "It is under no enchantment but its own," Aerimir replied.

Kolvar knocked another arrow and aimed in the same place. He drew and let it loose. Again, it whistled as it went, and when it hit the target, it split the previous arrow in two, right down the middle.

"I am not the greatest archer, but I have a feeling this is making me a better one," Kolvar said.

"Perhaps, but we best talk to the Ashwalkers soon," Aerimir replied, picking up an arrow from Kolvar's quiver.

The two of them walked out of the city and to the forest of Ashbeard. Descending into the forest and into a clearing, Kolvar grabbed the horn off his belt and blew into it. The booming sound that came from the horn echoed for miles. Kolvar and Aerimir waited for the Ashwalkers to arrive.

The loud stomping sounds surrounded them, and the Ashwalkers came from all directions out of the woods.

"Kolvarrrrrr, you have requested usssss," the Ashwalker said, lowering his head down toward Kolvar.

"I have. The reason I have called for you all is to inform you of what is to come." A storm has been brewing, and soon, a battle will occur, and if my hand is forced, you all must be ready," Kolvar said.

"Of courseeeeee," the Ashwalker said. "I do not know what preparations you must make, but I would make them," Kolvar replied.

"Will Ashbeard himself fight?" Kolvar asked.

"I do not know. We only do what he asksssss," it replied.

"Can you take me to him? I would like to talk to him," Kolvar asked.

"I am afraid I cannot do that Lord Kolvar. Ashbeard would not approve of such a thinggggggg," the Ashwalker said.

Kolvar replied with a shrug, and then he and Aerimir left the clearing and made their way back to the Elder Branch.

It was about midday when the two returned. Kolvar called his council for a meeting in the war room.

"Thank you all for coming. I have gathered you all here to plan our preparations for the battle to come," Kolvar said.

"I would like to start by asking, how many men do we have, Rion?" Kolvar asked.

"Roughly one hundred and fifty thousand, but I have communicated with a few different people back home, and they are willing to send reinforcements," Rion replied.

Kolvar nodded. "Very good. I don't believe we will require any reinforcements. In other words, I have thought of a plan. I say we go to Lokfur's wall on the border of the Greenlands." Kolvar paused briefly. "I know it is a bit run down, but we have the resources to rebuild it, and I would like to have men stationed somewhere in the eastern lands to let us know when the battle is beginning."

"A fine plan, my lord. When shall we go to Lokfur's wall?" Thaedra asked.

"Within the next week, I would like to be there, Rion. Will you see to it that men are sent out to the easterner's land? With enough food and a messenger bird or two," Kolvar said.

"It will be done, my lord," Rion said, then standing up and bowing to Kolvar and exiting the room.

20

DRANGAR'S MARCH

The day had finally arrived. Every single Viking was gathered outside Ravenhall. Vigrod was on his horse at the front of his army, about to give his speech before they started a month-long journey across Yrfel. Vigrod wanted them to go through the middle of Yrfel instead of around.

"You all have been waiting for this moment. I feel I should say something profound, but you all know why you are here." He paused and raised his fist. "To the start of our great conquest!" Vigrod yelled.

All his soldiers cheered back, and Vigrod lifted his axe and pointed forward, and off they went.

Vigrod rode proudly at the front of the army. The Wolf Lord and Brodir were at his sides. Vigrod's army contained thousands of soldiers, a third of that was calvary, and they brought siege equipment with them, a large battering ram with the head of a bear.

The days slowly came and went. All the horses and people slowed them down, but the journey wasn't a drag. The moral of every soldier was good, Vigrod noticed.

Later that night, the wind started to pick up. The snow blew in their faces and unsettled the horses. Vigrod sat in his tent, and the whole tent started to sway back and forth. The entrance to the tent was blowing back and forth fiercely, annoying Vigrod.

He looked up at the roof of his tent. As he was slowly drifting off to sleep, he started letting his thoughts run wild. He imagined standing at High Yrfel, holding Nathan's head, and he threw it down into the crowds below. Vigrod walked down a pathway and got on to his dire wolf, which he found in the Frostlands in a cave. The dire wolf was gray and white with dark blue eyes and was larger than a horse. He rode over to a house and walked inside. There sat a woman and two boys. The woman walked up to Vigrod and wrapped her hands around him. She then took a step back and pushed Vigrod onto the floor. He then fell into an abyss of black.

He was woken up to the site of Brodir standing over him. Vigrod walked outside and called for a dozen men to pack his tent up. Vigrod's horse was brought to him. He climbed up on his horse and waited a few minutes with the Wolf Lord and Brodir.

The army was mobilized, and they were off again. They were three days into the journey, and they were out of the Frostlands and out into the plains.

The afternoon sun arrived, and Vigrod strolled at the front. He felt the wind against his face, and he watched as the grass and trees waved back and forth. Birds flew overhead. Vigrod took notice of them, and he stared at them. As the flock came closer, Vigrod saw the red ribbons tied at their feet.

"Our little flock has returned," Vigrod said.

"What's that?" Brodir asked.

"Those birds that I sent out some time ago, it seems they are returning to Ravenhall," Vigrod said.

"Why did you even send those out, if you don't mind me asking?" the Wolf Lord said.

"Just in spite of Nathan, I suppose," Vigrod replied, shrugging his shoulders.

The traveling went a bit faster since the army was out of the Frostlands. Even though the environment didn't affect them much individually, the army slowed everyone down. A few more days came and went, and they came up to the Hall of the Lords.

Vigrod stopped the army and got off his horse. "What is it, Highlord?" the Wolf Lord asked.

"I would like to pay my respects. Tell the army to set up camp. We will stay in the area for the day," Vigrod said.

Vigrod pushed the doors open and walked inside, closing the doors behind him. He walked up to his father's statue and sat down on the floor in front of it.

"Soon, this will all be over. All of Yrfel will be mine, just know that I did it for you, Father," Vigrod said, staring at the blank eyes of Rhagnar's statue.

Vigrod stuck around for a minute or so longer. He walked back outside and started helping his soldiers set up tents and such.

The next day, the army started early and trudged along for hours on end, going until they could see the sun setting behind them. A week passed for them traveling on the road from the hall to High Yrfel, the lord's road the easterners called it.

"Here we are," Vigrod said.

Vigrod ordered for them to set up camp. They were a mile or two away from the front gate of High Yrfel, but it was still in view from there soon to be camp site.

Vigrod called for a gathering of all the high-ranking people in his army. "I have come up with a plan. While we were on the road, I want our best scouts to go into the mountain range from the far side away from High Yrfel and map it out," Vigrod said. "Then a force of ten thousand men, led by Brodir, will find another way into High Yrfel while the main force keeps the easterners occupied," he added.

"Surely, there will be a gate around the back side of High Yrfel," Brodir said.

"If ten thousand people cannot break a gate down, a gate that will be most disappointing, take a battering ram. We have three," Vigrod replied.

"Now get these scouts going. Tell them they have as much time as we need. We won't be going anywhere," Vigrod added.

21

LOKFUR'S WALL

Kolvar and the Elven army had been held up at Lokfur's wall for the past few days, watching their borders and waiting for a message from their scouts in the mountain range.

Lokfur's wall was constructed under the orders of Lokfur Keawynn, who at the time was Lord of the Elder Branch. They built it years before the first war. When just the Elves inhabited Yrfel, the wall itself took years to build; after all, it did stretch from one end of the island to the other.

The wall was refurbished by the elven builders, patching up the holes and such, making a large wooden door to prevent anyone from just walking into their lands, and it was now stationed by thousands of soldiers.

Kolvar stood along the ramparts, along with Commander Rion and Thaedra, when a soldier approached Kolvar with a letter.

"From our scouts in the eastern lands, my lord," he said, handing over the letter and then bowing to Kolvar.

"Thank you," Kolvar said, giving the soldier a nod. He opened the letter and read.

Lord Kolvar,

The Vikings have arrived. They have set up camp a good distance away from the gates of High Yrfel. The battle will be beginning within the coming days.

"The Vikings have arrived and are camped a distance away from High Yrfel," Kolvar said, relaying the message.

"What does that mean for us, my lord?" Thaedra asked.

"Nothing yet. I would like us to stay out here until their fight has concluded to ensure safety. But if our hand is forced, then it will mean something," Kolvar said.

"How will they force our hand?" Rion chimed in.

"If they come to close to the wall for my liking, then we will make our move," Kolvar replied.

Kolvar then walked down the stairs behind them, leading down to the camp. The camp they set up was like a town of its own, tents of green and yellow cloth stretching as far as the eye could see, and of course, Kolvar's tent was set up in the very middle.

The three Elves walked inside their makeshift war room, which was just a large tent set up close to Kolvar's. All the tent contained was a table with the map of Yrfel on it and seats all around.

Kolvar, Rion, and Thaedra walked in to find the rest of the war council already inside although Kolvar had not called for a meeting.

"I have not requested a meeting, I suppose, but since you are all here, I would like to discuss some things with all of you," Kolvar said.

He got his responses in nods and bows.

"The Vikings have arrived in High Yrfel, and the battle will be commencing soon," Kolvar said "Has the wall been rebuilt to its former glory?" he added.

"Down in this area, the walls are fully rebuilt, but toward the western side, our builders are still working their way down there, my lord," Ailvyr, commanding officer of the elven builders, replied.

"Is the army organized, Rion?" Kolvar asked.

"It is, my lord. Everyone is accounted for, and the horses are well-fed," Rion replied.

"Very good," Kolvar said. "Well, that is all I wanted to ask. Now all we have to do is wait."

22

THE CALM BEFORE
THE STORM

When the traveling was all said and done and their few days of camping, it was December twentieth, of the fifth summer, and the sixth summer would soon be upon them.

They left their camp where it was just to bring the injured back when the battle was over. Vigrod was riding over to Brodir.

"My friend," Vigrod said, giving him a firm pat on the back.

"Highlord," Brodir replied.

"Your first command, how does it feel?" Vigrod asked.

"I feel a bit nervous, but no matter," Brodir said.

"It's good that you are nervous. The nerves will keep you alive," Vigrod said, giving Brodir a nod, then riding off to join the main force.

Brodir's force of ten thousand then trotted off to the north to get to the far side of the mountains. The path that the scouts found would take Brodir's army about a half hour to get to the gates of High Yrfel.

Vigrod and his army waited about an hour to really make sure that Brodir and his company were there. Vigrod commanded his army to come with him. The battle was about to begin.

They slowly approached the gates of High Yrfel, and then Vigrod noticed something.

"Is no one up there?" Vigrod said.

"I think so. What is it they mean to do?" the Wolf Lord replied.

"Wait, do you hear that?" Vigrod said.

"Is that screaming?" he added.

"Shoot up the flare!" the Wolf Lord yelled out.

The one archer they had had his arrowhead lit up and shot it up toward where Brodir and his company were.

Before the battle started, the plan was that Vigrod and his army would shoot a flare-up, and eventually, they would receive the same reply.

"Quickly, get the battering ram up here!" Vigrod yelled.

The battering ram was grabbed up off a cart, and it was run up to the gate. Two dozen men hit the gate repeatedly till it fell over, and Vigrod ordered them quickly to follow him into the city.

They followed the path over to where the screaming was. All the men and women on foot were still filling in, following the people on horses.

The army arrived at a horrific scene. The eastern army was charging Brodir's force. Meanwhile, bottles were being thrown down at them from the mountains, which instantly enveloped whatever it hit in the fire.

"Charge!" Vigrod yelled.

They completely forgot the plan and rushed to Brodir's aid. Vigrod rode headfirst, axe held high, ready for what was to come.

The Viking army rode in, being followed by all the Infantry on foot. The eastern army was in the middle of an ambush on Brodir's force by the time they arrived.

Vigrod rode out onto the path to regroup with Brodir's force, trying to avoid the fire and swords. Riding his horse hard, he finally got over to them, riding into a sea of steel armor, swinging his axe around, taking multiple eastern soldiers out. Vigrod tried to get out, but the eastern soldiers were starting to surround him, and his horse was shot from a distance. He fell, hitting the ground hard and trying to get back up.

Vigrod looked up and started bear-crawling away until he eventually got up onto his feet. He fended off several soldiers until a few soldiers on horses finally came to his aid. Vigrod turned to see a great site, thousands and thousands of Viking soldiers running into the fray.

Vigrod stood in awe as his army ran to help Nathan's army. Vigrod noticed that the eastern army was receding back toward the mountains. Vigrod ran up to the large pack of Viking soldiers and called for them to hold where they were.

The fire had stopped being thrown at them; it had already claimed thousands of Vikings alone. The Viking army was all held up in a large clump in the middle of an open area surrounded by mountains.

Suddenly, a few hundred yards away from them, Nathan's army reappeared, reorganized.

"Walk with me now! Slowly!" Vigrod yelled out. He led the way as they crept closer and closer to the eastern army. "Infantry in the front, cavalry behind!" Vigrod yelled.

He stood alone while his army started to form itself.

"Is this how it's going to end!" a voice yelled out across them.

Vigrod instantly recognized it as Nathan's.

"It is!" Vigrod yelled back.

"Are you ready to die!" Nathan yelled.

Nathan's army cheered for him. Vigrod needed to hear no more, he turned back to his army.

"This may be our last day in this world. Let's make it a good one!" Vigrod yelled out.

The army cheered back.

He turned back around and pointed his axe at Nathan.

"Charge!" he screamed at the top of his lungs, and the battle was truly about to begin.

23

THE BATTLE BEGINS

The world seemed to slow down. The two armies ran at each other, screaming, with weapons held high in the air. When they finally collided, a large sound erupted from the mountains that stretched for miles.

Steel collided with steel, and the immense bloodshed had started to cover the gray ground and started to turn it red. Bodies started falling and piling up, and the two armies pushed back and forth against each other, fighting for the ground and their lives.

Vigrod was at the front. His army was armed with axes and swords, and they pushed against the stiff shields of the eastern men.

The Viking force pushed and stabbed, breaking down the eastern line. Some of the Vikings tripped over the eastern bodies as they continued to push back against them. The two armies were locked with each other, pushing back and forth for quite some time. Every few minutes, the momentum would shift back and forth. Both sides were motivated to beat the other.

Vigrod started to tire. He couldn't think of a way the battle would end.

"We hold here!" he yelled out breathlessly. "We back up as one! Now!" he added, with their weapons held up, backing up slowly, trying to avoid all the bodies, which were in small piles.

Vigrod just thought about how he had not seen Brodir. He started to worry. What if he was dead, for he had no idea. He tried to focus, but the thought was looming in the back of his mind while his army was held up. The eastern army stood their ground while the Vikings slowly crept back.

"Vigrod!" someone yelled out.

Vigrod looked back to see the Wolf Lord walking toward him, going around all the soldiers.

"What is it?" Vigrod asked while staring down toward the eastern army.

"Brodir, he had been found," he replied.

Vigrod quickly snapped his head to look at him. "Where, where is he?" he said with a concerned look on his face.

"He is hurt. He is being tended too, but he is being brought back to the camp," he said.

"Damn it, is it serious?" Vigrod said.

"He has multiple burns. Even his icy skin could not hold off the type of fire they were using. There is a chance he may survive," the Wolf Lord said.

"Thank Thalmer," Vigrod replied.

Vigrod was now even more motivated to win this battle and Yrfel as a whole. He felt the whole world was against him, and he knew somehow, he could win.

"Back, fall back to the camp!" Vigrod yelled.

Quickly, Vigrod's remaining army ran and rode back out into the open. Vigrod looked back as they were running. They were safe for the time. He could only wonder what Nathan was planning.

"Quickly! Come on!" Vigrod yelled, trying to motivate his army, but he didn't feel it had any effect. They got out into the open, running out of the front gate of High Yrfel, passing the castle and the mage's tower. They went out to the left side of the gate, getting ready to get the eastern army to the Greenlands.

"Hurry, form a line! Infantry in the front, cavalry in the back!" Vigrod yelled out.

The army shuffled quickly about, trying to form a half-decent formation. The line was formed, not very organized, but it was decent enough for Vigrod's standards.

Vigrod and his army sat quietly. He listened for any sounds at all, but in the distance, he heard hooves moving rather fast.

"Here they come!" Vigrod said.

Suddenly around the gates poured out thousands of eastern cavalries charging around the corner toward them.

"For Drangar!" Vigrod yelled, pointing his axe at the sea of horses charging toward them.

The two armies clashed. Vigrod avoided the horses charging at him and tried to pick off the soldiers on the ground. He kept trudging through, trying to keep his head, but the sea of horses had no end in sight.

As the day went on, the battle rolled on as they crept toward the Greenlands, toward the ever-growing wall on the borders. Vigrod had kept pushing forward. He had not seen Nathan the whole day, and the sun was starting to set.

Vigrod cut down man after man. The whole head of his axe was bloodied, dirt, and sweat covered his face. Even though they still had been pushing the eastern army toward the Greenlands, the mages had been a problem for them. There were several of them. Vigrod couldn't count how many. He had nearly caught a bolt of lightning to his head.

He looked to the side to see bolts of lightning flying everywhere and men screaming. Vigrod made his way over, trying to avoid anyone. He saw his men trying to get one of the mages, but this one had fought his men off with ease. With no hesitation, he charged in. Bringing his axe back over his head, he released it, putting everything behind it. It flew straight for the mage, and it was buried deep in the man's chest. A few straggling bolts of lightning crept from man to man.

The staff left the mage's hand. He fell to his knees, and his eyes started to glow with a large burst of light. Vigrod was blinded, and a shockwave emerged from the mage's body. When he came to, Vigrod was on his back, and everyone close was as well. He stood up and ran over to where the mage was. He looked down to see nobody, just the robes that he was wearing and his axe on top of them.

He picked up the axe and staring down at the sight of the empty robe. Looking up, there stood Nathan, just a few feet away from him. Nathan walked over to Vigrod. Vigrod was confused about what he was doing. Nathan then pushed Vigrod out of the way. Vigrod watched as Nathan fell to his knees and buried his head in the mage's robe. He could hear him crying. Vigrod stood and watched, doing nothing. Not even the men around him did anything.

Nathan stood up and looked at Vigrod. "The closest person I have to family on this island gone because of you," Nathan said, shrugging his shoulders.

Vigrod said nothing. He just waited for Nathan to do something, but he did nothing. He just stood and stared at Vigrod.

"I saw something in a dream," Vigrod said.

"What was it?" Nathan said somberly.

Vigrod could tell that killing that mage had taken the fight out of Nathan. Vigrod felt guilty.

He had to kill the mage, but he was a dear friend to Nathan.

"I was standing right up there," Vigrod said, pointing back to the castle of High Yrfel, which was barely in view now. "I was holding your head," Vigrod said.

"Were you now?" Nathan asked.

Vigrod nodded. "How about instead, I kill you now, remove your head from your shoulders, and mount it on a spike somewhere?" Nathan said, pointing a sword at Vigrod.

Vigrod did nothing, just stood with his axe at the ready. Nathan slowly walked toward him. Nathan quickly struck at Vigrod. Vigrod blocked it but had to watch out for the other sword Nathan had.

No one else did anything around the two of them. Nathan and Vigrod were locked in combat, going blow for blow, and one could not outdo the other.

The sun was now set, and only the light of the moon shone upon them. Vigrod had his army surround Nathan's, forming a large wall, blocking them from getting back to High Yrfel.

"Get a few men back to the camp to gather supplies. I want barricades made and everyone to be watchful. No one shall get past us," Vigrod said to a group of soldiers.

Nathan had taken his army further toward the Greenlands. They had set up a small camp and made a few fires.

"What are we to do?" Commander Aedric asked, the man who, during the battle of Ravenhall, fought Vigrod himself, lost, and was badly injured but has since recovered.

"Tonight, we stay here. These trees will provide us with some cover," Nathan said.

The humans were held up in a forest-like area, but they were not yet in the Greenlands.

"We have no supplies and no food," Aedric said.

"I do not know what to do," Nathan said nervously.

"We cannot go at them, that is for sure. Surely, there are some beasts around," Aedric said.

"If you say anything you can find then, birds, beasts, it matters not. Split it up however you can, but set the rest on watch," Nathan replied.

Aedric bowed and left and went away into the dark.

*****

Kolvar was awoken by the sound of people bustling around. He walked out of his tent to see men in armor walking up to Lokfur's wall.

"You there," Kolvar said, grabbing one of the passing soldiers on the arm. "What is happening?" he asked, letting go of the man's arm.

"Commander Rion has told us that the battle has arrived and to get to the gates and wait for you, my lord," the soldier said. "I see," Kolvar said, turning back and walking into his tent.

Grabbing his armor off the stand, he began to put it on, piece by piece, and tightening the straps. Kolvar's armor was quite exquisite, gilded steel, just like any other elf, minus the helmet, but with a large tree sigil on the breastplate. Picking up his sword, which was laid on a table next to his bed, and then putting it around his waist.

Going up the stairs to the top of Lokfur's wall, he found Commander Rion and Thaedra already there.

"Lord Kolvar," Rion said, both him and Thaedra giving a bow.

"Commander, Thaedra," Kolvar replied.

Kolvar turned and looked out toward High Yrfel, and there, just a couple hundred yards away, were both Vigrod and Nathan's armies, continuing their fight from the previous night.

"So they have finally arrived. Can't say I expected anything else," Kolvar said.

"Well, my lord, what are your orders?" Rion asked.

"Get the men outside the gates. I will be down in a moment," Kolvar said.

"At once, my lord," Rion said with a slight smile, hurrying off down the stairs, where the large line of elves waited for him, which seemed to stretch on for miles.

"Will you be fighting with us?" Kolvar asked.

"I will not be my lord unless you say otherwise," Thaedra said.

"Very well. You can stay or return to the Elder Branch if you wish," Kolvar replied.

"I would mean to stay," Thaedra said.

Kolvar responded by reaching out and hugging Thaedra. "In case I never see you again, you have been a true friend, Thaedra," Kolvar said.

"Likewise, my lord," Thaedra said.

"Goodbye, my friend, until our next meeting," Kolvar said, patting Thaedra on the soldier and walking down back to the camp.

Kolvar's horse was brought to him. He then rode outside the gates, where his army was waiting for him. All set up in a formation, rows upon rows of elven soldiers.

Kolvar turned to his soldiers. "People will remember this day for ages to come, the day that the elves of the grove took Yrfel! So with me now, let us finish what is set out before us!" Kolvar said, pointing out toward the ongoing battle.

"Charge!" Kolvar yelled, and off they went into the fray.

24

THE BATTLE CONTINUES

Vigrod was leading his forces against the eastern host when something caught his eye. Backing away and taking his focus away from the battle for just a moment, looking up, he saw thousands and thousands of horses riding in the distance, swords high.

"Everyone! Fall back!" he yelled, and his army started to scatter around.

They got a bit of distance between Nathan and the rest of the east. The easterners stood their ground, but they realized what was behind them all too late. Seconds later, the elven army pounced on the eastern army, and then Vigrod took his army back into the fray.

The real fight was beginning, the greatest war on Yrfel for many a year. The battle raged on for hours on end. The sun was high in the sky, and the fighting continued. Vigrod found this fight difficult from all the others. Every way he looked, someone was trying to kill him. He could only get a second's rest when an elf or a human didn't look his way.

Vigrod noticed Nathan from a distance. He saw his opportunity to take out his enemy, and he went to make his move. He charged toward Nathan, picking up speed, and Nathan didn't realize it until it was too late. Vigrod tackled Nathan and pinned him to the ground. Nathan quickly reacted by punching Vigrod in the jaw and shoving him off to the side.

The two of them stood up and stared at each other. Kolvar then suddenly rode in from the side, getting off his horse, and the horse then bolted away.

"Well, here we all are," Kolvar said.

Vigrod and Nathan said nothing. They just waited for someone to do something.

Nathan made a swift move toward Vigrod, a high strike toward the head that Vigrod easily blocked. Kolvar went for Nathan's side, which he blocked with his second sword.

The three of them were locked in combat. None could outdo the other, swing after swing, parry after parry, just continuously draining the energy out of each other. Vigrod went for Kolvar, and the two of them went for each other while Nathan hung back, waiting for an opportunity to strike. Kolvar almost got Vigrod with a low slash to his leg, but Vigrod jumped over the attack and got hold of Kolvar's arm. Vigrod noticed, out of the corner of his eye, Nathan running back in to try to finish him off. So quickly, he threw Kolvar with all his remaining strength at Nathan.

Nathan felt all the force of Kolvar landing on top of him. Nathan shoved Kolvar off him and then backed away, looking back to see the circle that was created around them. It was like the battle was completely halted for the three of them.

Seconds had passed after the three of them stopped glancing at the sight of hundreds of thousands huddled around them. Once again, the three were locked in combat. Nathan was going for Vigrod, pushing against him relentlessly. Kolvar joined in on the fun, kicking Vigrod in the stomach and swinging for Nathan's head.

Suddenly, Kolvar backed away from Nathan, taking enough steps away to be safe for the time being. He then grabbed the horn of wood from his belt and blew into it. The sound that was emitted from the horn blew loud and clearly. It stretched on for miles.

Everyone stared at Kolvar in awe, for they had no idea what he just did, save the elves. The whole field was silent. Hundreds of thousands of people stood in silence, waiting for something to happen. A minute or so later, there was a sound of rumbling in the distance. The Vikings and easterners all started panicking, but the elves and Kolvar stood still calmly.

A voice out in the crowd let out a scream, and there they were. The Ashwalkers had arrived in full force. Instantly, the Vikings and Humans dashed to find somewhere safe, but there was ultimately no escape. For once the Ashwalkers got to the battle, there was no escape. The fighting had also started again. The elves fought with the Ashwalkers, but there was really no fighting back.

The three lords still stood in a triangular formation. All three of them, staring at the Ashwalkers, causing chaos around them.

"I never thought they were real," Nathan said.

Vigrod just shrugged his shoulders. They nearly forgot why they were there and were completely caught in the wonder of the ancient beasts.

They said no more, Nathan pointed a sword directly at Vigrod's heart, and they were again fighting.

The day was coming to an end, and the battle was still raging on. The Ashwalker still terrorized the humans and Vikings, and the three lords were still battling. One could simply not out due the other. They were perfect matches for each other, but it would only take one mishap.

Vigrod was pressing Nathan, bringing his axe over top of his head and bringing it down with all his strength. Nathan blocked the strike, but it knocked him to the ground. Vigrod then quickly went to Kolvar, grabbed him by his sides before he could react, and tossed him to the side. Before Nathan could get up, Vigrod was already standing over him again.

Vigrod picked Nathan up by his neck, lifting him high into the air. Nathan struggled, gasping for air. Vigrod held him there, just waiting until life was relinquished from his body. Nathan tried to punch Vigrod, hitting and kicking his stomach, but Vigrod was not fazed by it. Nathan was on his last legs. With all the strength he had left, he brought down his elbow on Vigrod's forearm, making sure to use some of his bracers. Vigrod winced in pain, backing away. Nathan fell to the ground, gasping for air.

Vigrod stood covering his wound, stumbling back, then falling to the ground, his head bouncing off the dirt. He looked to the sky into the deep blue sky. Then he saw no more.

DRANGAR'S RETREAT

Vigrod awoke to the sight of one of his soldiers standing over him. He picked his head
up to realize he was being carried in a ham-
mock. He looked down toward his wound. It was
wrapped in cloth. He could see the blue blood stain
showing through the white cloth.

"Where are we?" Vigrod asked, with a lot of
pain in his voice.

"We are out on the Rose Road, Highlord," one
of the men carrying him answered.

Vigrod was confused. Why would they go to
the complete western side of Yrfel?

"The Rose Road?" Vigrod said.

"Yes, Highlord, the army came to a consensus
that we would want to have a nice view on the way
home after a defeat," the man responded.

"Very good," Vigrod said, lying his head back, staring up at the sky. "What is your name, sir?" he added.

"My name is Rune, Highlord," he replied.

"A fine name," Vigrod said.

"Thank you, Highlord," Rune said.

Vigrod just gave a grunt of approval.

Night was upon them. They camped just off the side of the Rose Road. The border of the Frostlands was just ahead, but they wouldn't dare venture forth with tired bodies.

Vigrod was propped up on a rock and facing the ocean, looking out upon the calm waves. As he sat there, his thoughts started to run away, going all sorts of places. He thought back to his dream about Nathan, about his father, and about what his mother was doing back home.

Vigrod started to doze off, but eventually, the subtle sound of the wind and the night put him to sleep.

He opened his eyes, and he was in another place. Instead of being surrounded by the night, he was in a snowy place.

It was an empty place with the crescent moon high in the sky. The snow fell onto the already snow-covered ground. Vigrod stood up and looked around. The place was empty. Just a snow-covered plain, but he noticed something. He looked down, and his wound was gone. There was no sign of it any-where on his body.

"Hello!" he yelled out.

Vigrod was greeted by the sound of silence. While looking around, something caught his eye. There was a man walking toward him. Vigrod saw a silhouette in the distance.

Vigrod started to walk over toward him. When he finally came into view, Vigrod noticed the man was wearing very exquisite clothing and had a face he didn't recognize.

"Hello, friend," the man said.

"Who are you? And where am I?" Vigrod said quickly.

"My name matters not, but you are in the Viking heaven," the man said.

Vigrod took a step back. "I am dead!" Vigrod yelled out.

"No no no. Calm yourself," the man replied.

"Then how am I here?" Vigrod asked.

"Some people have the ability to dream of this place. Apparently, you do too," he responded.

"So this place is real," Vigrod said.

"So it is," the man replied.

Vigrod had a million questions. "When did you get here?" he asked.

"I died some time ago after the gray human rebellion," the man replied.

Vigrod didn't really know how to respond. He had a dumbfounded look on his face. The man just laughed and started to guide him toward something.

As they walked across the snow-covered plain, something came into view, an abnormally large hall in the distance. The top of the building seemed to scrape the sky.

"Thalmur's halls," Vigrod whispered.

"That is right," the man replied.

"Is my father there?" Vigrod asked sincerely.

"Find out for yourself," the man said, holding his arm out and putting the other around Vigrod's shoulder.

Vigrod felt something come over him. His eyes started to grow heavy. He tried to keep them open, fighting a great battle with his eyes, struggling, but all for not, his eyes closed.

26

THE DUST SETTLES

Nathan strolled around the battlefield, looking upon the thousands upon thousands of corpses. Nathan hated the stench of death, but over the past few days, he had gotten quite used to it.

It was a day after the battle. Nathan was still quite hurt in body and mind, but still, he was there with the shrouded to get rid of all the casualties of the battle.

The whole of the Shrouded was there. Only three hundred of them were there. They built large pyres, trying to stack all the bodies up. Nathan did not condone their actions, but it was the only option.

They built three hundred pyres. All three hundred stacked high with the fallen from the battle. Nathan stood in the center with Commander Aegis, also Commander Aedric, and a few of Nathan's personal guards.

"If you wouldn't mind, Commander, I would say some words over the fallen," Nathan said, looking at Aegis.

He simply nodded.

"I thank all of you for serving faithfully and laying down your lives for mine. We hope that we can keep you all in our thoughts, so your great sacrifice will never be forgotten."

Nathan thought about the Vikings and elves that were scattered around throughout each pyre. He said a little prayer for them and continued.

Nathan raised his hand in the air. The members of the Shrouded all lowered their torchers down into the thistles and weeds, and it lit ablaze. Commander Aegis then walked over with a torch to the last pyre and put his torch down below the wood until it caught fire, then walked back to Nathan.

Nathan awoke the next day and got dressed in all black. Today, they would be having a funeral for Tymirial. He walked out of the castle and down the hill to find all his people already gathered there.

Tymirial had affected multiple people's lives, from Nathan to his apprentices, to the soldiers, and to the common folk.

The mages approached Nathan at the foot of the hill. Together, they walked through the sea of people all in black. They made their way to the mage's tower and stopped outside the front door but just off to the left of the door was something Nathan had made just yesterday.

"It is a great tragedy that we are gathered here today, for a great friend was lost to us just a few days ago, Tymirial Lamarius. Tymirial was one of the greatest men I've ever met. I met him when I was young, and he had advised me every day since, helping me become the person I am today. I am sure, in some way. He had helped some of you, for Tymirial was the type of man that would put everything aside to help anyone he could." Nathan paused and looked at the large object covered in a large cloth right next to him. Nathan grabbed the cloth and pulled at it with some force, and it unveiled a large marble statue of Tymirial in a strong and proud stance.

"We will all miss you, Tymirial Lamarius. This cruel world took you away from us too soon. Now, please, a moment of silence," Nathan said, bowing his head.

In silence, they stood for two minutes. Not even the wind spoke.

*****

Kolvar Keawynn was out in the city of the Elder Branch, celebrating the victory they had just two days prior. Kolvar had decided that they would celebrate until the week was over, and the day was only Thursday.

All around could smell the strong wine, grape as pungent as ever, and the great foods, such as chicken, turkey, and elk. The people were happy, playing and singing songs to the tunes of the harp and flute.

Kolvar knew that the threat of Vigrod and Nathan was still present. They were greatly diminished, and the result had made the elves quite happy. Kolvar had never been to a party of this scale, not for many a year. All he did was walk, talk, eat, drink, and sing, which were quite enjoyable for him.

Aerimir approached Kolvar. "Enjoying another day of partying, my lord?" he asked with a slight laugh.

Kolvar took a sip of wine. "Why, yes, old friend, very much," he responded.

Kolvar spent the rest of the night with the most enjoyable company, soldiers and citizens alike, meeting new people and sharing stories, singing songs, and drinking the finest wine. Truly, elven parties were not to be missed.

*****

Vigrod awoke, and he was in his bed back at Ravenhall. When he gained control of himself, he looked down toward his wound. It no longer gave him any pain, yet it was still wrapped in cloth. He got out of bed and pushed open the door, the light hitting his eyes like a slap in the face. He stepped forward onto the walkway. Everyone who passed by him gave him a slight bow or a "highlord," with a nod.

He made his way down to the great hall, pushing the large doors open; he found inside an abundance of his army sitting and chatting.

Everyone inside's heads turned toward Vigrod immediately. "If you would all please come out to the courtyard," he said.

They all stood up and followed him out. Vigrod walked onto the ramparts.

"Everyone, gather round, for I have something to say!" he said.

People started to file in, and multiple were getting pushed out to the barracks.

"Although our loss was great, I would just like to say that I am sorry for letting you all down. I led you into lands unknown to some of you. And I hope you can find it within yourselves to forgive me," Vigrod said.

Some of Vigrod's army kneeled, but others did not. Others were not as forgiving as some. Many lost friends and some family in a battle that they did not completely understand. Vigrod took notice of this. He had no idea how he would win back their favor, but he knew he should do it sooner rather than later.

Vigrod cleared his throat. "But after all that fighting, I could use a drink!" he yelled loud enough to make sure all could hear.

He was met by a loud roar of cheers, but he looked around to see some of his army not cheering.

This scared Vigrod, for he didn't want there to be tension within the stronghold his father was responsible for.

Many casks of ale were brought up from their cellar, and they proceeded to drink deep into the long, dark night.

THE MANY KINGDOMS

Book 1

PART 2

PROLOGUE

E ver since the great defeat of the Vikings, just not that long ago, Vigrod Frostbane had grown sick of himself and didn't think himself a worthy leader. He declared that since their forces were so decimated, they would sail home back to Drangar to gather their strength and return later. Vigrod also thought that with all the tension after their last battle, he thought that letting all his army return home would be the best course of action.

All the warriors of Drangar were in the stronghold of Ravenhall, starting to move supplies to the frozen harbor. Meanwhile, Vigrod sat in his quarters, slumped in a chair next to a window, while the shadow of his almost seven-foot-tall figure loomed behind him. Then suddenly, the door opened, and Vigrod turned to look and see who was behind him, and there stood his longtime friend, Brodir Bothvar, who was still partially wrapped in cloth from his previous injuries, most of which had healed due to his cold and icy body.

"Highlord, we are to be leaving for home soon," Brodir said.

"Alright, Brodir. Hand me my axe, please," Vigrod said with obvious sadness in his voice.

Brodir took the great axe of Clan Frostbane off the wall and handed it to Vigrod. Vigrod looked at the axe he had inherited from his father. "I don't deserve this axe. I thought we would win that battle," he said. "My friend, those flaming trees destroyed nearly all our forces. Thalmur was not on our side."

It had been an entire month since the battle, and it was now January twenty-third of the sixth summer in the year three hundred one, and Vigrod was still dissatisfied with their loss.

Vigrod stood silently and put his axe on his back. He and Brodir started to walk toward the harbor. When they had reached the boat that they were to depart on, Vigrod saw the Dark Bird and the Wolf Lord on the boat, and the Wolf Lord went to greet Vigrod, and the Dark bird did not (he was, after all, blind and in a wheelchair). But Vigrod went to greet the old man.

With the raising of Vigrod's hand, soldiers raised the anchors, set their sails, and they were off to Drangar.

*****

Kolvar sat on his wooden throne, accompanied by Aerimir and Thaedra, when, suddenly, Rion strutted into the throne room with a joyful look on his face.

"My lord, a report has come in from our scouts in the north. Ravenhall is completely abandoned," he said proudly.

Kolvar responded with a dumbfounded look on his face and replied, "Abandoned? That doesn't seem like something Vigrod would do. Are there any signs that they still linger anywhere in the north?"

"The scouts have seen no trace of them," Rion said.

Kolvar saw this as an opportunity to gain a foothold in the north. All he had hoped for was that Nathan did not retain this information before him.

"Send five hundred men. Command them yourself. Capture Ravenhall for the west," Kolvar said.

"At once, my lord," Rion said, bowing low and leaving the throne room.

*****

Nathan was in his war room, studying the map of Yrfel, hoping a plan would come to mind. Then the door burst open, and Aedric stepped into the room.

"High King, our men in the Frostlands have just sent us a message. Ravenhall is completely abandoned," he said, holding up a letter.

"Well," Nathan said in a low tone, "that is something, isn't it? Leave it be. I would put up a fair amount of gold that Kolvar has figured this out before us."

Aedric had a confused look on his face. "Shall we do nothing, High King?" he asked.

"Would you question me?" Nathan replied, still in a low and now irritated tone.

"Of course, we shall do something. Take a few hundred men, capture the surrounding villages, and take them yourself so I do not have to see you in my halls," he said, raising his tone as he spoke.

"As you command, High King," Aedric said, leaving the room swiftly.

*****

In the month that followed the battle, three Shrouded scouts traveled to the island in the south, sent by Nathan to report anything going on there after Kolvar had brought it up during their meeting at the Hall of the Lords.

They had finished their month-long journey and were finally landing on the shores of the southern island (which had no proper name).

"Finally," one of them said, "how much food and water do we have left?"

"Enough for the return journey. We can't afford to eat anymore while we are here," another scout said.

The shores had been teaming with life, birds, beasts, trees. But when they walked further into the forest, they came out into a hill, and the life that they just walked by was completely gone. The land was completely bare, and there were gray humans as far as the eye could see.

There were giant holes in the ground and large wooden machines surrounding them. The scouts went to hide behind rocks to just look and see what was happening. They edged closer and closer to the gray humans, getting close enough to where they could see but far enough to where they were still safe.

"What do you think they are doing?" a scout said.

"Preparing," a scout replied.

"For what?" one of them asked.

"War."

RAVENHALL ABANDONED

Commander Rion led his group of Elves to Ravenhall, the abandoned stronghold in the north of Yrfel.

Rion had been a commander for the Keawynns for nearly seventeen years, but this command felt special to him. Being able to waltz into a stronghold that not even the easterners could take gave him a warm feeling.

The elves' journey was complete. They had reached Ravenhall after a brief two-week excursion, and the day was February 6 of the sixth summer.

Approaching Ravenhall, Rion looked from one end of the stronghold to the other.

"A few of you scale the walls and get this gate open. Then I want the entire stronghold searched. Our scouts say one thing, but our eyes can say another."

The commander stood atop the ramparts, looking out onto the frozen wasteland the Drangarians called home when one of his men came up to him.

"Commander, we have found someone. He got two of ours before we got to him. We found dozens of human prisoners in the dungeons below," he said.

"Take me to him. We will see to the other situation in a moment," Rion replied.

The soldier took Rion over to the barracks, which was more than half of the stronghold. It was like its own city, housing thousands upon thousands. Rion was introduced to the lone Viking that did not leave with the rest of his kin.

"What are you doing here?" Rion asked.

The Viking breathed heavily and spit a wad of blood onto the ground.

"The Highlord sent thousands of my people to their graves. I realized that this was not a Drangarian war but a Frostbane war, and I now refuse to follow him," the Viking answered.

"Was it only you that stayed behind?" Rion said.

"Yes, but plenty of my people share my views. They are bound by honor, but I am not. To what do I owe, Vigrod Frostbane?"

"Perhaps he can be of some use to us," Rion said, looking around at his soldiers and being met by nods of agreement.

"I will be of no use to you, elf. I fought your people too. Best not forget."

"Kill me. I would not be thrown in a cell," the Viking said, staring Rion directly in the eyes.

Rion stood in silence, trying to decide. "I killed two of yours. It is only fair you repay one of them," the Viking said, interrupting Rion's thinking.

Rion then unsheathed his sword and appreciated the whistling sound it made. He scanned the blade from top to bottom and shoved it right into the Viking's chest.

He pulled the sword from the man's torso and wiped it clean. "Bury our dead and throw this one in the sea. Then get comfortable. We are going to be staying here a long while."

2

THE VILLAGE IN
THE NORTH

Commander Aedric led his band of soldiers, capturing the surrounding villages of Ravenhall, demanding a tax and housing. After all, the villagers were refugees from Drangar and could not withstand the combat skills of fully trained knights of the east.

The company was down to about one hundred, and there was one more village that needed to be taken. Another day had passed, and the company had just passed the icy tomb of the long-dead ice giant, and the village was in sight. They traveled in the night so they would not be seen, but they did not need the element of surprise.

"A few more hours. It's not like these people will resist," said Aedric.

His mother and father had thought it would be great for their son to be named after two legends of history, but as Aedric grew older, it seemed to make him hated. He was talented with a sword, a spear, an axe, any weapon, and he was just as skilled at making those weapons, just like the people he was named after. Nathan had a sort of dislike for Aedric, for he felt that the name Aedric belonged to his family.

But none of his companions had disliked him. There really was not anything to dislike about him, nothing except his name.

The soldiers had reached the village, and they were greeted with open arms. They were all taken to the inn, which was quite large for a village so small.

"Come, my friends. Take off your helmets. You are all welcome here," said the innkeeper.

"We hereby declare that this village now belongs to Nathan Eastmoore!" Aedric yelled.

"Oh, the High King of the east could have come himself. I would have quite liked to meet him," the innkeeper said.

"You would not resist my decree?" Aedric questioned.

"No, no one here is a fighter, except Gunir over there. We are all just looking for a new opportunity here."

Aedric turned his head to the corner where the innkeeper was looking to see what looked to be a giant, and Aedric's jaw dropped to the floor.

"The great eagles were so large that they covered entire castles, and they were made by Aella herself, goddess of light," Gunir said. He had a very deep voice, and when he smoked his pipe and breathed out, there was much smoke.

"Am I dreaming?" Aedric said. "No, Gunir came to this inn one day and started sharing stories of the outside. He drinks our ale and smokes his pipe," the innkeeper said.

"You do know that the whole army of Drangar has fled back home?" Aedric asked.

"Oh yes, but as I am sure you have gathered, we have no correlation with the Highlord and his army, and them with us, we are just simple refugees," he said with a long sigh.

"Well, the king is welcome here. I invite him to drink our ale and eat our food."

"Your company may stay for a while, the inn holds one hundred, but the night is still young. Let us eat and drink our fill," the innkeeper added.

Aedric took off his helmet and set it on the table in front of Gunir, "So you are Gunir the Giant?" Aedric said.

"I am. Who are you, small one?"

"I am Aedric, commander of this company."

Gunir's eyes widened. "Aedric Eastmoore? I thought you were dead. You are the second Aedric, aren't you," Gunir said.

"No, that is just my name," Aedric said.

"I should have guessed. You don't have the black hair and blue eyes the Eastmoores do, and Aedric Eastmoore has been dead for years," Gunir said.

"Well, I hear you know much of our world," Aedric said.

"You would be correct. Would you like to hear something about this world?" Gunir asked.

"Tell me, tell me about the things outside Yrfel," Aedric said.

"Well, I could talk about the leviathan," Gunir said.

"The leviathan, have you seen it or something?" Aedric said.

"I have seen him, of course," Gunir said. "He lives far in the south, surrounded by large rocks, and there he dwells, eating the sea snakes that come near his home," Gunir said.

"Wouldn't he try to kill you?" Aedric asked.

"He did. That was until I fed him something."

And the two laughed.

"Wait," Aedric said. "How did you get to the leviathan's den?" Aedric asked.

"I sailed there, of course," Gunir said. "I built a very large ship, for I am quite a large being."

"I thought giants spoke in the old tongue. How do you know the common one?" Aedric asked.

"I learned it during my travels."

"Well, Gunir, I am going to join my company," Aedric said.

"Go, enjoy yourself, my lad," Gunir said with a smile.

The rest of the night, the group of eighty ate, drank, smoked, and sang until they fell on the floor sleeping.

PART 1

Drangar

1

HOME

The day was February thirteenth of the sixth summer, and three weeks had passed since Vigrod Frostbane and his army of Vikings had departed from Yrfel to their cold home of Drangar. The day of arrival was upon them. Drangar itself was just ahead.

Vigrod took a deep breath in.

"Here we are, home."

Brodir gave him a pat on the back. "It feels good to be back even though I seldom remember the place," he replied, and the two shared a laugh.

Although they both were born in the Frostbane's ancient home of Frosthaven, the two friends had spent most of their lives on Yrfel, both going over with their fathers when the first war started just over sixteen years ago, Vigrod being around four, and Brodir being about six.

They had docked on the harbor. The Frosthaven harbor was large enough for dozens of ships to dock. Once they had fully stopped, Vigrod stepped off the ship onto the dock, breathing in the fresh air—the air he had not breathed for some time.

He looked around, taking in the scale of the harbor, looking up and down as all the ships docked and they unloaded all their cargo. Walking up the dock itself onto the land and into the small town that had been placed just next to the dock, seeing the bleak Drangarian architecture gave Vigrod a sense of comfort. He truly felt at home again.

Helping everyone he could to get their supplies off the ships and helping the Dark Bird to get onto the land, Vigrod was bustling around, trying to make himself useful, but then he started to smell something, and it smelled like something was burning.

"Brodir," Vigrod said, "do you smell that?" Brodir paused for a moment.

"It smells like…smoke," he replied with a terrified look on his face.

When Vigrod turned to see what Brodir was looking at, his heart dropped down to his stomach, a cloud of smoke coming from Frosthaven.

"Get the women, children, and elderly back on the boats! All who are willing to defend Frosthaven with me now!" he screamed.

Frosthaven was just a few minutes' walk away from the harbor, and thousands of Drangarians raced across the snow-covered ground back to the ancient Frostbane home.

They reached the colossal gate of Frosthaven, which had been broken in. Rushing into the city, Vigrod noticed what was happening. He saw Vikings but without the icy-blue skin that he had, wearing dark gray. Vigrod was in shock at what he had been witnessing. He could seldom believe it. *The clan that had been banished to the mountains centuries ago by my forefathers. Is it truly them?* he thought to himself.

Vigrod rushed headfirst into the fray, finding a Viking with dark gray clothing on and planting his axe right into his back, saving the life of two young men.

"Are you two alright?" Vigrod asked them. They could only nod their heads. The two boys were no older than fifteen. "Hurry, get out of the city. Find me when this is over. Do you both understand?"

The boys nodded and ran off into the distance. Vigrod watched them as they did, making sure they were safe.

The battle did not last long. The Frostbane army was too overpowering compared to the mere couple thousand Vikings that had invaded Frosthaven.

The sun was setting, and the city was in ruin, blood, and debris everywhere. Vigrod went around, trying to help everyone he could, but he was looking for one person in particular, his mother.

"Has anyone seen Lady Frostbane?" he called out. "Has anyone seen my mother?" He was helping with some of the wounded when he heard a voice, "She took some of us into the great hall, Lord Frostbane. We have not seen her since."

Vigrod instantly rushed down the road, running to the steps at the foot of the great hall.

He pushed the large doors inward, being greeted with the most horrid sight he had ever seen in his life. Corpses were everywhere. The hall was stained with Drangarian blood.

"Mother!" Vigrod cried out. He heard no answer, calling again and again, still hearing nothing.

"Freja!" he screamed, and still, no answer.

Vigrod went over to the corpses spread throughout the great hall, looking at each face with sadness, yearning to find his mother. He then looked up to the large table at the back of the hall, and there was someone slumped in a chair in the center of the large horizontal table. Slowly walking over to it, he then saw his mother lying dead in the chair.

He let out a scream so loud it could've been heard in Yrfel, his last parent, that he had truly gotten to know, ripped away from him. Vigrod felt immense pain, first his father, now his mother.

"Highlord, are you alright? What has happened...? What has happened?" Brodir said.

"They killed her. My last parent, our last parent."

Freja Frostbane had been a mother to both Vigrod and Brodir. Brodir grew up without a mother and only a father. Before the two of them went to Yrfel, Freja was a mother to both.

Brodir walked over to Vigrod, stepping over the corpses and witnessing the horrid scene at the back of the hall. Brodir grappled Vigrod into a hug. Both were crying.

"I am sorry, brother. I am sorry," Brodir cried.

Vigrod noticed something else. There was a letter in his mother's hand, and the seal was something Vigrod had never seen. He opened it and read it aloud to Brodir.

"Welcome home, Frostbane. We have killed your mother. We have ruined your city. We have ruined your people. Drangar will burn and be born anew. I will come for you. You are not safe. Welcome home, Frostbane."

"I am at a loss for words, my friend," Brodir said.

"A blue letter, and there is no signature. This will be dealt with, but for now, we need to tend to our people and to her," Vigrod said, taking one last look at his mother.

MANY GOODBYES

A new day had risen on Drangar, and Vigrod and Brodir started their day with the funeral of Freja. They walked down to the shore of Drangar behind Frosthaven, carrying Freja, who was wrapped in cloth.

They had arrived at the shore, where the grave of Rhagnar was waiting for them. Setting her down on the lone birch tree, the two of them began to dig her grave. It only took them a moment to dig a grave big enough. Vigrod then picked up his mother and gracefully set her down.

Vigrod tried to say something, but he choked on his words and started to cry. Brodir comforted him but succumbed to tears all the same. They started to bury her instead of giving her the traditional Viking pyre. Vigrod found a little bit of peace in it.

Once the grave was filled, Vigrod grabbed a branch from the birch tree and placed it on the freshly placed dirt. Together in silence, the two stood while precious memories filled their heads while the wind blew and birds flew overhead.

*****

Vigrod and Brodir made their way to the main gate, where the two clans that had set out from Drangar to help them win Yrfel just a few months ago were preparing to leave.

"Ready to leave?" Vigrod asked.

"Almost. Our journey home will be long," the Wolf Lord said.

Vigrod and the Wolf Lord looked at each other, then hugged. In the past few months, they had been through a lot together, and they had become good friends.

"I wish you well on your travels. Goodbye, Ulfir."

Vigrod shed a few tears. Ulfir was the Wolf Lord's name. In fact, all the Wolf lords' names were Ulfir because it means Wolf in the Viking language, but they just preferred Wolf Lord. Brodir also said goodbye to the Wolf Lord.

Vigrod knelt in front of the Dark Bird and put a hand on his knee.

"Goodbye, my old friend," Vigrod said (they weren't actually very old friends, Vigrod just said that because the Dark Bird is old).

"Goodbye to you, young Vigrod. May your mother be welcomed into the heavens above," he said.

The Dark Bird then held out his hand. Vigrod grabbed his hand with both of his.

"Goodbye, my friends. If the enemy is at your gates, send a messenger."

Brodir also said goodbye, but it wasn't as sincere as Vigrod's, for they didn't talk too much.

Vigrod and Brodir stood side by side, watching their allies depart from Frosthaven, and it only took a few minutes before they completely vanished from view.

They were back inside Frosthaven, which in its current state was a ruin, debris everywhere. Some of the citizens were hurt. Vigrod was at a loss. He called for everyone to meet him at the stairs leading into the great hall.

"Everyone!" he yelled out. "I know our losses today were great, but we must not mourn what we have lost. We must look to what is ahead. Our great city is in ruin. Our friends and family are hurt. We must band together to work toward rebuilding, not only this place but ourselves. I am deeply sorry for not being here when you needed me most. I vow to be here for you always, from this day and for all days to come!"

His people started to flock to him, to give him thanks and praise. Vigrod could not help but smile. He thought his people still doubted him, but now he realized his people still loved him, and he loved them.

REBUILDING

The day was February fifteenth of the sixth summer. A day had passed since the attack on Frosthaven. The city was still a ruin, and today would be the start of the Viking rebuild.

Vigrod was bustling around, helping where he could and giving orders where he thought he should. His idea was that they would use the debris and break it down into something they could reuse and only have a forest and quarry (which were both growing scarce as it is)

As he was standing and talking, he started to backpedal when he bumped into something. He turned and saw a boy, much smaller than he was, which, of course, was to be expected. The boy had short brown hair, a lanky figure, and peculiar blue eyes.

"I am so sorry, Highlord. Please forgive me," the boy said.

Vigrod chuckled. "There is nothing to forgive, my boy."

"Is there anything I can help with?" the boy asked.

"Come with me, young man," Vigrod responded.

As they were walking along, Vigrod decided to continue their conversation. "What's your name, my friend?" Vigrod asked calmly.

"My name is Eirik. Like Eirik the Wolfslayer, my parents named my brother and me after the legends in your family."

Vigrod had a confused look on his face.

He was amazed that someone would name their sons after his forefathers.

"Really? Eirik, I have always loved that name. What is your brother's name?" Vigrod asked.

"Thalmer, like Thalmer the pious," Eirik replied.

This small interaction had lightened Vigrod's mood drastically. "Where is your brother?" he asked.

"I am not sure. He might be with my mother," Eirik said.

"Eirik!" a high-pitched voice yelled from behind them. "What are you doing? Bothering the Highlord," the lady said.

Vigrod guessed that this was Eirik's mother, and accompanying her was who he assumed to be Thalmer.

"He is no bother at all, my lady. He is helping me," Vigrod said.

"Good, I did not raise my son to be lazy," she replied.

Vigrod eventually found out that her name was Val. She was a shorter person, with flowing brown hair and blue eyes that her sons both had. Thalmer was not that tall either, but he had a stout, muscular figure with short blond hair and blue eyes.

Vigrod continued to make more small talk with the three of them but eventually decided to end their conversation, saying, "If your boys would like to wield a weapon in my army, you send them straight to me," Vigrod said.

The sun started to set, and Vigrod began to send people back into their homes, telling them the same process would continue until the city had returned to its former glory.

Days and days rolled by the people of Frosthaven were hard at work. But today was a particularly special day. Today was the date of Vigrod's birth, and the day was February twentieth of the sixth summer.

Everyone in Frosthaven knew the occasion. The streets were packed to the brim with people celebrating. Inside the great hall, it was even more crowded. All that could be heard was the sounds of drums and loud talking. Barrels upon barrels of mead and ale were brought up from the cellars, and several types of meat were as well.

"This party of mine was not planned very well," Vigrod said with his eyes fixated on his guests that were being randomly flung up in the air.

"We are Vikings, Vigrod. Did you expect any less?" Brodir replied.

Someone approached Vigrod, who was sitting in the center of the table where he had found his mother just a few days before.

"Highlord!" the man yelled.

His words were slurred. Vigrod could tell the man was very drunk.

"Yes, my friend!" Vigrod yelled back.

"Allow me to challenge you to a drinking contest!" the man said.

Vigrod stood up. "Grab two barrels of ale!" he yelled.

Vigrod watched as a few Vikings carried two barrels of ale into the center of the room, which was cleared out enough to give Vigrod and the man some space.

Vigrod and the man were both handed a mug and sat down in chairs, and the fresh barrels of ale were opened.

They filled both of their mugs to the brim. Then another man stepped in between them.

"Ready? Drink!" he said.

Instantly, Vigrod tipped his mug to the ceiling and let the ale go down his gullet. He finished his first mug in a second.

Vigrod was no stranger to ale, but he noticed he was clearly outmatched as he looked over to see his opponent had three empty mugs next to his seat.

As time passed, Vigrod was into his seventh mug, and he was starting to feel the ale taking hold of him. He looked across him, and the man had downed thirteen mugs of ale.

"Are you still alive?" the man asked, bobbing his head and speaking with a slur.

"I am more alive than ever!" Vigrod yelled back as he chugged another mug of ale.

He then threw his mug to the ground, and then he could feel himself start to tip over. He then fell backward out of his chair onto the ground.

He was then met with a roar of cheers, and then he fell into a very comfortable sleep with the biggest smile on his face.

CHAPTER

4

THE ECHO OF THE PAST

A day had passed since the celebration of Vigrod Frostbane. Vigrod sat in the great hall at the high table in the back of the hall, still feeling a bit drowsy from the night before. A few people had been walking around in the great hall going about their everyday business.

For the past few hours, ever since he woke up, Vigrod had a thought in the back of his mind, and it kept repeating itself in his head time and time again.

Why did the enemy attack now? If they really are the ancient enemy of my clan, I should know more about them.

It had been a month since the Vikings had returned home and Frosthaven's rebuilding, and the city was nearly rebuilt. No word had come from Ulfir or the Dark Bird. Everything had seemed so calm.

Vigrod looked at the door that led to the library under the great hall. He stood up, walked to the door, and started down the stairs. Vigrod heard a faint mumble from upstairs, probably asking where he was going. The stairs went down and down. Then finally, they ended. Vigrod grabbed a torch and opened the door to the library.

He opened the door to find rows and rows of books and barely any light in the room. He walked down the aisle to a large table in the middle of the room. On the table sat a large scroll that read the name of every book in the library. He looked at the paper to find the section about the history of Drangar.

Walking to the right into the row with all the books about the history of Drangar, he walked far down the row to get to the BAV books. Most of the history books had dates on them, for example (years 0–100). When the enemy was banished to the mountains was before the elves started keeping track of time.

Vigrod took out the first few books that were dated before year zero. He walked back to the table and put his books down. He opened the first book and started reading. He skimmed through the pages, looking for a mention of the enemy. Vigrod should have started in the second book. The very first book was mainly about the great frost and how the Giant united the clans of Drangar.

He put down the first book and picked up a new one. He looked at the first page, and it was about what happened years and years ago. Now this clan was not in rebellion like the gray humans were. No clan looked down upon them, but when the Giant had united every clan of Drangar, big or small, they refused.

The enemy had refused to be ruled by the Frostbanes. Then the Frostbanes invited them into Frosthaven to try to negotiate terms. But when the enemy was welcomed under their roof, they slaughtered hundreds of Frostbane soldiers, breaking a strict Viking law. Then the giant had killed their leader and banished them to the mountains in the far north of Drangar.

But the book goes much further in-depth about them. Vigrod had no idea who had written this book. Possibly someone who was with them joined Clan Frostbane when the rest of them had been banished.

Vigrod had not read too far into the book. There was much more to read about, and Vigrod did not want to read about it in the dark library. Vigrod took his book and went to the door, completely forgetting about the other books he had taken out.

Vigrod knew that any books from the library were forbidden to be taken out of the library. So he made no effort to hide the book. He was the Highlord, so Vigrod didn't really care. He walked up the stairs, and his hands went to his eyes immediately; he had not seen light in a while.

Again, only a few people had been walking around the hall, but one of the elders had been walking through the hall toward Vigrod.

"Highlord, you know books from the library are forbidden to be taken anywhere else," the old man said.

"I know, but this is for the safety of all the people of Drangar," Vigrod said.

"Let me see this book," the elder said.

He opened the book and looked through it. "I see why you have taken this. Based on recent events, take it. Lucky for you, I am the only one of the elders in the great hall."

"Thank you, my friend," Vigrod said.

He walked to the front of the hall and up the stairs toward his old room. He opened the door and sat down on his bed, and he began reading.

THE CLANS OF DRANGAR

Traveling from Frosthaven to the Bloodhall had taken a month. Just a few days ago, the Darkwings had gone separate ways from the Bloodwolves toward their home in the southern part of Drangar.

The Bloodhall was in the western part of Drangar. It was a smaller city, but the Bloodhall was on a hill. The rest of the city was on the ground, and gates surrounded the city. All the denizens who lived in the Bloodhall were warriors. It was a requirement of the clan to learn to fight, or they would be given up to the wolf god.

The only people who had stayed behind were Ulfir's parents and their personal guard. Remarkably, Ulfir's parents were still alive. They were older than most at the Bloodhall, but they could still fight.

The Bloodwolves had reached the city's outer gates, and the gates were opened. Ulfir issued a command for the soldiers to go to their homes. The city had been mostly empty since almost every person had gone to Yrfel.

Ulfir walked up the path to the Bloodhall, and he looked at the large wooden doors. He thought about what his parents would say since they lost the battle. Victory in combat earns lots of respect among the Bloodwolves, and Ulfir lost the battle.

After a minute of thinking, Ulfir mustered up the courage to open the doors. The doors slowly opened, revealing the large fire and the tables, the throne at the end of the hall, and the wooden pillars. Ulfir walked to the throne. It was a large wooden chair with designs, and it was shaped like a wolf's head, and most of the wood, except the chair part of the throne, was covered in wolf fur. On the throne sat Ulfir's father to the side sat his mother.

"Son! You've returned," Ulfir's father said.

He stood up, and they hugged. "I heard about what happened in Yrfel. I am saddened by the loss, but I won't be disappointed in you because you lost in a battle you had a small chance of winning."

"Father, how could you have heard about the battle? No one was here to tell you," Ulfir asked.

"Vigrod sent a messenger from Frosthaven. It arrived quite a while before you."

Ulfir turned to his mother to hug her.

"Mother, you look well," Ulfir said.

"Ulfir, I am glad you've returned," she said.

"Well, did Vigrod tell you what happened at Frosthaven when we returned from Yrfel?" Ulfir asked.

"Yes, I want you to have guards stationed at our walls at all times and make sure no one is outside the walls after dusk," Ulfir's father said.

"I will see it done. I seldom care about winning Yrfel now that the enemy has returned."

*****

In the southern part of Drangar sat the mystical Dark Nest, surrounded by the vast dark forest of Delthir, home of the Darkwing clan. Like the blood wolves, the journey home from Frosthaven had also taken two weeks.

The Dark Nest was a smaller town with peculiar architecture. The residences were sort of stacked on top of each other, and the purple and black paint was splattered all about the walls. The Darkwings found a certain beauty in the mess of paint.

In the heart of the town, the Bird's Nest towered over the rest of the town. It was a tall, ominous, dark-colored tower. That gave off a strong aura of fear and mystery.

The Dark Bird and his assistants entered the tower. On the inside of the tower, the purple and black raven flag hung nearly everywhere. There was a plethora of books and maps and tools of observation.

There was a staircase that would take whoever was using it to the pinnacle of the tower, but since the Dark Bird was crippled, the Dark Wings designed a small pulley system to carry him to the top.

Once the three of them were at the top of the tower, they were greeted by the rest of the important heads of the Darkwing clan, Hilthar, Gelthir, and Magthar.

Clan Darkwing was set up as a sort of oligarchy, but the Dark Bird really had the most power, and the other three heads, while still holding a lot of power and status in the clan, were ultimately at the Dark Bird's whim.

"Dark Bird, good to see you," Magthar said in his low, cold tone.

"Ah yes, Magthar, thank you, are the other two here as well?" the Dark Bird replied.

"Yes, my lord, we are all here," Hilthar chimed in with his smooth and energetic voice.

The Dark Bird then nodded in reply, then turned his head to the open window, where he could feel the cold air hitting his face.

"Well, it would seem that some old friends of ours have returned. I would request that our defenses be improved tenfold, more traps throughout the woods, more patrols, and so forth," the Dark Bird said waving his hands.

The Dark Bird felt around with his hands, touching his wheelchair, then feeling the air coming in from the open window. "Bring me the book of the

Darkwings. Perhaps there will be something about this enemy that we shall find within its pages."

A few minutes later, one of the assistants of the Dark Bird, her name was Idunn, came back with the book of the Darkwings.

"Where would you like me to start, my lord?" she asked. "What we are looking for should be in the beginning, my dear," the Dark Bird replied softly.

Idunn opened the monstrous tome and began to skim through the pages until she found something of note.

"Here, my lord, the book says that the clan was banished for practices of necromancy and other sorts of forbidden magics, as well as breaking a sacred law of hospitality," Idunn said.

"Anything pertaining to us specifically?" the Dark Bird asked.

"No, my lord, nothing at all," Idunn replied.

The Dark Bird sat, pondering. "Other sorts of forbidden magic," the Dark Bird said. "Ah, but of course, blood magic."

Everyone's heads turned. "Blood magic?" Hilthar said.

"Yes, blood magic, magic more despicable than necromancy, torturing the body for its blood to fuel rituals and incantations. The spilling of blood for the use of magic was forbidden long ago," the Dark Bird replied.

"What are we to do about this enemy, my lord?" Gelthir asked.

The Dark Bird took in a deep breath of fresh air. "I suppose all we can do is wait and be ready. Perhaps the Highlord will summon us again. Unfortunately, we are playing their game now."

CHAPTER

6

THE DEFENSE OF DRANGAR

The day was March sixteenth of the sixth summer, and Vigrod Frostbane sat in the great hall of Frosthaven, accompanied by Brodir and the rest of his council.

Vigrod, for the past several weeks, had been thinking about what he would do about his enemies, and now that Frosthaven had time to pick herself back up, the Highlord thought it was time to enact his plan for the defense of Drangar.

He stood up. "My friends, it has been nearly a month since we came home to our home in ruins. Now I think it is time we got our revenge. Brodir, send four of our finest scouts to the mountains in the north with four of our fastest horses to hopefully find our enemy. Then when our scouts return, messengers will be sent out to every clan in Drangar, big or small.

And if it all works, we shall march on the mountains together, with Drangar in full behind us."

"It is a bold strategy, my friend, but I will play my part to see it done," Brodir said, standing up and then exiting the great hall.

"Highlord, I suggest instead of messengers, we light the bonfire," one of the elders at the table said.

"The bonfire! I nearly forgot. I haven't heard mention of it since my youth. It hasn't been lit in how many years, nearly fifty?" Vigrod replied.

"You would be correct, Highlord, fifty years since the bonfire has last been lit."

The bonfire was a place of meeting like the Hall of the Lords. It was in the center of Drangar, and as the name suggests, it was a bonfire placed on a tall tower, and the collection of wood was the size of a giant, so the fire could be seen from anywhere. But unlike the hall in Yrfel, it could be invoked whenever the liege lords of Drangar wished, and the liege lords of Drangar were the Frostbanes.

"How much time will it take me to get there?" Vigrod asked. "From Frosthaven, only a day, but waiting for the rest of Drangar will take many."

Vigrod scratched his head and thought. "I am not sure how much time we have until we are attacked again or if we will even be attacked again. But I will make the journey."

Vigrod left the great hall and went and found Brodir in the barracks with the scouts that had been selected.

"These are the four, Brodir?" Vigrod asked. "Indeed, Highlord. I've dealt with them before. You won't find any four finer than this lot," Brodir replied.

The Highlord paced slowly, eyeing up Brodir's scouts. "I know I ask a great deal of the four of you," he said as he looked at each one of them.

He noticed that one of the scouts was wearing a hood and mask.

"You, why the disguise? There is no need to hide your face, friend," Vigrod said. "It brings me a sort of comfort to be concealed, Highlord," the scout replied in a very low tone.

Vigrod gave a grunt of approval. "Now I need you four to travel to the mountains and gather whatever information you can. Once your task is a complete ride to the Bonfire, I will be there waiting for you."

"The mountains are a weeklong journey, yes?" the masked scout asked.

"You would be correct," Vigrod said.

"The sun is setting. I would like you four to start your journey in the morning. Get some rest, all of you," Vigrod said.

Then the four of his scouts went back to their respective bunks.

"I don't trust the one in the mask, Brodir," Vigrod said quietly. "Don't trust him. I only selected him because he is good at what he does, but I can have the other three keep a close eye on him," Brodir replied.

"Very well, something about him just seems... odd."

JOURNEY TO THE MOUNTAINS

The sun rose on a new day in Drangar, and already, the four scouts, Einar, Stigandr, Beckett, and Haldor, were awake, packing their things, preparing for the journey ahead of them.

They left the barracks, and the cold wind hit their faces like a punch in the face. Then they made their way to the stables where the finest horses in Frosthaven were being kept for them.

Mounting their horses, they made haste out to the gate and called up to the gatekeeper to open the monstrous double door. Once the gate was open, out the four of them went. Faster than a bolt of lightning, they raced down the road toward the mountains.

Not a word was said between the four of them, the sun had barely risen, and the group was still drowsy and fatigued. All that could be heard was the clicking of hooves.

The main road of Drangar was not a very scenic one. It was very plain and barren land, covered in a white blanket, with a few birch trees sprinkled throughout. Occasionally, a bird could be seen flying overhead, or the howl of a wolf could be heard echoing for miles.

The day started to drag on. The group stopped after only an hour of riding, trying to save their horses' legs for the rest of the day.

They stopped and made their way over to a little crowd of trees; it was a place where they could tie up their horses and be concealed from the world around them.

"Haldor, grab that skin of water," the masked scout Beckett said.

Haldor reached into one of the pouches on his horse's saddle and revealed a large leather skin of water and tossed it to his companion.

Meanwhile, Stigandr grabbed a fresh loaf of Drangarian bread, which had something in the yeast to keep it warm for hours on end in the harsh cold environment. Stigandr broke the loaf up into four pieces and split it among the group and Beckett passed around the skin of fresh water.

After their small breakfast, they were back on the road, riding hard and stopping only when they thought their horses were tired, which they rarely were. The light of day came and went. The journey to the mountains was a quiet one, considering the harsh environment that is Drangar.

The day was March twenty-second of the sixth summer. When the sun rose, the group of scouts rose along with it. The four of them stepped outside their tents, which they had slept in the night prior when they arrived.

"Come on, lads. Let us make this quick, aye?" Stigandr said, motioning his hands toward the mountains.

The group walked to the mountains, gazing upward, noticing how the mountains scraped the gray sky. Continuing to the eastern side of the mountain range, Drangar was all quiet. It was as if life was scared to venture near the mountains.

Beckett was at the front of the pack, a few yards ahead of the others, and suddenly, he stopped dead in his tracks.

"What is it?" Haldor asked.

"Look at this," he replied.

The other three scouts jogged to where Beckett was, and when they reached him, they realized why he had stopped so suddenly.

Lodged in this mountain was a large stone door. It was as tall as a giant and as wide as a catapult. The door was carved with designs, but they were the exact opposite of elegant like the Frostbanes were. The designs were scenes of war and bloodshed, strange symbols, and glyphs.

"How will we get inside? We can't just barge in," Haldor said.

"We might just have to. What else are we to do?" Beckett replied.

They searched the area for a few minutes, looking for an alternative way in, but they found none. The four of them approached the door and pushed it using all their might. The door started to budge, and it opened slowly with a loud skidding sound. The darkness that they were welcomed to on the inside was almost hypnotizing.

"Well, come on, we can't sit here all morning," Beckett said, "and grab a torch from the camp," he added.

Moments later, they were ready to enter the swallowing darkness. Beckett stood at the front, holding the torch. They crept in slowly. Nothing inside the cave could be heard, not even the winds outside nor the subtle shuffling of their feet.

Beckett noticed out of the corner of his eye an archway that contained a set of stairs. "Look, up there," he said, motioning to the barely visible stairway. "We could get a better look at things from up there."

Sneaking up the stairs slowly, they noticed there was light at the top, so Beckett blew out the torch's light, and they continued onward.

They reached the top and sneaked out into the light. They veered their heads left and right and saw a large walkway stretching from end to end of the mountain. But once they looked downward, their eyes were greeted with quite an unpleasant surprise.

Masses upon masses of Mountain Clan warriors, the four scouts stood on the walkway high above the crowd in awe, for no one had realized in the hundreds of years since their banishment that they had made a civilization inside a mountain.

"We have to get back," Stigandr said.

"I agree. Quickly before we are spotted," Beckett replied.

As they were beginning to leave, the loud voices of the crowd silenced, and suddenly, there was a low chant starting among them. The four of them crept back over to the railing to see what was happening. The horde of Vikings were in ranks and were on their knees.

"Look at those few walking through the lot. They don't look or dress like ordinary Vikings," Stigandr said, trying to point out who he was talking about to his comrades.

The four strange-looking ones he mentioned were not dressed like traditional Vikings. They wore no weapons on their side and were wearing a red cloak that covered their faces. The four-robed Vikings walked to what appeared to be a throne to the four of them, but what sat upon the throne, they could not comprehend. This thing took the shape of a Viking, twice the size of Vigrod, but on the throne sat a being that clearly was not living. It might have been a person once, but now, its flesh was ripped from its body, only showing flesh in some spots. Mostly, bones were showing. It was grotesque. They could see inside it. There was just a collection of glowing atrocities.

The four-robed figures surrounded the throne and lifted their hands. The motion silenced the chanting of the crowd. At the foot of the throne sat a large bowl stood on top of a pedestal. The robed figures approached it and then took a knife to their palm and let their blood pour into the bowl, then they started chanting, and a red stream rose from the blood and went into the thing's chest. The being started to rise, slowly standing up from its monstrous chair once it fully stood up and stared at its loyal army. One of the cloaked figures revealed a crown from under their robe. The monster knelt so its mage could place the crown upon its head.

The crown was placed upon the bare skull of this horrific monstrosity. Once it was crowned, it stood again and let out a roar, and his army responded with a cheer of its own.

The four scouts instantly booked it for the exit, getting out of there as fast as they could while the clan was occupied. Sprinting back to their camp and swiftly packing up their camp, leaving no trace that they were there, saddling up and riding off into the distance.

BECK AND CALL

The scouts had ridden hard to the bonfire, the large meeting place at the center of Drangar, where Vigrod was waiting for them.

The four of them got off their horses and ran over to meet Vigrod, the large tower holding up the monstrous bonfire looming behind them.

"Highlord!" Stigandr said breathlessly.

"Stigandr, lads," Vigrod said, nodding to the other three.

"In the mountains...our enemy...danger," Stigandr said, still trying to catch his breath.

"Catch your breath, then continue," Vigrod said with a slight laugh.

Stigandr paused for a moment.

"In the mountains, the enemy has created their own sort of city but not like that of High Yrfel. Their city was inside the mountain the place was completely hollowed out. There were thousands of soldiers, but their leader was twice the size of you, Highlord, and he looked like a skeleton. It was an undead monster being fueled by blood magic. We saw it all happen, and if they revived their leader, then they could be amassing for an attack," Stigandr said.

Vigrod stood in awe of what was just said. After all, who wouldn't be? "What? I am at a loss for words." He turned to Brodir. "What do you think we should do?" Brodir had no response, just a shrug. "And how many did you see? Give me your best guess," Vigrod said.

"Eighty thousand. Maybe more," Stigandr replied.

Vigrod scoffed at the reply. "Our forces are shattered by Yrfel, and I do not think we alone have the strength to defeat such a foe."

Vigrod put his hand on his chin as in deep thought. "Do we think that the other clans would help us? After the battle at Yrfel?" he said, looking around at the four of them.

"I do not see why not. You are the head of the greatest clan in Drangar. Should they not answer the call? It should be viewed as treason," Stigandr answered.

"Well then, I suppose it is time to light the fire then," Vigrod said.

Vigrod walked into the tower, grabbed a torch off the wall, and then began his ascension of the long spiral staircase. When he made it to the top, he glanced at the large collection of wood, putting his torch to it and waiting for it to catch. The fire suddenly roared up, and Vigrod quickly took a few steps back. He then turned to look out into the Frozen waste of his home, hoping that soon clans would come harking to him.

In the month that followed, the clans of Drangar rallied to the call of Vigrod Frostbane, which in his mind was a shocking revelation. Vigrod did not expect the clans to stand behind him following his defeat in Yrfel.

All the clans were gathered around the tower of the bonfire, and the sun was setting on the day of April twenty-ninth, the sixth summer.

"Friends! I know you have traveled long and far to come here, but what I have gathered you for is something you all need to hear. The mountain clan, the clan who was evicted from this part of Drangar centuries ago, has returned! They have already attacked my home, killed my people, and… my mother." Vigrod made a slight pause. The crowd lowered their heads at his last remark. He picked up again. "I ask you now to stand with me and fight back this threat. Whatever it holds for us, we, the people of Drangar, must be ready!"

The crowd gave their nods and noises of approval as they always did, but Vigrod still felt a little bit of doubt in the back of his mind. He had to say one more thing, just something to win them over for sure.

"The plan is quite simple. We meet them out in the field, then do what we do best!" Vigrod cheered loudly, so all in the city could hear.

He was met by a tidal wave of cheers and roars. To Vigrod, a motivated army was everything, and getting them excited shot his confidence to the moon.

In reality, Vigrod had no plan. He had no idea where the enemy would be and when they would be there. Somehow, they had to be drawn out. Vigrod knew that they were after him, and he would have to use that to his advantage. Vigrod gathered all the clans and took them back to Frosthaven. Now having an army of over one hundred thousand soldiers, Vigrod felt ready for the battle to come.

The next morning, the heads of all the great clans of Drangar, Brodir, the elders, and Vigrod met in the map room of the great hall back at Frosthaven.

Vigrod was at the head of the map table, looking around at all the other prominent figures in the room. He took a moment to think before he broke the silence. He stood from his chair.

"We know that the enemy is large in number, and I have a feeling that they know that all the clans combined outnumber them ten to one. Does anyone have any ideas as to what we should do?" he said.

"They would be foolish to meet us in the field. I'd be willing to wager they would attack us while we aren't prepared," Ulfir replied.

"Perhaps we can draw them out somehow," said Dane Giantsfoot, leader of the Giantsfoot clan.

The Giantsfoot clan were close relatives of the Frostbanes. After the Great Frost, when the "Giant" Frostbane had united all the warring factions, the giant's brother, who was called Giantsfoot, started his own clan, and although the Frostbanes are much more prominent, they keep very close together.

"They're after me, I am sure of it. They probably have some sort of scouting party surrounding Frosthaven," Vigrod said.

"We must also remember that even though we outnumber them, they use blood magic," Brodir said, standing behind Vigrod.

"You are right. Perhaps we should draw them out. We could go to them with all our strength. I don't think they could resist the open challenge."

"Now if you wish, you all may take your clans back to your home and wait for my call," Vigrod said.

The conglomerate of Vikings seemed to agree with him on his ideas, for there was not much else offered when it came to battle plans.

"For now, I want our patrols to double, triple even, I don't want to take any chances."

A YOUNG PROMISE

After the meeting had concluded, Vigrod left the great hall to get a breath of fresh air. He looked down the stairs to see two young men at the foot of them. Vigrod instantly recognized who they were, Eirik and Thalmer. He was pleased to see them but was a bit confused as to why they were there.

"Highlord, we have come to learn how to fight," Eirik said.

Vigrod remembered the promise he had made to their mother, teach the boys the art of the sword should they feel the need to.

"Very well. We start right away. I hope you're both excited. We have a long road ahead of us."

Vigrod took the two boys to the barracks, where there would be a ground for them to train. The training yard was nothing marvelous, a large, square, dirt area with a few training dummies throughout. Vigrod grabbed the two boys training swords, along with one for himself.

"Now can either of you tell me what the most important aspect of fighting is?" Vigrod asked.

"Uh…footwork?" Eirik answered.

"Very good. Now for your first test. Land a hit on me," Vigrod said, taking a step back to give himself some room.

Eirik rushed Vigrod quickly. His swings were good, but Vigrod's footwork was much better, dodging all his attacks. Thalmer tried to ambush Vigrod, but it was to no avail. For a man of his stature, he was still too fast for the two boys. Their little game continued for a while longer until the boys were out of energy.

"Too slow, lads. I hope I showed you the importance of knowing where to step," Vigrod said laughingly.

"Give us a moment, Highlord. We will show you," Eirik replied.

He then turned to his brother and started to whisper.

"You boys are better than I thought. You are coordinated. You put pressure on me, but we will work on your skills," Vigrod said.

"Thank you, Highlord," they both said.

Vigrod walked back to the foot of the stairs of the great hall. "That will be all for today. Come back tomorrow, same time," Vigrod said.

The boys bowed, then walked away into the bustling streets of Frosthaven. Brodir sneaked up behind Vigrod, surprising him with a pat on the back.

"How did it go?" Brodir asked. "They're better than I thought for being that young," Vigrod replied.

"We were only that young a few years ago," Brodir said quickly.

The remark got a laugh out of the two.

The next day came. It was Tuesday, a cloudy one. The weather was getting cold. Winter was upon them. Vigrod and Brodir stood at the bottom of the stairs. They saw Eirik and Thalmer walking toward them on time.

"Welcome back, boys," Vigrod said. "Let's begin," he added.

They walked over to the courtyard, and they stood in the center of the yard.

"Today, we do something different. Follow me," Vigrod said.

Vigrod took the two young boys outside the city gates and into the Forest nearby. There was a little clearing that Vigrod led them to, where he had rocks set up as weights.

"I want you two to lift these rocks as many times as you can. I will tell you when to stop," Vigrod said. They were decently sized rocks.

Eirik, who was fifteen, and his brother, who was fourteen, were both tall and respectably strong. The two boys started to lift. They started out good. They lifted and threw down the rocks over and over for about ten minutes. Then they started to tire. Thalmer tired out first. He could barely lift the rock off the ground, but he tried. Then Eirik, he got one more lift then couldn't anymore.

"Alright, that is enough. Better than I expected," Vigrod said.

The boys were drenched in sweat. Their brown hair looked almost black. Their dark blue eyes were barely visible.

"Take a short break, then get back to it," Vigrod said.

Brodir threw Eirik a water flask. Eirik took a long sip, then passed it to his brother.

"You know the real reason I brought you two out here?" Vigrod asked

The boys sat there dead silent. It was quite an awkward scene, all quiet in the clearing of the small Frosthaven forest.

"You know, you are allowed to talk," Vigrod said, laughing.

Eirik shrugged, then went back to drinking the water.

Vigrod sighed. "The real reason I brought you out here isn't just to help make you stronger. When Brodir and I were your ages, perhaps just a bit younger, my father took us to these stones and told us that when you lift these stones. Think that every time you lift it is an improvement. Teach your mind to take you one step further. Let this rock be a stepping stone to a better you."

Another few minutes passed until they started lifting rocks again. Vigrod even went and got some other rocks for him and Brodir to lift.

The four Drangarians trained deep into the night, lifting, then taking a break, then more lifting.

"Perhaps it is time we head back. I am proud of both of you for the strides you are making," Vigrod said. They walked back to Frosthaven and went to bed, ready for training the next morning.

For the next several days, they trained, rocks, then swords, then rocks, then more swords until Vigrod felt they were ready to go up against him again. The day was May 4 of the sixth summer.

"After all your training, I think you two are finally ready to face me again," Vigrod said. "You think so?" Eirik said.

After the relationship between him and Vigrod grew, he became more confident and actually talked.

"Ready, boys?" Vigrod asked.

"Are you ready?" Eirik said.

Vigrod gave a slight laugh. Vigrod started advancing toward them. He noticed that the boys started making hand signals. Thalmer charged first and took two swings before Eirik went in and took swings of his own. Vigrod was almost hit. Their speed and coordination had improved.

Eirik made another hand signal. This time, he charged first, took a swing, and he locked blades with Vigrod. Then Thalmer came in. Vigrod was ready to

AIDAN TAUTIN

parry his strike, but something happened Vigrod did not expect.

Thalmer took a fake swing, but Vigrod went to parry, but there was nothing to parry. Eirik quickly struck Vigrod on the arm. Vigrod backed away.

"Well done, lads, a fine move," Brodir said. "I don't think he's been hit by a warrior since the battle on Yrfel," he added.

Again, the two rushed, and again, more hand signals were made. This time, Eirik got on his knee with his hands cupped. Thalmer ran and jumped, and Eirik gave him a boost. Thalmer was in the air, falling toward Vigrod. Thalmer used all his might to swing at Vigrod in the air. Vigrod parried his attack and pushed him away. Eirik caught his brother and got him back on his feet. Immediately, Thalmer rushed Vigrod and swung, again and again, faster and harder than Vigrod had ever seen him. Vigrod was genuinely surprised.

"Wait!" Vigrod yelled. Thalmer stopped. "Brodir, take Thalmer's sword and give him two short swords," he added. Brodir walked, grabbed the short swords, and took Thalmer's old one. "Alright, same speed and same power," Vigrod said.

Thalmer did just that, and Vigrod was still surprised. He thrived with two blades. They went back and forth until Thalmer finally hit Vigrod. He made a stabbing motion and was parried, but while that was happening, Thalmer got Vigrod on the arm.

200

Thalmer retreated to his brother. Vigrod saw them talking. Thalmer came back running at Vigrod with Eirik running directly behind him. Thalmer broke off to the left and started to fight with Vigrod, but then Eirik, with all his might, threw his sword at Vigrod and hit Vigrod directly in the chest.

Vigrod knelt on the ground. "Very impressive," Vigrod said. He stood back up. "But this is just the beginning of your warrior journey."

A few hours later, Vigrod was back in the great hall; he went to the elders to take care of something that had been on his mind. Brodir was accompanying him on his mission, and the two found the elders in their study.

"Elders," Vigrod said. All of them turned and faced Vigrod. "Someone, write down what I say, for this will be my new will. I, Vigrod, of the Clan Frostbane, declare that if I should fall in battle or die from any cause of nature, the boy Eirik should inherit my name, my lands, and my titles."

This deed had been on Vigrod's mind for quite a while. He was not focused on having any sons now, and he figured that Eirik was old enough to accept responsibility if it came to him.

Vigrod looked around at all the elders seriously. "Keep that somewhere safe. Make no mention of it to anyone, and if the time comes where I should die, he is the rightful heir of Drangar."

SWORDS IN THE NIGHT

The day had passed since Vigrod had his tremendous battle with Eirik and Thalmer, sitting at his desk in his room, studying over the book that he had grabbed from the library long ago.

Vigrod had an eerie feeling. As he skimmed through the pages, a thought lurked at the back of his mind, creeping forward slowly. He read on and on, just retaining what he could although he wasn't very focused on his reading.

Suddenly, the door opened, Vigrod jumped at the sound, but it was just Brodir.

"Sorry to scare you, my friend," Brodir said.

"It is fine. Is something wrong?" Vigrod asked.

Brodir looked confused. "No? I just came to check on you."

Vigrod sat back in his chair, a bit calmer now. "Right, good, something just seems wrong, but I can't quite put my finger on what."

Vigrod and Brodir continued to talk for a while longer, but then the sounds of screaming jumped into their ears. Vigrod ran to his window to see what was happening.

Fire, blood, ruin, Frosthaven was under siege by the enemy from the mountains. Vigrod and Brodir sprinted out of the great hall out into the city. The two were waylaid by the opposition. Vigrod and Brodir stood back-to-back, hacking and slashing away.

The battle was a scrambled mess. Vigrod, in his mind, was still trying to process what was happening. He let his mind numb and let his axe do the work. Blood was scattered along the walls from Frosthaven and Mountain clan both, and the fire was starting to build up around the city.

Vigrod looked around frantically, trying to focus on the battle in front of him, but the fact that his home was being ruined in front of his eyes was taking his conciseness away from the fight. He drove his axe through the chest of the man attacking him. As the lifeless corpse of his enemy was flung off his axe, he saw, in the distance, Eirik was being chased.

The boy was under immense pressure from a stout warrior from the Mountain clan. Vigrod sprinted over. When he was within reach of the man, he leaped up and reached out to tackle him. Vigrod punched him repeatedly and then shoved his axe into the man's skull, and when he ripped it out, blood splattered on the wall in front of them.

"Are you alright! Are you hurt?" Vigrod yelled, checking Eirik for any wounds.

"No, no, I'm alright," Eirik replied breathlessly.

Vigrod picked the boy up and hugged him. Over the course of the training, the two had become close friends, and Vigrod also could not imagine what Eirik's mother would do if something happened to the boy.

"Where's your brother?" Vigrod said.

"I...I don't know. I lost him," Eirik stuttered.

"Come, quickly now," Vigrod replied.

The two fought their way through the crowd. Vigrod had to do most of the work, but Eirik was holding his own. Eirik yelled out for his brother. He yelled again and again. There was a small yell back, but it was very faint. Vigrod and Eirik tried to get closer to Thalmer's yelling. They continued to fight their way through, and eventually, Thalmer came into view.

Thalmer was with a few other of Vigrod's men, trying to hold off an oncoming wave of Mountain clan. Vigrod and Eirik jumped into the fight, helping their brethren to fend off the attackers.

Eirik and Thalmer reunited as Vigrod continued to help his men, and then he saw something in the distance his eyes could barely fathom. It was the most disgusting thing he had ever seen; it was taller than he was, armed with a large sword.

Vigrod walked out to challenge the creature. He could tell this was the leader, and he knew he was plenty capable of killing it. They stood a few feet away. The creature approached Vigrod, taking a few long strides and then raising up his sword. The strike was easily dodged by Vigrod. He then struck back, and his axe was lodged in the side of the creature. It didn't even seem to faze the monster, but blood spilled out its side. Vigrod had to be quick on his feet, moving out of the way from the slow and powerful swings of his enemy.

Swiftly, Vigrod rolled under an attack and grabbed his axe from the side of the creature, but the move couldn't get Vigrod far enough away. The monstrous hand of the creature grabbed Vigrod by his neck. Instantly, Vigrod dropped his axe, and he tried to loosen the grip on his neck.

He was quickly losing air, struggling to loosen the tight grip. But suddenly, a sword went through the chest of the creature. Vigrod was dropped to the ground. He looked up to see Thalmer on the creature's soldiers. The creature then reached up, grabbed Thalmer, and flung him toward the ground. On impact, the cracking of bones could be heard.

The creature fell to the ground, it started to crawl away, but eventually, it ceased. Once it finally stopped, the Mountain clan started to retreat. Dozens of troops grabbed the body of the creature and carried it out of Frosthaven.

Eirik ran to his brother and held him in his arms. "Brother, no. Please no. Don't go," Eirik started to break down. He couldn't hold back his tears.

Vigrod came over. "Why, son? You can't leave us now," Vigrod said, succumbing to tears himself.

Thalmer took a few breaths. "You...would've done the same for me."

Vigrod couldn't even respond. The tears were flowing so fast.

"You're a hero, Thalmer. You can rest now," Vigrod laid a hand on the boy's face as he took his last breath.

Thalmer's back was broken, and his head had lost too much blood. There was nothing they could do.

Eirik let out cries so loud they could be heard from the other side of Drangar. He held his brother long into the night. Vigrod sat next to the boy. He had no idea what to do. They had won the battle but lost a pure soul.

THE VIKING TOLL

The next morning, every man, woman, and child in Frosthaven was gathered out into the street where Thalmer's act of heroism had taken place.

The boy's body was placed on top of a large pyre. Eirik and his mother stood next to it, staring at the wooden foundations that held up Thalmer.

When Vigrod arrived, he came down from the great hall, splitting the large sea of people to get through to the pyre. Vigrod greeted Eirik and Val both, not with words but with a comforting hug, taking them both up in his arms.

Eirik motioned for the Highlord to come close, so Vigrod knelt and opened his ears.

"All he wanted…was your approval. You were his idol. He may not have shown it, but training with you meant everything to him," Eirik whispered.

"I am glad I was the idol of someone so self-less. But your brother paid the Viking toll. He gave an honorable death and received one in return. He will get the hero's welcome in Thalmur's halls above," Vigrod whispered back.

Vigrod turned and faced the crowd. "I thank you all for coming. The previous night's events have taken a toll on all of us. I was unprepared. I did not suspect such an attack. The battle could've been lost had it not been for this boy!" Vigrod yelled out, pointing to the pyre.

"Thalmer Frostbane, for he has earned the name, saved my life, and he saved all of yours as well."

Vigrod walked slowly, letting his large fur cloak drag behind him, over to Brodir, who held the torch.

Vigrod handed the torch to Val. She then slowly put it into the kindling, letting it all catch. Val then gave the torch to Eirik. He looked the pyre up and down, then threw the torch in, watching the flames slowly rise and creep up toward Thalmer.

The dark clouds and slow-falling snow added to the somberness of the funeral. Eirik and Val said their final goodbyes as Thalmer Frostbane was put to rest.

A feast was held in honor of Thalmer. It was not very organized in truth, but it was enjoyable for the people of Frosthaven. Vigrod kept Eirik and Val close to him the whole night, trying to be a source of comfort for them. Songs were sung, ale and mead were drunk, and stories were told. The festivities continued long into the night.

Vigrod eventually retreated to his bed after the feast started to die down, taking off his cloak and changing into more comfortable attire. The Highlord then crashed into his bed, letting his head sink into his feather pillow, and in mere moments, he drifted off to sleep.

Vigrod opened his eyes to see he was back in that empty, snow-covered place, the crescent moon still high in the sky. Vigrod looked around. The last time he was here, a man greeted him. He wondered who would be here for him this time.

In the distance, Vigrod could see a silhouette, but this wasn't the large one he saw when he was here last. This was a small one, significantly smaller than the last.

The silhouette came into view. It was Thalmer. Vigrod could barely believe what he was seeing.

"Thalmer?" Vigrod said.

"Hello, Highlord, it is great to see you," Thalmer replied.

Vigrod knelt so he could be at eye level with the boy. "You have my eternal gratitude for saving my life and my people. You are a Frostbane now. Do not ever forget it."

Thalmer couldn't help but smile. "Thank you, Highlord."

"So how are you enjoying the hall," Vigrod said, looking behind the boy's shoulder for a brief second. "It is amazing. I have met so many legends from years long past."

The two continued their conversation for a bit longer, but then Vigrod could feel his eyes starting to grow heavy.

"You paid the Viking toll, Thalmer Frostbane, and you will always be remembered."

Vigrod hugged the boy, trying to instill every feeling of approval and trust into him before his eyes closed shut.

12

AT THE HARBOR

It was a beautiful day in Drangar on May 7 of the sixth summer. The sun was in the sky, and for once, there were no clouds in sight.

Vigrod and Brodir were sitting at the table in the great hall, reminiscing over their childhoods, as they often did when they had the time. The doors to the great hall suddenly opened, and one of the elders was walking in with a letter.

"For you, Highlord," he said, handing the letter to Vigrod and exiting with a bow. Vigrod examined the letter. It was stamped with the tree sigil of House Keawynn. *Why is Kolvar sending me a message?* Vigrod thought.

He opened it and started to read.

Vigrod,

I have requested a meeting at the Hall of the Lords, but as far as I know, you are still in Drangar. So if you would be so kind as to return for this meeting on the twentieth of June, I would very much appreciate this.

You, along with your armies, must return to Yrfel, Nathan and I are now the least of your concerns.

I hope this reaches you well,
Kolvar Keawynn

Vigrod rolled the letter back up and set it down with a dumbfounded look on his face.

"What does it say?" Brodir asked. "Kolvar requested a meeting at the hall on the twentieth of June, and he wants me to bring back all our armies. He also mentioned that Nathan and himself were the least of our concerns," Vigrod replied.

The dumbfounded look then found its way onto Brodir's face.

"What shall we do then? I feel he is asking for too much," Brodir said. "At the very least, you should attend the meeting, but I would advise caution," he added.

Vigrod stared off, pondering over the letter and his friend's advice. "We do not know when the Mountain clan will return, and I cannot ignore a meeting at the hall. Perhaps we leave a small force here, maybe a thousand, then we call Ulfir and the Dark Bird. They will come with us to Yrfel. I will not lead us undermanned into something even I am unsure about," he said.

"A sound plan. I will leave Helmar in charge, and I will get the elders to send word to the other clans. Should I tell them to send it to your cousin as well?" Brodir replied.

Vigrod nodded. Brodir then turned and left the great hall.

The day was May twenty-fourth of the sixth summer. Everyone had answered Vigrod's call. Bloodwolves, Darkwings, and Giantsfoots alike had arrived at Frosthaven, ready to make the journey to Yrfel.

Vigrod and Brodir were already at the harbor, watching the preparations for their departure take place.

"Friends! Wonderful to see you both," said a voice from behind them.

The two turned to see Ulfir with his arms stretched out and a smile on his face.

"Ulfir! Ha! Good to see you," Vigrod replied.

Brodir gave his greetings also, but he did not take part in the bear hug the Highlord and Wolf Lord were doing.

"Ready to go back?" Vigrod asked.

"We are. I am deeply sorry for not being here during the attack," Ulfir replied.

"Do not let it trouble you. You could not have known," Vigrod said, giving his friend a pat on the back.

The Dark Bird then approached them, being pushed in his wheelchair by his assistant.

"Here is Lord Frostbane, my lord," the assistant said.

"Highlord!" the Dark Bird said.

"How are you doing, old bird?" Vigrod replied.

"I am still here!" the two shared a laugh.

The time rolled by, and finally, they were ready to depart on the three-week voyage back to Yrfel.

As they set sail, Vigrod turned and looked back at his home. Thoughts of doubt crept into his mind, and anxious feelings crept into his heart. He hoped with every ounce of his heart that he would see his home again, and the next time, he saw it that it wasn't on fire.

PART 2

Yrfel

VIKING'S LANDING

The three-week voyage back to Yrfel had finally reached its conclusion. The Drangarians docked and got all their supplies and such unpacked. As the conglomerate of Vikings marched toward Ravenhall, Vigrod noticed something.

"For fuck's sake," he said.

After the voyage, Vigrod was in quite a grouchy mood.

"What is it?" Brodir asked concerningly.

"The flags, look at them," Vigrod replied.

Brodir then glanced up to where the usual Frostbane flags would be on the turrets on each corner of Ravenhall and instead saw the flag of House Keawynn.

Brodir let out a large grunt. "Surely, there aren't many of them. We can make this quick if it comes to it," he said.

217

Vigrod could hear the mixed opinions among his troops. Some wanted battle. Others didn't, but for once, he wanted to decide for himself.

"No, just let me talk to them. I wouldn't make such a move only a few days before I see their lord," Vigrod said.

The army approached the gate. A few elves were on the ramparts to meet them.

"Who goes there?" one of the elves asked sarcastically.

"Vigrod Frostbane, can you let us in, please?" he yelled up.

The elves did not reply, and Vigrod was growing impatient. "What do you value more? Your honor or your life?"

Another elf poked their head out. "Highlord Frostbane! Welcome back. I am Commander Rion, leader of this company. Please come in."

The gates slowly opened, and the Vikings started to flood in. Lots of loud moans and groans of sore Vikings could be heard. Rion approached Vigrod and Brodir. He had a very welcoming look on his face. It gave Vigrod a bit of a nervous feeling.

"Highlord, if you please follow me. We have matters to discuss," Rion said.

Vigrod gave his signature grunt of approval. Rion took them to the great hall. The long table was full of Elves, and Vigrod's tired mind had to take an extra second to process.

A few elves got up to make room for the three of them. Rion made a motion with his hand, and within a few moments, three plates of food were brought to them. The plates were full of bread, chicken, and elk, along with large flagons of ale.

"So what brings you back?" Rion asked.

"Funnily enough, your lord did," Vigrod replied.

"He called for a meeting at the hall in a few days, and my business on Drangar has been taken care of for the time being," he added.

"Ah yes, a messenger arrived here a few days ago. Lord Kolvar had said when you return that we would escort you to the hall, along with who you choose to bring, of course."

Vigrod looked at Brodir for any input. Brodir simply gave a shrug. "Fine with me. We can leave tomorrow, but we send word to Kolvar now that when we get there. He brings back the prisoners that we sent him a year ago to make sure there be no ill will."

"Very well, and the eastern prisoners in your dungeons below. What about them?" Rion said. "Set them free. They can go wherever they please," Vigrod replied.

Vigrod finished his meal and went off to his old room. Rion occupied it but gave it back to Vigrod without much hesitation. The stress of leading had started to ware on Vigrod's mind, but he tried to drown the stress out with sleep. It took a little bit, but eventually, the Highlord dozed off to sleep.

THE UNEXPECTED
MEETING

The day of the meeting had arrived. Vigrod and his companions, along with the company of elves made it to the hall. When they got there, they found that, to no one's surprise, Lord Kolvar was early, and High King Nathan was not there.

Kolvar had honored Vigrod's request to release the prisoners. When he saw all his comrades, Vigrod let out a sigh of relief. The Highlord got off his horse and went over to greet them.

"Lord Kolvar," Vigrod said.

"Highlord," Kolvar replied, extending his arm for a handshake.

"Thank you for honoring my request, my lord."

"Of course, we didn't keep them in our true prison in the roots of the Elder Branch with the true criminals. We kept them fed, unarmed, and working," Kolvar said.

Vigrod went over to his soldiers, thanking every one of them for what they had done for their people and for him.

By the time Vigrod was done with his thanks, Nathan had finally arrived, and the three walked inside the hall to begin their meeting.

The three walked in. Nathan took one look at Vigrod, and his jaw dropped.

"Vigrod? When you get back? Are you here, or am I just dreaming?" Nathan said.

"No, I am here, sitting down in front of you," Vigrod replied.

The joking quickly ceased. Nathan unsheathed both his swords and walked over to Vigrod. "I would kill you right now for what your soldiers did to Tymirial, but I would not shed blood in the hall our fathers built," Nathan said. He walked over to his seat and sat down.

"Kolvar, you called my people and I back to this island. Why?" Vigrod said.

"Nathan, tell him."

Nathan let out a sigh. "The gray humans have returned,' Nathan said slowly.

Vigrod's head snapped like an owl to look at Nathan. "What? Are you sure?" he asked.

"Undoubtedly, a few of the Shrouded members investigated their island for me. Sure enough, they are still kicking. They say that they had five times more soldiers than all our armies combined," Nathan said.

"That is why I said that Nathan and I are the least of your concerns. Now I propose a treaty although we all want Yrfel for our own reasons, we should be at peace until we have eradicated this threat whenever they arrive on our shores," Kolvar said.

Vigrod and Nathan were both in agreement with the idea of a treaty. Kolvar then left briefly, returning inside with a quill, ink, and parchment.

"Of course, you came with an ink and quill," Vigrod said with a slight laugh.

"What can I say, Highlord? I like to come prepared," Kolvar replied.

The elf lord then began to write. The room was quiet for multiple minutes. All that could be heard was the scratching of the quill onto the parchment.

Kolvar then put down his quill and began to read. "On this day of June, the twentieth of the sixth summer, the treaty of Yrfel is in effect from this day until the end of time. Peace between north, west, and east is now forevermore. Should one of these break this peace, they are relinquished from this pact and shall be viewed as an enemy. Should one of the three standing lords die, their next of kin will take their mantle of lord."

Kolvar then put the finishing touch on the treaty by signing his name.

"Gentlemen, do we have an agreement?" Kolvar said.

Vigrod gave his usual grunt of approval and signed his name under Kolvar's. Nathan then gave a nod and signed under Vigrod's name.

"Before we conclude, there is one more thing I would like to bring up," Vigrod said.

He then took one long breath in and out. "Long ago, when the giant brought together all the clans of Drangar, there was one clan who refused. He invited them into Frosthaven to try to negotiate terms. But when they were inside the great hall, they slaughtered hundreds of Frostbane soldiers, breaking one of the strictest laws of Drangar. The giant then killed their leader and banished them to the mountains in the far north of Drangar. It is forbidden to speak the clan's true name."

"You tell us this. Why?" Nathan asked.

"They returned and ambushed Frosthaven during the night. Their leader was an abomination. I could see his bones and his glowing organs. He was taller than me, fueled by blood magic. I tried to kill it. In truth, I almost died doing it, but I was luckily saved by a son of mine. He sacrificed himself for me." Vigrod took a quick pause. "I am worried that perhaps they try to make a move while we are away. Perhaps they even try to ally with the gray humans. Nothing is out of the question with them."

"If you defeated them, I would not be so quick to worry. They will be dealt with. This, I promise to you," Kolvar said.

"Thank you, my lord," Vigrod said.

"Vigrod," Nathan chimed in. Vigrod looked toward Nathan. "You know of Gunir? The giant who lives in one of your villages."

The Highlord nodded. "Speak to him. Perhaps he could help us in the wars to come."

"Very well. I take my leave now. Safe travels," Vigrod said, getting up from his seat.

"Good luck with the giant. Safe travels," Nathan replied.

"Goodbye, Highlord," Kolvar added.

Vigrod nodded, then walked out of the room.

"We need to sail home. Bring back what forces we can. If they were snooping around this place, then I think they are bound to start their assault here," Kolvar said.

"Agreed. Send me a messenger when you depart. When I receive it, I will leave for home."

The two lords stood and said their goodbyes, then exited the Hall of the Lords.

3

A GIANT'S HELP

Vigrod, Brodir, and Eirik had traveled to the village in the Frostlands, where Vigrod knew Gunir was holding up. The village was still occupied by Nathan's soldiers. On the outside, Vigrod didn't have a problem with them, but on the inside, it bothered him just the slightest bit.

The three entered the inn. The residents who were from Drangar gave Vigrod the upmost respect. To the villagers, it was like Thalmur had come to visit them.

Vigrod said hello to all the Drangarians in the inn. Then he turned to see Gunir sitting in the corner, smoking his pipe and telling a story to a few easterners who were sitting with him.

"Gunir," the Giant's head shot up to look at Vigrod.

"Ah! Highlord Frostbane, to what do I owe the pleasure?" Gunir asked.

"Unfortunately, I come bearing grave news. Our old enemy in Drangar has returned, along with the gray humans. I would ask for the support of you and any other giants that live here in Yrfel," Vigrod said.

Gunir let out an angry grunt. "It displeases me to hear this. The last time I saw the enemy with my own two eyes, I was only as tall as you and perhaps the same age."

"But no matter, come with me, Highlord."

The four journeyed out into the woods, going out toward the shores of Yrfel. They traveled a short distance before Gunir had stopped them. The group had arrived at a cave. It stretched far down beneath the surface, and Vigrod couldn't see the bottom.

Gunir then cleared his throat and looked down into the dark cave. He then began to speak the old tongue, something that only Giants understood.

Vigrod imagined he was saying, "*It is I, Gunir. I have come on urgent business. May I please see you?*"

Nothing happened at first, but suddenly, the ground started to rumble. The rumbling sound got closer and closer until a large hand had reached itself out of the cave and climbed out. This giant was extremely large. It was taller than Gunir, who was sixteen feet tall. It wore fur clothing made of bears, wolves, deer, and who knows what else, along with fiery red hair. Vigrod assumed that this was the leader, and he was astonished by what he was witnessing.

"This Highlord is King Gromir, the first and only of the giant kings," Gunir said.

"Gunir, please translate everything I say. I am Vigrod Frostbane, leader of the Drangarian people. I have come to seek your allegiance to help us in a fight with an old adversary."

Gunir translated what Vigrod said to Gromir.

The king then spoke back, "Vigrod only wished he could understand. Something about the old tongue had intrigued him greatly."

For a moment, Gunir and Gromir started conversing in old tongue, and to Vigrod's surprise, the king knelt in front of Vigrod.

"You have their allegiance Highlord. Gromir and his tribe is at your command from this day until their last day," Gunir said.

The ground began shaking again, and one by one, Giants started to pour out of the cave below. It took some time, but twenty giants emerged from the cave. They surrounded Vigrod and his company, and one by one they all knelt.

GOING WEST

Kolvar was in his quarters, packing all his things, preparing to go home. Kolvar hadn't been to the ancestral grove in years. Kolvar had come to Yrfel when he was fifteen. Now he was twenty-five. It was the year three hundred and one, and his father had disappeared eleven years ago. Kolvar was too young to fight in battles. But he was not young to rule. That is why Kolvar was smarter than most rulers, he had been doing it for a long time.

It would take about two weeks to sail to the grove, and it would take a lot longer to gather all the Elves to Yrfel. The day was June thirtieth, of the sixth summer.

There was a knock at the door. "It is Thaedra, my lord."

"Come in," Kolvar replied.

"Our ship is to leave in an hour," Thaedra said.

"Very well. I am leaving Aerimir in charge, and speaking of Aerimir, tell him to send messengers to Ravenhall and High Yrfel, saying that I am leaving for home to unite the Elven people," Kolvar said.

Thaedra nodded and walked out the door.

A few minutes more and Kolvar had finished his packing, he opened the door and started down the ramp. As he was rushing down, he felt the cool summer breeze, but Kolvar had a feeling he would return by the beginning of winter.

Kolvar walked into the throne room to say his goodbyes to Aerimir. He approached the throne, where Aerimir was sitting.

"I see the throne suites you," Kolvar said.

"I wouldn't say that it may just be the comfort of the chair," Aerimir replied with a slight laugh.

"I wish you well, my lord," Aerimir added.

"Thank you. I don't assume I'll be back anytime soon. Uniting the Elves will take time," Kolvar said.

"I agree, but our militia back home is larger than the one here, so it will give us a fighting chance in the wars to come," Aerimir said.

"It will, but I best be off. My ship leaves quite soon, and one more thing, get a messenger to Nathan that I am leaving," Kolvar said.

"At once, my lord, but you best hurry now," Aerimir said.

Kolvar exited the throne room when he saw an elf approaching him with his horse. "Thank you, my friend," Kolvar said.

He mounted his horse and rode off to the harbor.

Kolvar reached the harbor in no time at all. The elven city was quite close to the edge of Yrfel. Kolvar got on his horse and walked along the dock. He walked to the very edge to find his ship waiting for him.

Kolvar's ship was among the largest ships in the world. Elven ship craft was unmatched. He got on board to be greeted by Thaedra and the rest of his crew. He then signaled for the anchor to be raised and the sails to be lowered. Kolvar hadn't been home in ten years. One thing he'd hoped for was that he'd be accepted back home.

PART 3

The Ancestral Grove

CHAPTER

1

A WARM WELCOME

The journey west was coming to an end on the day of July eleventh of the sixth summer. The elven harbor was a great beauty, with markets and towns. The harbor was its own city. They docked and exited the boat, and they were greeted by the harbormaster.

"Lord Kolvar, I am surprised to see your ship coming into our harbor," he said. "I have come back to unite all the elven people and bring all the warriors I can back to Yrfel. The gray humans have returned," Kolvar said.

The harbormaster laughed. "What! The gray humans haven't been around for three hundred years," he said.

"Believe me, harbormaster. It is true," Kolvar said. "I ride for the golden spire, good day," Kolvar added.

Kolvar and Thaedra were given horses. Kolvar mounted up and turned to his crew.

"Stay at the harbor. I will return when my task is finished," he said, then rode off for his home, the golden spire.

An hour passed, and the sun set as Kolvar and Thaedra approached the golden spire. The setting sun shined upon the city, making it glow brighter than the stars.

The two young elves approached the gate of the city, looking up at the gatekeeper.

"Who goes there?" he said.

"Kolvar of House Keawynn, lord of the Elder Branch," Kolvar replied.

"Kolvar!" the gatekeeper yelled back. "Lady Keawynn is expecting you!" he added.

The gates opened, and the two started strolling through the illuminating city.

They looked all around, Kolvar remembering all the things he had seen years ago. The golden spire was split up into districts, the market, the residences, the military, and the spire. The three districts surrounded the spire.

They continued for a few minutes longer until they were at the gates that surrounded the spire, Kolvar told the gatekeeper who he was, and he and Thaedra were let in.

The spire was a large stone tower with designs of gold. It was almost as tall as the Elder Branch and every bit as marvelous.

Kolvar and Thaedra approached the doors to the spire. Someone approached them to take their horses, and then they walked to the doors of the spire.

The guards approached them.

"Lord Kolvar, you are expected," the guard said.

The two guards then opened the large double doors, and it opened to the throne room. The doors closed behind Kolvar and Thaedra. They then started walking toward the throne. Kolvar looked around at all the pillars and windows. They had magnificent designs shown upon them.

Kolvar and Thaedra walked around the large spiral staircase going up the entire spire. They then stopped at the foot of the stairs that led up to the throne.

"Kolvar, welcome back," Lady Keawynn said.

Her name was really Liara, but everyone referred to her as Lady Keawynn. Kolvar started walking up the stairs to reach the throne. Kolvar reached the top of the stairs seeing the throne, his mother, and the large stained-glass window behind her.

"Mother, it is good to see you," he said.

Lady Keawynn regarded her son with a nod. "How goes the war in Yrfel?" she asked. "It's going fine. We won a great battle, and we have signed a peace treaty," Kolvar said.

Lady Keawynn was drinking a fine elven wine that she spit out of her mouth when she heard the words, peace treaty.

"A peace treaty? Why?" she asked.

"The ancient enemy of Drangar has returned, along with the gray humans. I have come back to unite the Elven people and bring warriors back to Yrfel," Kolvar said.

"Unite the elves, please, Kolvar. We haven't been united since the gray human rebellions," she said.

"Mother, they are a real threat. You have to trust me," Kolvar said.

Lady Keawynn stood up to look at Kolvar. "Why we would bring everyone to Yrfel?" she asked.

"Why would they take every island in the world? It would spread them too thin, and we could just go around to each island with the largest force in history to destroy them. But if we are all at Yrfel, we can face them with all our forces," Kolvar replied.

She sighed. "It is going to be quite a task to unite every elf in the west."

"I know, but if they want to live, they will come to Yrfel," Kolvar said.

Lady Keawynn then hugged her son. "I am glad you are home, Kolvar."

WHISPERS IN THE NIGHT

K olvar was standing on the balcony at the top
of the golden spire. It was three in the morning. He'd been up thinking about how he was
going to complete his task.

He looked out and saw the sea, the two other
elf cities, and everything a person could see anything from the top of the spire. Kolvar just stood and
stared, looking, and thinking, then he heard something coming from the floor below. Kolvar wondered
who or what could be up at this hour. He trod carefully down the spiral staircase.

All the lanterns and candles were not alight. It
was quite hard to see, but the bright moon gave a
little light. As he looked down on the floor below, he
saw two figures by a window. One was hooded; the
other was cloaked by darkness.

Kolvar got closer and closer, still being careful not to get caught. He hid behind a pillar, still looking at the two. Kolvar then started to hear what they were saying. It was all faint whispers, but one of the two sounded like Kolvar's mother. Kolvar was confused, but he thought nothing of it. A lot of elven women have higher-pitched and soft voices. Kolvar then moved a bit closer, hiding behind a desk.

Kolvar listened to the women talking. He heard her say, "They know what you are preparing for."

Kolvar was so confused, preparing for what he wondered. Kolvar then listened to a man talking. Kolvar could tell by the deep voice he talked in.

Kolvar heard him say, "It doesn't matter if they know. They won't be able to handle what is coming."

What was happening was something about to happen to the golden spire was someone important going to die. Kolvar had no idea. He listened for a bit while longer. He heard the women say something about Yrfel and the man saying something about Drangar. The two figures then went their separate ways, the man going down the spiral staircase and the woman going up.

Kolvar watched this happen. He figured he was a bit late to the conversation. The two had no idea that Kolvar was right in front of them. Kolvar waited for the sounds of walking to disappear before he walked back up to the balcony.

Kolvar thought about what just took place, perhaps it was just a regular conversation, but at the latest time of night and what they spoke about, Kolvar found the chances for it being a regular conversation unlikely.

Morning arrived. Kolvar was still out on the balcony. He decided not to sleep that night. Kolvar then walked down the staircase, out the spire doors, and to the stable inside the inner gates. He then rode out to the residence district, where Thaedra was. Lady Keawynn had given Thaedra a nice place in the richer part of the district. Even though Thaedra's kin were not well-liked by Lady Keawynn, she still treated him as an honored guest.

Kolvar got off his horse and approached the doors, he knocked, and Thaedra answered. Thaedra had a surprised look on his face.

"My lord, to what do I owe the pleasure?" Thaedra said.

"May I come in?" Kolvar asked.

Thaedra nodded, escorting Kolvar to his living room. "My lord, you look like you haven't slept in a week," Thaedra said.

"I didn't sleep last night," Kolvar said, and it showed.

His long hair was messy, and there were bags under his eyes.

"Why?" Thaedra said.

Kolvar sat down and sighed. "I was up thinking about how to go about this task, then I heard something. I then walked down to the lower floor to see two people conversing. It was so late in the night. I was confused as to why they were there. I listened to their conversation. They said something about preparing, and someone wouldn't be able to handle what the man was preparing. They talked about Yrfel and Drangar, then they left."

Thaedra gave Kolvar a pat on the back.

"My lord, who knows who those people were. They could've been speaking of anything," Thaedra said.

Kolvar then looked up at Thaedra. "Why would they converse of such things at three in the morning?" Kolvar said.

Thaedra then nodded. "Good point, but we should start worrying about the task at hand," he said.

"Fine, I should most likely start with the people here. I would tell my mother to call every elf in the city to come to the spire. I would make my speech there," Kolvar said.

"Very well. We probably should go then," Thaedra said.

The two then walked outside. Kolvar mounted up and waited for Thaedra to get his horse.

They soon were at the spire. The two then entered the throne room. Kolvar walked up to his mother.

"Kolvar, where did you go earlier? I was surprised not to see you at the spire," Lady Keawynn said.

"I went to get Thaedra," Kolvar replied.

Lady Keawynn then looked at her son's appearance. "You look like you've just had a sleepless night," she said.

"Indeed, but I would request you call the people of the spire to the inner gates of the spire," Kolvar said.

"Why?" Lady Keawynn asked.

"To tell them about what is coming and get ready to sail for Yrfel," he said.

"Fine, but if they do not agree with you, I won't tell them too," Lady Keawynn said.

Kolvar then laughed. "What?" Lady Keawynn said.

"You know, I am father's heir, so technically, I should rule the spire. The only reason you do is because we left for Yrfel," Kolvar said.

"Hmm, I hadn't thought of that. Well, son, here is the throne," Lady Keawynn said, standing up. "But I guess then you give the commands," she added.

"I would still request you gather everyone here. You've been their ruler for the past ten years. They would more likely listen to you," Kolvar said.

Lady Keawynn started walking down the stairs. "I will see it done, Lord Kolvar." She then turned around and bowed.

Kolvar started laughing. "Get the militia to gather everyone in two days," he said.

Thaedra then walked up to Kolvar. "What would you do now?" Thaedra asked.

"I will wait till night to see if those people are here again," Kolvar said.

"My lord, you need sleep," Thaedra replied.

"I know, but I need to know if they are there again," Kolvar said.

"You also won't see me tomorrow," Kolvar added.

"Why is that?" Thaedra asked.

"Because I will be sleeping."

Night fell. He again stood out on the balcony, and he waited. Kolvar knew what time it was. All elves were taught as children how to use the sun and moon to tell time. It was one in the morning. He then started down the spiral staircase, checking to see if anyone was there with the coast clear Kolvar went to the desk he hid behind last night.

He waited and waited when, finally, he heard something. It was the sound of walking. They were light footsteps. Kolvar could tell it was the woman. A few more minutes passed, and he heard heavy footsteps. The man had arrived.

"Good to see you," the woman said.

The man's response could not be heard by Kolvar. "Anything to say about him?" the man asked.

Kolvar then peaked his head out a little bit. The woman then looked out the window.

"He plans to start his mission in a day."

Kolvar heard the man grunt. He would not expect this behavior from any elf.

"We plan to sail within the next year or so," the man said.

"Sail where? Remember, they plan to get everyone to Yrfel," the woman replied.

"I know if there is nothing else you would tell me, I would take my leave," the man said.

"No, nothing else of importance," the woman said.

"He will reward you greatly for this, my lady," he said.

Kolvar eyes then opened widely. Who was this lady really? She had to be someone of importance to be referred to as my lady. He assumed that the mission they referred to be his own. But something the woman said piqued Kolvar's suspicions about the lady sounding like his mother.

The two left, and then Kolvar sat still for a moment, then he started talking to himself about what had just happened.

"If the man referred to this woman as 'my lady,' she must be someone important. But this lady knows of my mission and the plan to get everyone to Yrfel, and the only woman I told of this is my mother."

STARTING THE MISSION

The day had come, and Kolvar had delivered on his promise of yesterday of sleeping through it. But before Kolvar started, he had to talk to his mother. Kolvar sat on the throne, and his mother walked up the stairs to the throne.

"Kolvar, you wanted to see me?" Lady Keawynn said.

"Yes, I have a question for you," Kolvar replied.

She gave a nod back.

"Where were you last night, around one in the morning?" Kolvar asked.

Lady Keawynn's face showed surprise and worry. "I was sleeping. Where else would I be at that hour?" she said.

Kolvar then stood up with quite a serious look on his face. "Possibly awake, just up going on a stroll throughout the spire, or talking with someone," Kolvar.

Kolvar could tell Lady Keawynn grew more worried with each word. She slowly backed away, standing at the edge of the stairs.

"Who was I talking to, and who strolls through the spire so late at night?" she said.

"Who else did you tell of my plans?" Kolvar asked.

"No one. Who would I tell? Certainly no one here," Lady Keawynn said.

"Well, if you will not say, or if you are telling the truth, perhaps I should prepare my speech," Kolvar said.

Walking down to the spiral staircase, where Thaedra was waiting for him, they then walked up the stairs into the library.

Kolvar and Thaedra sat down at the table. Thaedra handed over a quill and parchment to Kolvar.

"She was not telling the truth. You could hear it in her voice," Kolvar said.

"I think you are right. If the whisperers of the night appear again, it most likely is her," Thaedra replied.

Kolvar looked up at Thaedra. "What if it is her, but the thing that is on my mind the most, who is she talking to?" he said.

"I don't know, my lord. Perhaps work on your speech," Thaedra said.

"Yes, you are right," Kolvar said.

He started writing. It took Kolvar a few minutes to write. He was quite good at coming up with speeches, and there was not much to write about. He read over it a few times to get the words to stick in his head. Then he was ready.

Kolvar walked back down to the throne room when a guard approached him. "My lord, the people are here," he said.

Kolvar walked out to large doors to see thousands of people surrounding the spire.

Kolvar waved to all the elves then he started speaking, "People of the spire! I have come back after many years of being away, but I have come back to you to tell you something. Our enemies from long ago have returned, the gray humans. You may not believe it, but it is true. All warriors of the west must come back to Yrfel. I will unite our people and bring them to Yrfel, but I will need everyone to, to—" Kolvar stopped talking.

He saw something. He noticed everyone. All the elves with their fine hair of gold and brown. He spotted someone in the crowd. Someone wearing a hood and all black. Kolvar stared at the man. He knew this was the man he heard in the night. A guard came up to Kolvar and put a hand on his shoulder.

"Are you alright, my lord?" the guard asked.

"Yes, yes…," Kolvar replied. He couldn't see the man's face, but he noticed his skin was particularly gray. "That man in the hood, bring him to me," Kolvar said slowly.

Kolvar felt as if he had been put in a trance.

The guard looked at the three other guards behind him and made a motion for them to go with him. They started making their way through the crowd. All the while, Kolvar and the man stared at each other. The guards reached the man, and instantly, the man pulled out a knife and plunged deep into one of the guard's hearts. It tore through his gold armor. A fight broke out, the guards trying to get the man's knife. Slowly, all the people backed away while the guards used their shields to surround him. It didn't take them long; his knife wasn't too much use against the shields.

The guards subdued the man and brought him to Kolvar. The man's head was down, so his face was covered.

"Take off his hood," Kolvar said.

The guards did so. Every person inside the walls gasped. The man was a gray human.

His skin was gray and cracked, with spots of white throughout. He had no hair on his head, compared to Kolvar's brown hair and blue eyes, and smooth skin.

The guards turned the gray human around to face the people, then Kolvar stepped forward.

"Do you now see, fair elves! I am telling the truth. They are coming for us all!" Kolvar yelled.

After Kolvar was done speaking, all the Elves bowed to him. His mission was going well so far.

"Bring me, my mother. I would quite like to speak to her," Kolvar said.

One of the guards went back inside the building and came out an hour or so later. "My lord, I've searched the tower bottom to top and back again. She's gone."

Kolvar's sneaking suspicions were true. His mother was talking to a mysterious someone, who turned out to be a gray human. Still, they all stood outside the large doors to the spire. The citizens all surrounding them. The gray human still in chains.

Kolvar turned to the guards. "Throw him in a cell. I want guards at his cell at all times. He must not escape," he said.

Kolvar planned to question him after he found his mother. Kolvar looked at all the people of the spire.

"Stay calm, my people!" Kolvar yelled.

Kolvar and Thaedra walked back to the throne room. Kolvar sat down on the throne, his face buried in his hands.

"Well, this was not how I thought today was going to go," Kolvar said.

"Well, my lord, the mission is starting off well, and now it is confirmed that they have returned," Thaedra replied.

"Now we should head for your home, and you will have to do some work to help me convince them," Kolvar said.

Thaedra's eyes widened. He had not been home in some time. He came to Yrfel when his father had gone off to fight in the first war. Thaedra and Kolvar's fathers were good friends. Thaedra's father was a commander in the militia, so Thaedra and Kolvar became good friends while their fathers fought in a war.

"Very good, my lord. When shall we leave?" Thaedra asked.

"I plan to leave tomorrow. I will inform the militia leader to send a messenger if they find her," Kolvar replied.

"Yes, my lord, but it will feel good to be home," Thaedra said happily.

Thaedra left to go to his home in the residential district while Kolvar went to the military district to inform the commander of his orders.

Kolvar then returned to the spire to go and lay in his bed. For a while, he thought about everything that had happened today and everything that could happen in the coming days. Finally, after a few minutes of thinking, he finally fell asleep.

THE MISSION CONTINUES

The morning came, and Kolvar and Thaedra's horses were already prepared. Guards were out looking for Lady Keawynn, and soon enough, a fine breakfast was prepared for Kolvar and Thaedra.

It was a fine breakfast indeed, perfectly cooked bacon, bread, and a cup of wine. Some people wouldn't have a cup of wine this time, but for an elf, it is always a perfect time for wine.

Soon after, they were off, riding through the golden spire while the sun rose behind them. A few guards accompanied them and the gray human.

The guards were necessary. The wood elves were quite different from the elves in the spire. Thaedra's people were not on speaking terms with Kolvar's, so there was a chance they could be attacked.

A few minutes into their journey, they were riding through the lush plains of House Keawynn's lands, looking at the few hundred-foot-tall trees.

The elves rode west, under clouds and stairs, day after day, seeing all the beautiful things in the west. They decided to camp beside a large rock, they started a fire and took care of their horses, and they prepared a meal.

"We will be in the woodlands in a few days," Commander Alwin said, commander of the golden spire militia.

"Very good, Commander," Kolvar replied. "Thaedra, once we pass into the woodlands, I want you leading us. They will let you pass for certain," he added.

"Yes, my lord. We should keep him as concealed as possible. The wood Elves will most likely kill him as soon as they lay eyes on him," Thaedra said while staring at the gray human.

Commander Alwin then put out the fire, trying not to attract any hawks or forest prowlers. The group of elves was soon asleep, ready for the day ahead.

Morning had come. The guards were taking watch of the things around them and their prisoners. Their horses were ready, and they were off.

*****

Three more days of traveling, the group had entered the woodlands. The trees surrounded them, hundreds of tall trees. There were winding paths through the woods, up and down hills. The path was made of dirt, and sometimes the grass would cover it. They lost the path many times and were riding around for hours and hours on end. The sun started to set. They could see it through the trees. The light was starting to fade. When it turned completely dark, the path was lost.

"Should we stop, my lord?" Thaedra asked.

"I don't think we can. There has to be a village or inn somewhere," Kolvar said.

They kept riding, going north, then west, then south, then west again. The woods started making noises, birds, bugs, and otherwise.

Thaedra started to stroll off to the right, going further than the rest of the group.

"Thaedra! Wait just a moment!" Kolvar yelled.

"My lord, I see a light up ahead. I think we have found an inn!" he yelled back.

The rest of the elves rode up ahead to catch up to Thaedra, and he was right. There was the inn.

The group approached the inn; the architecture of the woodlands was quite different compared to the architecture of the spire. The buildings were made of dark wood instead of stone, clear glass instead of stained, and the inn had vines hanging from the sides.

They went to the stables next to the inn, then Kolvar and Thaedra went inside while the guards and the prisoner stayed out. The first thing they saw was the innkeeper. Behind him were barrels upon barrels of ale, wine, and beer. They also saw wood Elves talking, singing, drinking, and smoking. They went and sat down at a table in the corner. Then the innkeeper came to them.

"Welcome to the woodlands inn. How can I be of service?" he said.

"We are looking for a place to stay and directions to the hanging city," Kolvar said.

"We have room for you. Is this all your company?" the innkeeper asked.

Kolvar nodded in reply, "Very well. I will see you to your rooms in a moment," he said, then walked away.

Kolvar and Thaedra walked back outside to see the guards setting camp next to a tree. "We are going to be staying here for the night," Kolvar said.

"Yes, my lord, we will be fine camping out here," Commander Alwin replied. "Okay, we will be back at the break of day," Kolvar said.

The commander nodded in response, then Kolvar and Thaedra went back to the inn.

The innkeeper made a gesture for them to follow him. He took the two upstairs into their room. It was a cozy little place with two beds, a table and chairs, and a fireplace, where a fire had already been set for them.

"Would you two fine sirs request any food or drink?" the innkeeper asked.

"Two ales, and bread, thank you," Kolvar said.

Soon after, a server came and gave them their food and drinks. They had their meal and sat by the fire, telling stories all the while of the war, their childhoods, and anything they could think of. They then got into their comforting beds and were asleep almost instantly.

The morning came, and Kolvar and Thaedra had woken themselves up and went downstairs to find the innkeeper cleaning mugs and other things.

"Ah, I see you are awake. Take this map. It will give you directions to the Hanging city," he said.

"Thank you, sir. Your food and drink were excellent," Kolvar replied.

"I try my hardest," the innkeeper said, smiling.

Then Kolvar and Thaedra left to get the guards, who were already awake, getting the horses ready and packing up their supplies.

"The innkeeper gave us a map to the hanging city," Kolvar said.

Then Kolvar turned to look at Thaedra. "Thaedra, you used to live here. Don't you know your way around?" he added.

"I used to. There used to be paths and such. It is a lot different now," Thaedra said.

"Anyway, it's only a few hours away. We should be there by midday," Kolvar said.

Their journey started, going north on a not-so-visible path around the inn. But after they got over the hill behind the inn, the paths became a lot clearer and the forest more open. The path went forward and only forward for the rest of the journey.

The group approached a large hill, a very large hill. It was sort of like a mountain. They rode up the hill. It took them almost thirty minutes. When they got to the top, they finally saw it.

5

THE HANGING CITY

The group stopped at the top of the hill and stared. The hanging city was a great marvel. It was high in the air. It was suspended in the air, connected to great vines. Four trees were placed at each corner, each of them miles apart. The city itself was sitting on a large wood platform made from the tallest trees from the wood elf forest itself. The trees that kept the city hanging were protected by great vines that were stronger than any metal. No fire could burn it except grayfyre.

They rode up to the town that was at the face of the hanging city, and they were met by two soldiers with armor of wood made from the trees of the forest.

"Welcome to Vinecrest, the town of the hanging city. Where are you coming from?" he said.

The wood elves had long black hair and green eyes and darker skin than most elves.

"We were traveling from Woodtown at the other end of the forest," Thaedra said.

The wood elves did not trust outsiders, and the town at the south end of the forest was considered part of wood elf land.

"Well, it doesn't seem so. The guards in gold armor and man in all black, say otherwise," the soldier replied. "Where do you really come from?" he added.

Kolvar got off his horse and walked close to the soldiers. They put their hands on the hilts of their swords. Kolvar quickly punched the guard standing on the left in the nose, knocking him clean out. The other soldier took out his sword, and Kolvar ducked under it and tackled him. Kolvar took off the soldier's helmet and hit him in the head with it till he was unconscious.

"Well, let us make for the city," Kolvar said.

"Good job, my lord. I didn't know you were a proficient hand-to-hand combatant," Thaedra said.

"Well, when I wasn't doing things for the war, I would shoot Eldrin's bow or train with Commander Rion," he replied.

"My lord, did you bring back Eldrin's bow? I would like to see it, if you wouldn't mind," Alwin said.

"Unfortunately, no, I keep it somewhere safe back on Yrfel, but soon, I might have to take it everywhere," Kolvar replied.

Kolvar got back on his horse, and they made for the stables. Kolvar paid the stable's owner to keep their horses for a while.

To get up to the hanging city itself, there was an elevator made of wood and iron, and chains carried it to the top. The elevator could hold up to five hundred people. The group approached the elevator, and an elf approached them.

"Do you need to use the elevator? That will be five silvers for each of you," he said.

Kolvar agreed to pay, reluctantly. Five silver was quite expensive to use in an elevator.

They entered the elevator, and the man who just took Kolvar's money blew a horn. The elevator then started moving. Kolvar looked to the side to see hundreds of people pushing a mechanism that lifted them up. Minutes later, they were at the top, they got out, and the city was right there in front of them. There were no walls. The height and trees were the defense.

They walked through the city. It was longer than the spire, much longer. The houses were made of wood and wood only. The houses were made of different types of wood, and it was a very bustling city. People were working and trading, walking, and talking.

Thaedra talked all the while, saying how he remembered everything, which Kolvar quickly contradicted because Thaedra didn't remember the forest paths.

Thaedra stopped. They were past all the stores and businesses and were now in the residences.

"I need to go see someone, someone I haven't seen in a long time," he said.

"Who?" Kolvar asked.

"My mother," Thaedra said.

"Well, I will come with you," Kolvar insisted.

"No thank you, my lord. I don't think she knows you. She's never been outside the forest, at least since we've left," he replied.

Thaedra then walked off into the distance. Meanwhile, the rest of the group walked to the castle.

They spent hours walking the few miles of the hanging city when the sun started to set. They approached the end of the hanging city where Kolvar assumed the wood elf royalty would be. There was a staircase leading up to a platform. Up on this platform, there was a table for the royalty and tables for everyone else there, and it was shielded by a large tent.

They waited on the staircase for Thaedra. Time went on, and people started to go to sleep. The city was almost completely empty when Thaedra appeared.

"Thaedra, finally, we should probably find somewhere to stay," Kolvar said.

Commander Alwin had a confused look on his face. "If we stay at the inn, what will we do with him, it's too risky to leave him on his own," he said.

"Before I went to Yrfel, I would see people camping on the edge of the platform," Thaedra said.

"Hopefully, you are right. If so, we will have to ask someone to let us camp with them," Kolvar said.

They walked to the east edge of the platform, looking north and south, not seeing anyone. They started to walk south. Hopefully, they would see someone.

They walked and walked and walked, to no avail. No one was found. It was late into the night, and everyone was getting tired.

Out of the darkness came an elf from the city, and he came up to the group.

"You lost, friends?" he said.

"We are looking for a group to camp on edge with," Thaedra said.

The elf man came and gave Thaedra a pat on the shoulder. "Perfect! I and my partner were looking for a group to camp with," he said.

"Come with me," he added.

They walked to the west edge of the platform, following the man, and he took them to a campsite. It wasn't much, a small tent, two wooden chairs, and a campfire.

A woman came out of the tent to give her partner a kiss on the cheek. "You found a group to camp with us?" she said.

The man gave a nod.

They all sat down, the elf man and woman on chairs, Kolvar's group on the ground.

"So what are Elves from the spire doing here?" the man said. "We came here to see the city. Most of us haven't been out…"

Thaedra was saying when Kolvar stopped him. "I am Kolvar Keawynn. I returned from Yrfel to unite our people and bring warriors to Yrfel. The gray humans have returned," he said.

The two Elves gave a laugh. They laughed for quite a while. "Apologies, my lord. The gray humans probably don't even exist. A story, it was three hundred years ago," the man said.

Kolvar didn't respond.

"What's your story? You aren't dressed like an elf, and I don't think you are an elf," he said. Kolvar stood up.

"Since you don't believe in gray humans," Kolvar said.

He then removed the hood of the gray human. The man and women's faces were in shock. They had never seen a gray human. Kolvar assumed they were in shock because they had never seen something so ugly.

"This is a gray human. Since you don't believe they are real, here he is," Kolvar said.

The man got closer to the gray human, but not too close, even though the gray human was in chains.

"This looks like how they are described. Why would you bring us to Yrfel?" the man said.

"We are going to enlist every person in our world in our army to fight them," Kolvar replied.

"How do you know when they are going to attack?" the woman said.

"This one said it himself," Kolvar replied.

"But you don't rule here. How will you convince everyone here to follow you?" the man asked.

Kolvar was stuck in thought. The man had a point. He did not rule here, so why would the wood Elves follow him?

He then had an idea. "Gather every person you know in the hanging city. Bring them back to this campsite," Kolvar said.

"That is a good idea. Consider it done," the man said.

"Now I would like to get some sleep," Kolvar said.

The man and woman went inside their tent.

Commander Alwin got sleeping bags made of fur from their supply bags, and the group then fell asleep.

GATHERING CROWDS

The morning came. The two wood elves were gone. Kolvar assumed that they wanted to get off to an early start to gather some other elves. Or perhaps they had just left and gone about their daily business.

"What are we to do, my lord?" Thaedra asked.

"Wait until they come back. I don't think they would have left their camping supplies here if they meant to not do what I asked," Kolvar responded.

"If this does work, once we convince a good amount of people, we will approach the wood elf royalty, then send a messenger back to the spire," Kolvar said.

Commander Alwin replied with a nod. As the day passed, not much was said, they waited and waited until some people approached them.

Kolvar saw an elf walking through the buildings with a decently large group, twenty people or so.

The man from the previous night approached Kolvar.

"I've done what you asked," he said.

Kolvar stood up and gave the man a handshake.

"Thank you, sir," Kolvar said.

He then turned to the group. He made a hand motion for Thaedra to stand beside him.

"I am Lord Kolvar Keawynn of the golden spire. This is Thaedra, my adviser and a resident of these lands. I have coordinated a gathering today to announce that I will be uniting the elven people to fight against our common enemy, the gray humans."

Some people chuckled; some others held in laughter.

"I expected you wouldn't believe me, Commander Alwin! Bring the prisoner forward," Kolvar said.

Commander Alwin did as he was told. The gray human had his head down. Commander Alwin wasted no time in taking off the prisoner's hood and forcefully raising his head.

"This is a gray human. You now see the truth," Kolvar said.

A man in the crowd stepped forward.

"What would you ask of us to do?" he said.

"Gather more people. If our crowd gets big enough, I'm sure others will come as well," Kolvar answered.

As the day went on, more people flooded in. Kolvar went on explaining to the new people as soon as they arrived. Kolvar's prediction came true. More random people came to the crowd. Elves had a strong sense of curiosity.

When Kolvar felt he had got enough people, they walked together in a troupe to the end of the hanging city to approach the royalty. When they did reach the royalty's platform, guards came up to them.

"What are you doing here?" the guard said. "I've come to speak to your leaders," Kolvar replied.

Kolvar then looked at Commander Alwin. Alwin then knew to bring the prisoner to the guards. When the guards saw the gray human, they stepped back and had looks of fear on their faces.

"Come with us," he said.

The crowd came with them. It would make Kolvar's claims more believable if he had his believers with him.

The royalty stood up when the crowd flooded the royalty platform. "What is the meaning of this? Guards get them out of here!" the wood elf lord yelled.

"My lord, you will want to hear this," the guard said.

Kolvar approached the wood elf lord. Commander Alwin came with him.

"My lord, I am Lord Kolvar Keawynn of the golden spire. I have come to unite the elven people, the gray humans have returned, and I know you do not believe me, so I brought a living gray human to show you that they have returned."

"I...I...I don't know what to say. You are right. What do you need from me?" the wood elf lord said.

"Your soldiers, I plan to take all the warriors I can get back to Yrfel. How many can you provide?" Kolvar replied.

"We have forty-five thousand fighting men. When will you need them?" the wood elf lord said.

"I need a bit of time to think. In the meantime, can one of your advisers send a messenger to the spire informing them of what happened here," Kolvar said.

The wood elf lord gave a nod and gave his orders.

Kolvar thought of a genius idea. This would easily convince the last group of elves, the celestial elves.

Kolvar's plan was to take a large group of wood elves and meet up with a large group of spire elves and go to the bright city, home of the celestial elves. The wood elf lord strolled up to Kolvar.

"Have you thought of anything?" he asked.

"Yes, we will take a large group of wood elves and meet up with a group of spire elves, go to the bright city, and that's how we will convince the celestial elves," Kolvar replied.

"That is a good plan. They will see how many people believe you," the wood elf lord answered. "I will be coming with you," he added.

Kolvar looked at a wood elf standing next to the wood elf lord. "Excuse me, sir. Get someone to write a message to the spire. Tell them to gather a large group of citizens and come to the town at the south end of the forest," Kolvar said. The man looked at Kolvar.

"Who are you to give me commands!" he yelled.

Kolvar gave the man a look. Regardless of if he was an outsider, he had the trust of this man's lord.

"You speak to our guest in this way? Find someone to write the message, now!" the wood elf lord yelled.

The wood elf lord gathered more people. Kolvar requested about a thousand. Some people didn't even know what was happening, but they were coming. Once everyone was informed of what was happening, Kolvar decided that they would wait for a response, then leave.

*****

Two days had passed. It only took two days by messenger to get from the hanging city to the spire. Kolvar was the first person to read the response. Here is what it said.

Lord Kolvar,

We will be at the settlement of woodtown in hopefully two weeks, a large group will most likely result in a slow journey.

Aymar Elwynn
Lieutenant of the spire militia

Everything was going as planned so far. The wood elf lord went back to his chair at the royalty table. Kolvar was sitting right next to him.

"Lord Kolvar, I would give you a residence for the night. We will hold your prisoner at our prison down below in Vinecrest under heavy guard," he said.

"Thank you, my lord, but I can't accept. My prisoner is too valuable. I will not let him out of my sight. I can't risk having him escape," Kolvar replied.

"Very well. I will see you tomorrow morning," the wood elf lord said.

He then walked off, going down some stairs behind the royalty table. Kolvar assumed it was to his own personal space.

Kolvar's group went back to the camp a few days ago. The elf man and women were already there. They welcomed them to open arms. They were fast asleep. Commander Alwin watched over the prisoner, who did sleep. Even people of evil needed sleep.

The morning came, and everyone was awake. Kolvar met up with the wood elf lord, a large following behind him. They walked down to the elevator, going a few hundred at a time, going down to Vinecrest. Soon everyone was at Vinecrest. They started walking toward Woodtown, led by guides who knew the forest like the back of their hand. Kolvar's mission was soon complete. He hoped that Nathan was having the same success he was.

WOODTOWN

Woodtown was quite a large town. Nearly a thousand people lived in it until the rest of the elves arrived. The wood elves for the hanging city were staying outside, going in and out of town, waiting for the elves from the spire to arrive.

Kolvar and Thaedra were sitting at the table in the town hall. With the town master, he was quite nice, welcoming them as any good elf should.

"They should be here in a few days," Kolvar said.

"I hope so. With any luck, they haven't been held up by anything," Thaedra replied. "What is the plan for the bright city?" Thaedra asked.

"Probably what the wood elf lord suggested. If we arrive there and if they see that a lot of people believe us, maybe they will join us," Kolvar responded.

Commander Alwin walked into the town hall. "My lord, a message from Lieutenant Elwynn."

Kolvar was surprised. He had no idea that they brought messenger birds with them. Alwin gave the message to Kolvar. Kolvar opened it, then started reading.

Lord Kolvar,

We will be at Woodtown in a few days. We are moving at a quick pace for a group of a thousand elves.

Aymar Elwynn
Lieutenant of the spire militia

Kolvar folded the message up and put it down. "Very good. Inform everyone to start camping on the edges of town. We won't take up their space," he said.

Commander Alwin nodded and left the town hall.

*****

Around four days passed; the group had finally arrived. Kolvar and Thaedra left the town hall, which was where they were staying. They walked out to where Kolvar's troupe was.

"Now that we are all here, we will go to the bright city and convince the bright Elves to join us!"

They waited till morning. Everyone was ready to leave. Kolvar went back to the town master, accompanied by Thaedra and the wood elf lord.

"Sir, would it be possible to bring your citizens along with us? I feel the more we have, the more likely our chances of convincing the bright Elves to join us are," Kolvar said.

The townmaster nodded. There was not really much hesitation before he responded.

Every elf who was making the trip was gathered up. After they prepared enough food, water, and materials for camping, they started on their journey.

"I've never been to the bright city. How long will the journey be?" Thaedra asked.

"I asked the town master, it will take about a month, but with this group, possibly longer," Alwin replied.

The company was incredibly slow. Kolvar's militia on Yrfel could make better time, and the militia had over fifty thousand men. They went up and downhill, down riverbanks, and through small forests. Kolvar was waiting for night to fall. This journey was starting out terribly.

"We aren't making good time," Alwin said.

"I thought so. I'm not sure we will get there," Kolvar replied.

Everyone was tired. They camped on a riverbank. Some people didn't even finish setting up their tents. They just took a sleeping bag and fell right asleep. Kolvar was in his tent, trying to get some sleep, but he couldn't. Kolvar could not stop thinking about where his mother was. Kolvar hoped they had found his mother. He was yearning to ask her one question, which was, Why?

The next morning, Kolvar woke up and walked outside his tent, he stretched, and his eyes dilated to the bright sun. Thaedra then approached Kolvar.

"My lord! Good morning," Thaedra said excitedly.

"Good morning, my friend," Kolvar said slowly.

"Do you know what day it is?" Thaedra asked.

Kolvar raised his eyebrow. "It is your day of birth, Lord Kolvar."

"Ah, how did I not know that? Time is really getting away from me," Kolvar said, laughing.

The day was August twenty-second, and twenty-six years ago, Kolvar Keawynn came into the world.

Kolvar felt indifferent about the fact it was his day of birth, but he knew the last thing he wanted to do on his own day was walk any further.

BRIGHT LANDS

After two long months of traveling, they finally did it. They reached the bright lands. October of the year three hundred one was upon them. The leaves started to change color, but none fell off the trees.

The group was at the entrance to a town leading to the rest of the bright lands.

The town's name was Light's Point. They were stopped by guards, clad in armor made of regular-looking metal. That had a lining that looked like starlight. It was quite beautiful.

"What is your business?" the guard asked.

"We are trying to get to the bright city," Kolvar replied.

"Hmm, quite a large amount of people. Move along."

They passed through, all the people in the main street getting out of the way. Kolvar felt a sort of pride strolling through Light's Point. It took them several minutes for every single person to get out of the town and out into the road and grass of the bright lands.

They continued onward. There was a light breeze, the sun was setting, and Kolvar felt happy. The journey to the bright lands was miserable, the weather was hot, and everyone was walking extremely slowly.

They continued down the road, and they passed a sign that marked where Bright City was. Soon, they would arrive. The troupe arrived at a stone bridge that was placed over a river, and that river went on and on the right to the bright city. Kolvar looked to the left and saw the city.

The first thing he saw was the waterfalls going out to the river that they were standing over. He saw the large towers and bridges and the mountains surrounding the southern side of the city.

They continued over the bridge into a forest. Kolvar saw that there were lanterns hanging from the branches. *Quite a unique design*, Kolvar thought to himself. They followed the path out of the forest, then saw a large bridge. That was somehow illuminating. Kolvar had heard about the unknown ways the Celestial Elves manipulated light.

They started walking the bridge, soon approaching the front gate. That was open. The walls were also illuminating, displaying the same features the bridge did.

"Their gates are open?" Thaedra said.

"It seems so. Quite odd," Kolvar replied.

Entering the city, they saw interesting architecture and large waterspouts.

"Once they see what we are here for, me, you, and Alwin will go inside and talk to the royalty," Kolvar said to Thaedra.

Thaedra nodded in response, and they continued onward. Continuing forward, they saw many celestial elves. Wearing their finest clothing made from silks that Kolvar had never seen. The castle loomed in the back of the city; it took them several minutes to walk over to it.

The guards stopped them.

"What are you doing?" he asked.

"I have come to speak to your leaders about the returning gray humans," Kolvar replied.

Alwin already knew how to bring the prisoner forward.

"This is what they look like? They are uglier than described," the guard said while staring at the gray human's face.

Celestial elves had better sight than any living being. Their vision at night was unparalleled, so it was easy for them to see under the prisoner's hood.

"So these are your believers?" the guard asked. Kolvar nodded. "Well, I guess I can't refuse," the guard added.

He called for the gates to be opened. The two guards guided the four inside. The doors opened to reveal a large throne room, columns holding up the castle, and large chandeliers hanging around. They approached the throne. Sitting upon it was a young woman, only a year or so younger than Kolvar. She had brown hair, brown eyes, and pale skin.

"My lady," the guards said, bowing.

They left the castle to go back to the gates.

"My lady, I am Lord Kolvar Keawynn, lord of the golden spire and the Elder Branch."

"I know who you are, my lord. I am Lady Aerin."

"So why are you here, my lord?" she added.

"I am here to bring warriors back to Yrfel. The gray humans are returning, and we need every person we can to stop them," Kolvar said.

"Bring forth the prisoner Alwin."

Alwin did as he was told. Lady Aerin's face showed fear and surprise.

"I heard stories about them. Their appearance was not described correctly," she said. "Do I have your allegiance?" Kolvar asked.

"How will we get everyone to Yrfel? We surely don't have enough ships," Lady Aerin said.

"I'm sure we have plenty of architects. We will be fine, my lady," Kolvar replied.

Kolvar stepped closer to the throne. "Do I have your allegiance, my lady?"

Lady Aerin sighed. "You do."

"Good, if it is possible, get your army ready and out of the city within the week," Kolvar replied.

The guards stepped forward to escort Kolvar's group out of the castle and back to their troupe.

"Well, what happened?" Lieutenant Aymar asked.

"They are coming. We will leave tomorrow morning," Kolvar replied.

The sun started to set, and Kolvar's troupe was split up and given places to sleep. Kolvar and Thaedra were given rooms inside the castle.

Kolvar sat on his bed. The bed felt like a dream compared to what he slept on inside his tent when they were on the road. Every day, he still thought about his mother, wondering where she was and why she was working with the enemy. A thousand thoughts rushed through Kolvar's mind. He just wanted some sleep, and he wanted to get back to Yrfel. To Kolvar, Yrfel was like a second home that he had spent most of his life in, and he couldn't wait to get back.

HEADING FOR HOME

Kolvar was woken up by a servant of Lady Aerin. He exited his room to find Thaedra standing a few feet away. The servant escorted them down to the throne room.

"The guards will guide you to the front gates," the servant said.

He then turned around and left, then guards approached and guided them toward their destination.

He was met at the front gates by the rest of his troupe and several guards.

"Attention, everyone!" Kolvar yelled. Everyone's heads swiftly turned around to look at him. "I have decided that everyone will be able to travel at their own pace. Traveling with such a large number slows things down. Hopefully, this will speed up the journey back."

Kolvar was met with many responses, such as, *Great! And thank goodness.* Kolvar walked around to find Alwin, Aymar, and a few other guards.

"I don't want to waste any more time here. Let's go," Kolvar demanded. He led them out the open gates, and they started across the bridge.

"When we get to Light's Point, we shall buy horses, then discuss our route to return home," Kolvar said.

Exiting the bridge and back out onto the cobblestone road, they traveled a bit further and entered back into the small forest. The lanterns hanging from the branches gave off very little light this early in the day.

They exited the forest and crossed the river bridge. They moved on swiftly, the town of Light's Point in sight. The sun shone brightly on that day. The grass was greener than usual. Many birds and beasts were scurrying around.

The Light's Point guards welcomed the group back.

"Where is the town's stable?" Kolvar asked.

"Near the front of town on the left side of the street. You will know it when you smell it," the guard replied.

Kolvar bid them a good day, and they continued forward. The street was bustling. All the elves performed their everyday deeds, making no notice of Kolvar. They saw him as one of the many. His royalty didn't matter much in their land.

The stables had an odd smell. Kolvar knew it was horse manure, but he tried not to think about it.

Thaedra made a groan. "The smell of shit is unbearable," Thaedra said.

Kolvar looked at Thaedra, he had never heard Thaedra curse before, but to Kolvar, it was quite funny. Some of the guards even smirked.

"Thaedra, calm yourself. The stable's owner probably smells it all day, and if he heard you, he'd probably hit you harder than an Ashwalker could," Kolvar said.

Kolvar approached the stable's owner, grabbing his coin pouch.

"Excuse me, sir, how much for seven horses?" Kolvar said.

"Give me five gold per horse, and you have a deal. Please excuse the smell. My employees clean it every few hours," the stable owner replied.

Thaedra rolled his eyes. Kolvar gave him a little shove and smirked.

Kolvar reached into his wallet and pulled out thirty-five gold, and taking that made Kolvar feel that his pouch was nearly empty, but to Kolvar, fifteen gold wasn't that much to him. They lost their original horses in Vinecrest. When they went up to the Hanging City, they were taken somewhere.

The stable employees saddled the seven horses and brought them out to Kolvar. The seven of them mounted their horses, the prisoner riding with

Alwin. The stable owner then yelled at his employees to clean the horse manure.

"Now we have a choice to make, do we go back the way we came, or do we cut across the entire grove and to the spire," Kolvar said.

"Keep in mind. We need to go as fast as possible."

"I think we should go back the way we came. We would know where we're going, and we can still go fast," Thaedra said.

"I agree with Thaedra. We can find a guide at Woodtown to help us to get through the wood elf forest," Alwin said.

"But no one is at Woodtown. We took them all here," Aymar said. "But still, I agree with Thaedra."

"Well, that is what you three say. I agree with you," Kolvar said. He turned toward his other guards. "I'm sorry if you felt different, but we do have the majority of votes," Kolvar said with a slight laugh.

They were on their way out of the bright land before midday. Kolvar's craving to get back to Yrfel was growing. He was close now. He had a plan for when they got back. Everything was going according to plan so far.

10

THE WANDERER OF
THE WOODS

The journey back to Woodtown only took the group two weeks. They only stopped when they had too.

The emptiness of Woodtown gave Kolvar an odd feeling like they were being watched.

"Well, now what do we go around the forest?" Aymar asked.

"No, that would take way too long, even if we weren't trying to rush," Kolvar replied.

Kolvar looked around. He hoped someone would be there to guide them. "We still have to go through. Come on," Kolvar said.

They approached the forest slowly. They had no map, only one from the inn on the other side of the forest to the hanging city.

Suddenly, someone approached them. He was oddly dressed. He wore a large cloak, covered in leaves and dirt. He wore no shoes or anything. On top of his head, he wore something like a crown. It was decorated with an assortment of leaves.

Kolvar was startled. He unsheathed his sword and pointed it at this random man.

"Who are you!" Kolvar yelled. "I am the wanderer of the woods. I will guide you through the forest," he replied.

The wanderer lifted his staff, and his eyes started glowing green, along with the crystal at the top of his staff. He then started to guide Kolvar's group through the forest. Kolvar noticed that the staff seemed to guide them.

"Who are you really?" Kolvar asked.

"Most people know me by the wanderer of the woods, as I told you before, but in the days of old, most people would refer to me as a druid," the wanderer replied.

"A druid?" Thaedra chimed in. "I heard stories about them. I thought they didn't exist."

"Once there were many druids, but they died out a long time ago," the wanderer said.

"If they died long ago, how aren't you dead?" Alwin asked.

"I escaped. The elves back then believed that we were trying to rebel against them. It's quite a long tale," the wanderer said sadly.

"Please tell us. I'm sure we have time," Kolvar said to the wanderer then sighed.

"The druids were the first elves born into the world. We were the protectors of the forests even though all Elves were born to do so. We waited around for years and years, just enacting our purpose. We could have waited as long as Greenleaf wanted. Back then, elves were immortal. Then Greenleaf created more elves to start a civilization. As they developed, they learned how to make and destroy. They started destroying forests to build their homes. We, of course, stepped in to defend them, but we could not withstand the number of the rest of the Elves. I alone escaped. Then Greenleaf stripped away the immortality of the Elves. If they had known we were sent by him, I'm sure you few would be immortal as well."

"How did the druids all die?" Thaedra asked.

"We were in a battle. There were only ten of us left. One by one, we were cut down until I was the last one left. I ran. I've been avoiding every person living for hundreds of years and more. The ancient age of magic died out long ago. You few are lucky to experience the prime of this new age," the wanderer said.

When the wanderer ended his spiel, they were out of the forest, the sun was setting, and the group rode out a bit further. The wanderer stayed at the tree line.

"We need everyone we can to help out with this war. You should come with us," Kolvar said.

"No, my place is here. It always will be," the wanderer replied.

"Just think about all the other forests in this world. They will all burn under the heel of the gray humans. Come to the spire if you decide otherwise," Kolvar retorted.

The wanderer said nothing, then Kolvar's group rode off into the sunset.

BACK TO YRFEL

The group returned to the spire quickly. To Kolvar, their four-day journey felt like four hours. Kolvar's group was welcomed back to the spire. They were brought back to the harbor, where they saw many Elves building ships. As time passed, more and more elves filed into the harbor, wood elves, and celestial elves.

More time passed. Ships were finished. More elves arrived. Soon, they would be on their way to Yrfel.

Kolvar gathered his crew together. He wanted to get everyone ready early.

Kolvar's group got off their horses. They were taken by a stableman off into the distance. Kolvar's crew then boarded their ship. He asked them to get everything ready for the day of departure tomorrow.

When Kolvar was walking along the dock, he saw Lady Aerin in the distance.

"My lady, I'm pleased to see you here," Kolvar said.

"Thank you, Lord Kolvar. The Keawynn lands are quite beautiful," she replied.

"I would like to take you and the rest of your group as honored guests on my ship," Kolvar said.

"I would accept your offer. That's very kind of you, my lord," Lady Aerin said.

Kolvar turned away. "We leave tomorrow, my lady. For now, follow me."

Kolvar guided them to his ship.

The sun was setting, and all the elves were getting ready for the journey ahead, preparing ships and gathering materials.

Kolvar saw someone in the distance, just at the edge of town, he left his ship, and as he got closer and closer, the figure started to come into view. Kolvar approached him and saw it was the wanderer of the woods.

"Wanderer! Good to see you," Kolvar said.

"Good to see you, friend. I thought about what you said, and you were right," he replied.

"Well, come to my ship. We will be leaving for Yrfel tomorrow morning," Kolvar said.

"No, I don't need a ship. Just look for me in the forest of Ashbeard," the wanderer said.

He then walked away, leaving Kolvar wondering how he was going to get to Yrfel.

Nighttime was upon them; the town of the harbor wasn't as bustling as it was earlier. Kolvar and Lady Aerin were standing out on the deck, staring off at the sea.

"Have you ever traveled at sea, my lady?" Kolvar replied.

"No, my lord, until a month or so ago, I had never left the bright lands, and please call me Aerin," she said.

"Sorry, Aerin," Kolvar said with a slight laugh. "And please call me Kolvar," Kolvar added, bowing.

Aerin and Kolvar laughed together.

Aerin then stopped laughing and she had a serious look on her face. "What happened to your mother, Kolvar?" she asked.

Kolvar's face saddened, and he looked off to the distance.

"She left. I found out she was working with our enemy, and then she left. I haven't seen her in what feels like forever," he said.

"Oh, I'm sorry," she replied.

Kolvar didn't say anything. It was then that their conversation was over. Lady Aerin walked away, and Kolvar stayed out for a little longer.

Thaedra walked over to Kolvar.

"Are you alright, my lord?" he asked.

"Yes, I'm fine," Kolvar replied.

"Coming back here did not feel like a homecoming. I'm just ready to get back to Yrfel," Thaedra said.

"I felt the exact same way," Kolvar replied.

Thaedra put his hand on Kolvar's shoulder. "Not to worry, my lord. Soon, we will be home."

PART 4

The Steel Isle

HEADING EAST

Nathan was waiting in High Yrfel for an answer from Kolvar. Suddenly, Robb walked into the castle and approached Nathan.

"My king, I have just received word that Lord Kolvar has left for the grove," he said.

"Very good. Now we need to prepare to leave. Send a messenger to Vigrod telling him that we are about to leave. Soon after, we need to prepare our ships to sail. I want our army to go with us," Nathan replied.

"Very well, my king," Robb said.

He walked off to the other parts of the castle to find their writer. Nathan walked out of the castle. He then started down the hill to the barracks.

Nathan yelled at the top of his lungs, "All soldiers outside immediately!"

All the soldiers rushed outside and stood around with surprised and confused expressions.

"I hope that you are all glad to hear that. We are going home!" Nathan said excitedly.

Most soldiers were happy. Most soldiers just shrugged or grunted.

"Well, I won't waste any more time here. I want everyone ready by tomorrow," Nathan said.

The soldiers gave him a salute, and Nathan walked back up to High Yrfel.

Nathan went back into his quarters to pack his things. He didn't pack much, only his cloak, a few books, and a picture of his father and him that he took everywhere. Nathan looked out his window to see the sun setting. The orange setting sun shone brightly on the mountains. Nathan changed out of his fine clothes into something more comfortable. He looked into his mirror to see himself with some jet-black facial hair growing in. Nathan is just nineteen years old; he was waiting for his facial hair to grow; Nathan always wanted a beard like his father.

Nathan put out the candles and climbed into his bed. He wondered what was happening back at his home. He wondered how his mother was doing. He also wondered how his grandfather Brandon was doing. Nathan fell asleep, knowing he would get to see his family soon, all except his father, who he missed the most.

Robb awoke Nathan from his peaceful sleep, and Nathan jolted awake.

"My King, we will depart for the isles soon, a few more hours."

"Thank you, Robb. I will be down to the docks momentarily," Nathan replied.

Robb then moved his head closer to Nathan.

"I see you are finally becoming a man. You look like your father," Robb said, looking at Nathan's growing facial hair.

Robb left the room. Nathan then changed into his fine clothes, put on his armor, put his two swords on his belt, then wrapped himself in his fur cloak.

Nathan walked out to the throne room to find a few soldiers there to escort him down to the docks. The doors opened, and Nathan saw a bright blue summer sky, the sun and clouds, and a nice breeze on his face.

The mountain range was very long but not very wide. The trip to the docks was short. They passed through a few villages before they reached the docks.

Nathan felt a certain pride. Although he didn't want to leave Yrfel, he was proud that he was going to be out at sea and returning home.

He would also be returning home as a man. He left when he was sixteen, fought his first battle at Ravenhall when he was eighteen, then turned nineteen on November 3.

Everyone boarded their ships. Nathan yelled out for the sails to be lowered and the anchors to be raised.

"I don't think this endeavor will take all that long, my King," Robb said over the sound of the waves.

"What makes you think that?" Nathan asked.

"Well, our people respect your family more than any family living, your father most of all. You are all that is left of his memory," Robb replied.

Nathan nodded back, Robb was right, and Nathan hoped he was right about this task not taking long.

"I'm sure your grandfather and mother will also be a great help," Robb said.

"I hope so. I don't want this to take too long," Nathan replied.

"Don't try to force anything on them. They won't take that too kindly," Robb answered.

After their conversation was done, Nathan went to the tip of the boat and looked out at the sea. Although his family members were extraordinary blacksmiths, most of them also were excellent sailors and loved being out at sea, including Nathan.

REUNION CELEBRATION

The two-week journey to the isles was concluded, and July was just beginning. The eastern fleet was taken into harbor. They docked and left their ships, and many citizens came to the harbor to welcome back their soldiers. Once Nathan got off his ship, all the citizens at the harbor bowed to him.

The Steel Isle was made up of multiple islands, the main island (where Nathan was now) and the outer islands. There were no other extremely rich families in the isles. Everyone followed the Eastmoore family. No one had to, but they did anyway.

They started from the docks and made their way down into the town of Hammershire. It was a small town. Some people supply the blacksmith shop at the center of town. Some people run their own shop. As Nathan walked the gravel paths, many people greeted him. Nathan saw many Eastmoore banners as he strolled by.

Nathan approached the gates of his old home. In fact, his old home was half of the main island. The great city of the Steel Valley. The gates were opened, and Nathan went to the train carts to get down into the valley.

"My king, welcome home," the man overseeing the carts said.

"Thank you. I would request a cart straight to the castle," Nathan replied.

"At once, my King," the overseer said.

"Right this way," he added.

He stepped into the cart, along with Robb and a few others.

"Welcome back, High King," the cart driver said.

"Thank you, sir," Nathan replied.

The cart made a sound, and it started to move. The cart was made of metal and wood, and it was dragged along by the mechanics of the cart tracks. The trip down into the valley and into the city was long. Nathan could hear the wind pushing against the cart as they glided down the tracks.

Nathan looked out the windows to see his old home, and he felt good inside while he had flashbacks of his childhood. The cart stopped, then Nathan and company exited the cart, and the castle of the valley loomed over them.

The company was welcomed with open arms back into the castle. The throne room was filled with people, cleaning, talking, and drinking. When Nathan entered the room, everyone made way for him to get to the throne.

Nathan got closer to the throne, and two large Eastmoore flags hung high in the rafters and made large shadows covering the throne where his grandfather sat.

Brandon the third was a tall old man with a long white beard, long white hair, a frail body, and eighty-one years of age.

"James! My son, welcome home!" Brandon said. His voice was loud for a man of his age.

"Grandfather? Father has been dead for nearly a year," Nathan said.

"What? I...I...no one told me. What happened?" Brandon said.

Tears started to stream down from his eyes.

"He was killed by an assassin," Nathan said.

"No, no, no, but who are you?" Brandon said.

"Grandfather, it's me Nathan, James's son," Nathan said.

"Nathan, I forgot about you. In my old age, I am starting to forget everyone."

"It's okay, Grandfather. I still remember you," Nathan said, leaning down to hug his grandfather.

Nathan's mother, Ariana, sat right next to Brandon. "I'm so glad you are home, son," she said.

"I am too," Nathan replied.

The two exchanged pleasantries, and then Brandon started speaking. "Let us throw a feast for Nathan's return and for James's untimely death," he said.

"A great idea, Grandfather," Nathan said.

Ariana called over one of Brandon's servants. "Yes, King Brandon?" the servant asked.

"I want to throw a feast for my grandson's return and my son's death. I would like it ready by nightfall. Every person in the valley is welcome," he said.

The servant walked away, and Nathan noticed a particularly ugly look on the man's face as he walked away.

By night, the courtyard was fully decorated, tables were set up everywhere, and barrels upon barrels of ale were brought up from the cellars. Food was brought out in masses to be placed on tables, and Eastmoore banners were hung up at every corner. The Eastmoores sat at a table at the top of the courtyard, and soon, crowds of people flooded in to greet Nathan.

While the party went on, more and more people flooded into the packed full courtyard. Nathan had no space to walk to get food, and his servants just had to bring it to him. Brandon had an exquisite gold goblet of wine decorated with jewels and pearls. He grabbed his fork and hit it hard against his goblet.

"Everyone!" he called as loud as he could. It wasn't loud enough to attract everyone, but those who heard quieted the crowd. "Today, my grandson

Nathan has returned! We shall celebrate his return all through the night, but let us not forget those who we lost. Only hours ago, I first heard of my son Victor's death," Brandon's voice quivered. He started to sink back into his chair.

Nathan then stood up and yelled, "To the isle!" to get everyone's spirits up and truly begin the celebration.

Nathan feasted on the finely cooked venison; the many flavors were bursting inside his mouth. He washed it down with fine wine. Nathan thought the grape taste of the wine was a fine change to the taste of the ale he usually drank. Nathan tried to multi-task, eating and talking to everyone who greeted him. Nathan called aloud to get everyone's attention, "Everyone! I would like to welcome you all to this celebration."

"Even though this is a celebration, hard times lie ahead. Our old enemy, the gray humans, are return-ing. Soon, all the fighters in the isle shall go to Yrfel, and with the combined might of the west and north, we can defeat our enemy!"

Nathan stopped speaking, and most people gasped. Some people said nothing.

"Nathan is this true?" Brandon asked.

"Yes, Grandfather, I promise you," Nathan replied.

Brandon called for another drink, and Nathan's subjects threw every question they had at him, and he answered every single one. Nathan left the courtyard minutes later while some citizens left, and some stayed. Nathan strolled around the halls of the castle, looking at the blue drapes, potted plants, and paintings. He went up staircases and turned corners. He strolled and strolled.

Someone was walking toward him. Nathan couldn't tell who it was. It looked like a blur of black. The blur of black appeared to be one of Brandon's servants. The blue and gold cloths shone brightly, and Nathan realized what he was seeing.

"Is something wrong, High King?" he asked.

"Sorry, I am just…lost…," Nathan replied slowly.

Everything around Nathan faded to black, and he remembered no more.

BEDRIDDEN

When Nathan came to, the sun shone brightly through a window, and he removed the blankets covering him. Nathan looked left to see his mother standing at his bedside.

"What happened?" Nathan said.

"The servant said you were strolling the castle, and you saw him and fainted," Ariana said back.

"Perhaps I was a bit drunk, but I only had one goblet of wine," Nathan said. "Where is Grandfather?" Nathan added.

"Gather yourself, Nathan, and follow me," she said.

Nathan stood up, and he walked slowly to his window. He opened it and breathed in the fresh eastern air.

Ariana guided Nathan out of his room and through hallways and up staircases, and soon, they were at the top of the castle, at Brandon's quarters. They opened the door, and Nathan saw cloaked figures and smoke and bowls filled with liquids. Nathan smelled things he couldn't even name. Ariana stood by the door with her head in her hands. Nathan walked over to the bed to see what was going on.

Nathan moved one of the healers aside to see his grandfather covered with blankets and drenched in sweat. Nathan looked to one of the healers.

"What is wrong with him?" The healer leaned close to Nathan. "He has been poisoned. We have seen this once before. It has been made from a plant from the isle of banishment. It's called the steel grip. It grips the windpipe until the victim runs out of air."

"Is there anything you can do?" Nathan asked.

"All we can do is ease the pain. He only has a few hours," the healer responded solemnly.

Nathan didn't know how to react. He only had spent a day with his grandfather. Now he was being ripped away. Nathan remembered all the things Brandon, his father, and himself would do, but that seemed like a lifetime ago.

Nathan looked at Brandon. Brandon slowly tilted his head to see his grandson. "Nathan...my dear grandchild," he said. "Where is James now?" he asked.

"He is on Yrfel, overlooking the eastern sea. He looks toward home," Nathan said.

The tears started to stream out of his eyelids. "Can you take me there?" Brandon said.

"Of course, I can. Soon, we can all sit by the sea together," Nathan said.

"That reminds me of when you were much younger. Of all the things I've forgotten, at least my only memories are of my son and grandson," Brandon replied.

The healers took a bowl and put it in Brandon's mouth. "Will you spend these last hours with me?"

"Yes, Grandfather," Nathan replied.

"We will be leaving. Give him a sip every few minutes," the healer said.

"Thank you. You did all you could," Nathan said.

The healers left the room, and Ariana went and stood next to Nathan.

"I don't need any more of that medicine. It is only delaying what is to come," Brandon said.

"But…what is to come will come sooner," Nathan replied.

"It does not matter to me. I want to see my son again," Brandon said. "Do you have a dagger, grandson?" he added.

Nathan's head shot up to look at him. "What?" Nathan said.

"I will die my by hands, not by some poison," Brandon replied.

"Mother?" Nathan said.

"Give him the dagger, son," she said.

Nathan slowly drew his dagger and handed it to his grandfather. "Thank you, Grandson. Us Eastmoores will watch over you with pride," he said.

"Goodbye, Grandfather," Nathan said.

Brandon gave him one last smile, and Ariana and Nathan then left the room.

A day had passed since King Brandon Eastmoore the thirds death. Words were said over him for a successful transition into Aella's heaven.

Nathan stood by the altar where Brandon's body was laid. The church was as silent as a graveyard. Light shined in from the large stained-glass window at the back of the church, illuminating Brandon's body.

The healers and priests came to Nathan as he requested. "You called for us, High King?" one of the healers said.

"Yes, yes, I have. I have been wondering, how could my grandfather have been poisoned?" Nathan said.

"Most likely, the poison was made into a liquid and mixed with wine, and it was served to him," the healer answered.

"That was all I needed to hear. I would request you all to make the necessary preparations to move his body to Yrfel," Nathan said, leaving the church and heading for the castle.

Nathan ran into the castle and went to the kitchens. Nathan walked in and smelled many different foods and spices, but he wasn't there for refreshment.

"I want every servant that was at the celebration last night, specifically ones that were serving wine. Meet me in the throne room," he said.

All the servants were lined up, surrounded by Nathan and soldiers.

"I will give you all one chance to tell the truth. Which one of you poisoned my grandfather?" Nathan asked calmly.

He stepped closer to the suspects. He looked each one of them in the eyes, staring deep into their souls. He stopped at one of the servants who was wearing a very fine necklace with a beautiful ruby in the center of it.

"You always have an ugly look on your face, don't you?" he said.

Nathan slowly drew his dagger. Nathan leaned closer to whisper to him. "Try to run. Go ahead." Nathan stepped back.

The servant looked around and started running but was soon tackled by the soldiers.

He was brought to his feet and toward Nathan. "Anything to say?" Nathan asked.

"I have something for you, a letter." The guard reached into the servant's pocket and pulled out a letter. It was sealed with gray wax. Nathan slowly opened the letter then he began to read.

Nathan Eastmoore,

The ravens' blood will cover the snow. The forests will fall and burn, and your swords and hammers will break upon our shields. The world will unite under one black flag.

Nathan looked up at his grandfather's killer. "Take him away."

CHAPTER

4

DIGGING DEEPER

Nathan let his rage and emotions take over. He went to find his mother or a priest, someone more knowledgeable than his thick-skulled guards.

He entered the church and went to the first priest he saw.

"Excuse me," said Nathan.

The priest turned around to face Nathan. "Yes, High King?"

"The poison that killed my grandfather. Where does it come from?" he asked.

"It comes from the isle of banishment, in the outer isles," the priest said.

Nathan didn't even reply. He turned and swiftly walked out of the church.

The isle of banishment is where the riffraff and criminals were kept. It was in a chain of islands surrounding the steel valley. A prison that was made of layer upon layer of steel was the only building that was on the isle.

Nathan gathered a few guards, and they found a boat to take out to the isle. Nathan partially still being controlled by his emotions and partially by his brain, thought that there was some deeper meaning behind this poisoning. Perhaps there was a plot going on against his family, or the gray humans were somehow at work.

They reached the isle, the warden, Lukas Strong, along with a few guards, came out to greet Nathan and his company at the entrance to the prison.

"High King, what an unexpected visit. How can I be of service?" Warden Strong said.

"I need to talk to the murderer of my grandfather," Nathan replied.

"My guards will take you to him."

Warden Strong made a sharp movement with his hand, and the guards guided Nathan to where the killer was being held.

They entered the prison, and the wave of yells washed over them like a tidal wave. The prison was loud, and it stunk. Nathan had never been inside a place so vile. He was out of touch with the outside world, he had no idea what was happening outside the walls of his castles and war rooms, and he supposed it was this.

"Here we are. The prisoner will be brought in momentarily," the guard opened a large, barred steel door to reveal a small room with a table and two chairs. Nathan walked into the room and sat down. Then as the guard said, the prisoner was brought in a few moments later.

"Leave us. I will come for you when I am done," Nathan said to the guard.

"Who are you?" Nathan started.

The man sitting across him laughed. "I am just a piece in the game being played."

Nathan stood up, taking an aggressive stance to try to put fear into the man. "What game?"

The man continued his laughing and smiling. "Soon, you will see. Your grandfather was a player that needed to be removed."

Nathan walked over to where the man was sitting. He suddenly slammed the man's head off the table. "Why!"

The killer lifted his head up. "Soon, the heads of power around this world will be removed. It's like the letter said, the world will unite under one black flag."

"You're with the gray humans. How do you communicate with them? What are their plans?" Nathan said. He pulled his sword and pointed it at the killer.

"Do not worry about that. I know no more than my purpose, and that has been served."

Nathan sighed. He knew he was getting nowhere, and he had one last idea. "What if I killed you?"

"You may, but it will get you no closer to what you…"

Nathan didn't let the man finish his sentence before he chopped off his head, leaving only his necklace hanging from his severed neck.

5

A MEETING OF NORTH
AND SOUTH

The mountain clan had arrived on the shores of the gray human island. They had been summoned by King Dominus South, leader of the gray human people.

The blood mages were the true leaders of the mountain clan. They masked their strength in their leader, who could not even talk. It was just purely made for combat. It had taken them a while to revive the creature. Many rituals had to be done, and many ounces of blood had to be spilled.

Grayfire Citadel was in the center of the island, which was quite large. The Citadel was a marvel to behold. It was a terrifying site, bigger than Frosthaven, the golden spire, and the Steel Valley combined. Made of a fused black stone, the gray humans turned stone into liquid with grayfyre, fusing it to build their monstrous citadel.

The mountain clan all walked inside the throne room of Grayfire Citadel. Even the army of thirty thousand could all fit inside this throne room and still have plenty of space. The gray human banner was hung from every huge column holding up the ceiling, and the room stretched to be about one hundred feet tall. The king's throne was abnormally large, with massive steps leading up to the throne, made of fused black stone. He sat in luxury on beautiful red silks.

"Welcome in, honored guests. I am glad my associate could guide you to us," King Dominus South said in a soft tone that echoed throughout the room. "You have called us to you. What is it that you want from us?"

The Bloodweaver took responsibility for all his mages and all the soldiers in their army.

The king gave a small laugh. "I would propose an alliance, you seek revenge on your enemies, and I seek retribution for my people's mishaps long ago. We seem to have a common goal."

The Bloodweaver scratched his chin as if he was deep in thought.

"What is in it for us?" he asked.

"When the war is won, you will have control of Drangar, but ultimately, you will still answer me," Dominus replied with no hesitation.

The Bloodweaver turned to whisper to his other mages for a few moments. Then he turned back to face the king.

"We have an agreement."

The king started clapping, and his guards and all the other gray humans in the room followed suit. "Good, very, very good."

Then one of Dominus's servants approached him on his throne and then whispered in his ear, "Brandon Eastmoore is dead, Your Grace."

A smile crept over Dominus's face. "So he did complete his task. Soon, we will move on Yrfel."

THE YEAR OF THE KNIGHTS

Book 1

PART 3

AIDAN TAUTIN

PROLOGUE

A year had rolled by since the three lords of Yrfel declared their treaty and set off on their mission to bring home as many soldiers as they could.

The day was June twentieth of the seventh summer in the year three hundred two. The three lords stood out on Kolvar's balcony at the very top of the Elder Branch, looking out toward the sea, now a year older and a year wiser. Together, they had amassed an army of over four hundred thousand soldiers, along with King Gromir and his giants.

"What if they never come?" Vigrod said.

"They will. I have spent every day for the past year. Fearful of the day they will return, and an elf's instincts are rarely wrong," Kolvar replied.

"Have you received any word from Drangar, Vigrod?" Nathan asked.

In the year that had gone by, the high king and the Highlord's relationship had drastically improved, but they weren't best friends by any means.

"No, so I must hope that it is a good thing, and my enemy will not return in my lifetime and even longer after that," Vigrod replied.

They conversed for a while longer until the sun started to set when, suddenly, Kolvar's sharp eyes spotted something in the distance. In the year that followed, the three separate races had learned to set aside their petty grievances and prejudices because of the ever-looming threat of the southern gray humans. The three lords had forgotten all their ambitions, their plots, and their feelings for vengeance.

"What is that? It looks like a line of ink splattered across the sea, and it is getting closer," Kolvar said.

They continued to wait. The sun was almost about to go down.

"What is it?" Vigrod asked.

Kolvar took a long look. "Ships," he replied.

The three lords then immediately started to make their way down the Elder Branch, going as fast as physically possible because Kolvar Keawynn saw ships flying black flags on the horizon.

The day of reckoning had come, the gray humans had come, and their ships were a few hours away.

Godwin and Aegis sat together at a fire by their lonesome, staring into the flames in silence. The bells tolled in the distance, the stomping of feet and the clanking of armor, the united banners prepared for battle as the sun fell.

"This brotherhood might not survive what is to come," said Aegis in a low tone. "We can rebuild. After all, we stand in the shadow that the rest of the world casts for us," Godwin replied.

Aegis was worried about his small brotherhood; the forthcoming darkness was on the horizon, and he did not know what was to come.

"This world will need to be rebuilt when the fighting is done, regardless of who the victor is. The world will be left a very different place than it was before," Aegis continued.

"Commander, you should not worry so much. This has happened before," Godwin said, trying to be a voice of comfort to his anxious leader. "You are never this worried before you go into the field. What is wrong?"

"There has never been a threat of this magnitude on our doorstep. My parents used to tell me stories about them when I was disobedient to scare me," Aegis said. "My instincts are telling me something is wrong."

"Commander, think about what is in front of us, your instincts are right, but we must keep pushing regardless."

Aegis made a distinct loud whistling sound. Moments later, all the brothers of the Shrouded made their way to the fire.

"Commander, what is it?" Arthur Riverglade asked. "If we are all to die in a few hours, I'd like to spend these hours with you all," he replied.

An hour had passed since Kolvar Keawynn had seen the enemy ships coming toward the shore. The three lords, although out of breath, made it down to the bottom of the Elder Branch to try to assist their army in preparing for the battle to come.

They all went separate ways. Kolvar went to the forest of Ashbeard to look for the Wanderer of the Woods, but the druid from the Ancestral Grove had still not arrived.

He reached the forest and started calling out, "Wanderer!" he yelled repeatedly.

A short distance into the forest the rustling of leaves could be heard, and Kolvar went to investigate.

Walking into the forest, Kolvar looked around when, suddenly, the druid had just appeared out of thin air.

"Wanderer, you are just in time," Kolvar said.

The wanderer brushed off his cloak and looked up at Kolvar. "Good. Will you bring the inhabitants of the forest along with us?" he replied.

Kolvar pulled the horn of the Ashwalkers off his belt and blew into it, the loud booming rung out into the forest. The loud stomping sounds of the Ashwalkers could quickly be heard shortly after Kolvar called out to them.

"Ahhhh, Lord Kolvar, how can we help youuuu?" the Ashwalker sounded.

"It is time, my friend. Take your company to the beach. Our forces will meet you there shortly after," Kolvar demanded.

The Ashwalker simply gave a bow in reply, and together, they started to mosey their way over to the beach.

"Is this a fight we can win?" the wanderer said in a worried tone. "I do not know, but the world depends on us, so I am trying to push my doubt aside," Kolvar replied.

Vigrod went over to gather his Giants that had come down from the Frostlands. Gromir and the rest of his kin sat by themselves where they had enough space to sit comfortably. When Vigrod walked over, Gunir was the first to turn his head to see him.

"Highlord, good to see you," Gunir said.

"Likewise, my friend, the bells are sounding. It is time," Vigrod replied.

The giants shook the earth when they all stood up. Gromir looked at Vigrod and started speaking in the old tongue.

"What would you have us do?" Gunir translated for Vigrod.

"Gather on the beach just outside the city. We plan to make our stand there."

Vigrod pointed to where he was referring. Gunir gave Vigrod's orders to Gromir, and the giants then made their way to the beach.

Vigrod sought out all the leaders of the clans of Drangar. He jogged around looking for them when Brodir caught him and brought him over to where all the leaders were gathered. Dane Giantsfoot, Ulfir

Bloodwolf, Hilgar Ironhand, and Magthar Darkwing were who Vigrod was greeted to.

"How are they feeling?" Vigrod started.

"They are fearful, Highlord. They are worried we will not be able to handle what is to come," Ulfir said.

"If this is Drangar's last stand, then we should make it one worthy of songs," Hilgar Ironhand interrupted.

Hilgar was a stout baldheaded Viking with a yellow forked beard and the leader of the stubborn Ironhand clan. Hilgar and his clan all shared the same reluctance toward the feeling of fear, and they ached for battle like a hungry stomach ached for food.

"I agree. All we can hope is that there are still those who write songs when this is all over."

Nathan met with Aedric and the new archmage, Jarius Skyward, a dashing young man who had taken up the responsibilities of running the mage's guild when Tymirial was killed.

"Bring everyone to the beaches quickly," Nathan said to the two of them, then dismissed them both with a wave of his hand.

The young king made his way to the beach. The Ashwalkers and giants were already there, standing patiently facing out toward the sea. The feeling of fear made its way into Nathan's brain, giving him a headache. He felt the whole world resting on his back. He wanted nothing more than to end this threat here and now. He had been training with the sword his whole life, and he knew that it was for a moment like this.

The sun finally fell, darkness had swallowed the world, and the coming darkness was now here. The united army of three banners had marched its way out to the beach. Everyone was now at Nathan's back, and all they could do now was wait.

DARKNESS AT THE DOOR

Nathan watched as the southern ships slowed down and dropped their anchors. The world seemed to stand still. He could hear their small boats dropping into the water. The battle was here, and Nathan was ready to make the first move.

"Archers! Nock your arrows!" he yelled.

Nathan heard thousands of arrows being pulled from their quivers and placed onto the shelf of the bow.

"Draw!" Nathan yelled. The twanging sound of the arrows being released could be heard for miles. "Fire!" and he watched as a wave of arrows rushed toward the sea.

Nathan repeated his command for as long as he could, but finally, the gray humans reached the shore, and it was like a line of black paint had covered the shoreline. Thousands upon thousands of soldiers in sleek black armor charged toward the army of three banners.

The young man then unsheathed his two swords and pointed them toward their enemy.

"Charge!" he screamed.

Nathan ran as fast as his legs would carry him; his mind went blank. He drew closer and closer to them, and when he was in range, he drove one of his swords through a gray human's neck and his other sword through a second gray human's chest. Pure adrenaline is all he felt. Cleaving through his opponents, Nathan could not stop moving.

When he got a quick glimpse of the shoreline, more gray humans were spilling out of large wooden boats carrying hundreds of soldiers. The giants and Ashwalkers wiped away dozens of them. Nathan watched the large burning tree man walk to and fro, stomping on countless soldiers. Suddenly, Nathan heard a loud booming sound that rattled his ears. He saw cannonballs hurling toward the humongous trees. It sounded like someone was thrown down a flight of steps. *Boom, boom, boom.* Burning bark was flying everywhere. Nathan tried to avoid getting a piece in his eye.

Nathan cut through his enemies like he was carving a cake. Nothing could stop him. He then stood a few yards away from a gray human who wore very fine armor, sleek black with a red tabard, rubies filed throughout, and instead of a helmet, it wore a crown upon its head.

"So you must be the high king. I have heard so much about. It is nice to finally meet another monarch. I am King Dominus South."

In Nathan's mind, this was what all his training was preparing him for, here and now. He gave no response to Dominus and charged him, and he thrust his swords toward Dominus's chest and neck. The southern king easily moved out of the way of Nathan's attempts.

What ensued could have been described as the most graceful use of swords in history. It is like the two were linked with each other. Block after block, and parry after parry, and the sounds of their swords clashing was like music. One could not subdue the other. The fight turned into a dance with beautiful movement and elegant turns. Nathan was starting to tire out, and he knew Dominus was toying with him. He had never come up against an opponent with his level of speed and skill. Dominus eventually stopped playing with his food. Nathan went for his head, and he performed a counter move that disarmed Nathan, sending his sword high into the air and then crashing down into the sand.

Nathan gave one last effort going for a lower strike, but Dominus knew what Nathan wanted to do even before he did. Dominus used another countermove, and Nathan was completely unarmed. Nathan put his fists up to try to defend himself, but he was so exhausted he could barely see what was in front of him. The last thing he saw was a fist hurling toward his face. Then his vision went from blurry to black.

Dominus watched as Nathan's body hit the sand. "Ah, but, High King, I cannot kill you just yet. You can be at my side as I burn the world you have come to know."

The king then brought Nathan back to the boat that he landed on and left him there. Dominus stood and watched the fight from afar, taking pride in the revenge he was getting for his people.

Vigrod fought alongside his Drangarian brethren. The Vikings were in a large pack, pushing back their enemy. The onslaught of gray humans was relentless, and they started to break through the Drangarian lines. Vigrod could see out of the corner of his eye that Hilgar was standing on top of a pile of gray human corpses and killing more where he stood.

The Highlord saw his friend Brodir under heavy duress. Vigrod tried to fight his way over. Nerves were taking over. He swung his axe left and right, trying his hardest to get to Brodir.

He had almost reached his friend. Brodir was surrounded by three gray humans. Brodir Bothvar tried to fight off his assailants. He was slashed in the arm, and the arm went limp. He tried to defend himself with all his might, but it was not enough. Brodir was stabbed in the chest. The gray human ripped his sword out of Brodir's chest, causing him to fall to his knees, then face-first into the sand.

Vigrod could do nothing but watch as his friend was brutally killed just a few yards away. He then let out a scream that could've been heard in Drangar. Killing all the gray humans in front of him, Vigrod finally reached Brodir.

Picking up his friend, Vigrod held him close. "Brodir, say something. Come on. You're not gone yet. Say something. Brother, please, keep fighting. Thalmur isn't ready for you yet."

Blood covered his hands. His friend, whom he had been with all his life, was now gone. Tears poured out of Vigrod's eyes; the sadness eventually turned into rage. He put down Brodir's body and picked up his axe. Vigrod was controlled by his anger. He was fighting so hard that he was cleaving his enemies in half with a single swing. One by one, his enemies fell to him; he took a few cuts here and there, but they did not bother Vigrod Frostbane.

Vigrod cut through a few gray humans before he was face to face with an old enemy. The Mountain clan had made their way to the battle. Vigrod was confused for just a moment, but truly, he cared not. To him, they were just the next thing he could chop in half.

He had now come across their monstrous leader. He then grew even angrier. Vigrod now had a chance to avenge Thalmer's death. The Highlord let out a scream to get its attention. The creature turned to face him and let out a scream in response. Vigrod charged the creature, easily moving out of the way and parrying all its slow attacks. He had no idea how he had almost been killed by this thing before. Vigrod drove his axe into its stomach again and again. He gave it no mercy, using all his remaining strength. The second time around, this battle came very easy to Vigrod. With one final strike to its large neck, the creature fell to the ground with a large thud. Vigrod drove his axe into its back repeatedly, just to make sure it was dead.

Kolvar watched as the Ashwalkers and Giants were showered with cannon fire. He knew they were losing. They were being pushed closer and closer to the gates of the Elder Branch. Kolvar fought alongside his grandfather Aerimir, who, for the first time in a long time, wore a set of armor and had a sword at his side. The two Keawynns fought wonderfully together. It was a sort of chemistry the family members shared. Kolvar tried to motivate his troops the best he could. They had to keep fighting. The world as they knew it was at stake.

An Ashwalker fell right in front of where Kolvar was standing. They were losing momentum quickly, getting pushed back further and further. The logical side of Kolvar's brain would not stop telling him to retreat. The battle was lost. He had lost sight of Nathan and Vigrod, and their forces were scattered. The writing was on the wall.

Kolvar retreated into the crowd of elves that he was fighting with. They only had one place to leave, the gate back into the Elder Branch. Before the battle, the three lords agreed that if retreat was needed that they would meet at the Hall of the Lords, and the way things were looking, that is where they were going to be headed. He grabbed the horn of the Ashwalkers and blew into it thrice, signaling the retreat.

He yelled out to his allies. Kolvar sprinted toward the gate with his soldiers, running through the city, ducking and diving over objects. Thousands of soldiers passed through the open gate at the north end of the city out into the Greenlands. Now the battle was officially lost, and the end was now beginning.

SO IT BEGINS

The sun rose on a new day in Yrfel. The gray humans had won their "homecoming battle," and now the Elder Branch was theirs. They went through the city, taking down and burning the Keawynn flag and replacing it with the flag of the gray sword.

Dominus quickly acquainted himself with the throne room, getting comfortable on the wooden throne. He was followed into the throne room by his three generals, who were carrying Nathan around by his arms. Dominus's generals were Sirius, Gruk, and Chelmere, whose last names were also South. Gray humans did not believe in last names. Their history books only showed first names. To them, having the surname of their country was more honorable than winning glory for their own surname.

The southern king had reveled at this moment. His conquest was finally beginning. Finally, he could avenge his people for their humiliating loss hundreds of years ago. Dominus had no desire to rule the world. Vengeance was his goal. He wanted to show this world that his people were strong.

Nathan had his armor removed; he was put in a dark-colored garb. He could barely see a foot in front of him. His vision was still blurry from being knocked out.

"Nathan, you should be glad I did not kill you. Instead, you will get to watch as I burn the world, you know," Dominus said.

In his mind, he thought calling him Nathan would humanize him more and make him feel powerless.

"The gods will punish you," Nathan replied breathlessly. Dominus instantly busted out laughing.

"What gods!" he said, continuing his loud laughter.

"Where is there any evidence of gods in this world, boy? I've killed a thousand men and more, and how have our just gods punished me?" he continued.

Dominus then drew his dagger and walked over to Nathan. "Will Aella save you now?" he said.

Dominus repeatedly cut Nathan with his dagger. All Nathan could do was hold his tongue and try not to scream. Dominus was right. No help was coming for him.

"Drop him," Dominus said.

The generals did as they were told, and Nathan hit the floor. A light from the large opening in the tree shone upon him.

"They should have a war room somewhere. I think we should get started as soon as possible," said Sirius, who was the closest friend to Dominus, and the heir in line for the throne of the south.

"I agree. We shall search around. See that someone takes care of our guest here," Dominus replied, staring down at Nathan.

The four gray humans searched around the Elder Branch when they finally came across Kolvar's war room. They all sat down and began their planning.

"How should we look to proceed? Continuing upward, or perhaps we should look to eradicate our adversaries immediately," said Chelmere.

In the south, Chelmere was described to be the most frightening warrior in the entire world, with the size and strength of a bear but as dumb as a rock.

"We shall go slow, going further north and backing our enemies into a corner. They are most likely going to be held up here," Dominus said, pointing to the little figure of Ravenhall.

"We are going to send a message. We start by burning the forest of Ashbeard. Then we will move to conquer High Yrfel."

"I like this. We can burn the forest today. I think in a few days, we can continue forward. Let the men rest," Sirius said.

Dominus replied with a nod. "Very well. In time, we shall move. Let us tend to this forest."

They left the room and gathered a few men to go over to the forest with axes and torches. They started by chopping down tree after tree, lighting it on fire once it fell, and watching the forest start to catch. The screams of many a bird and beast could be heard, wolves ran for the grass, and birds flew high into the air.

Dominus stood with his arms stretched out. "I am right here, Greenleaf. Strike me down!" he yelled into the sky, laughing as he did.

To Dominus, he was the god of this world, no force that people believed in would save them from the wrath that he brought. Dominus could do nothing but smile. He had a terrifying grin that went from ear to ear.

SHADOWS ON THE WALL

The forces of the three banners had reached the Hall of the Lords. Shattered by the loss, morals were low, many were injured, and Nathan was not there. Kolvar took charge, helping where he could and trying to find Vigrod.

Kolvar tried to get everyone organized, putting the injured together to get them treated, letting all the giants relax by themselves, and getting all the important figures close to the hall so he could devise a plan with them. After lots of yelling, Vigrod eventually made his way to the hall, along with Ulfir, Hilgar, and Magthar. Aerimir, Rion, and Thaedra came to the hall quickly after Kolvar yelled for them. Aedric and the mages made their way around eventually. Then lastly, Godwin and Aegis made an appearance, hiding in the background of the group.

"All of you, listen to me, please. We are too vulnerable to be sitting out here, but we are too weak to go anywhere. You," Kolvar said, looking at archmage Jarius, "can your mages put some sort of spell over us to keep us safe?" he asked.

Jarius nodded. "We can put a concealment spell over the hall and around all of us, but regardless, we should try to move on as fast as possible."

"Very well. Do we have any knowledge of where Nathan is?" Kolvar paused for a moment. "Was he killed in the battle?" he added.

"I saw the high king briefly. He was locked in combat with their king by the way it looked, but I never saw him die. He must be alive. They could've taken him captive to get more leverage over us," said Commander Aedric.

"Where are his Shrouded?" Kolvar asked.

Aegis and Godwin then stepped forward into the eyes of all those who were present.

"You two, I need you to do something for me," Kolvar said. Aegis did not reply, but his body language showed that he was listening. "You two can sneak into the Elder Branch and try to rescue Nathan if he has not already been slain, there is no easy way in truly, but if you are masters of your craft, it will be easier for you."

"It will be done," Aegis said, and the two then left the scene, vanishing into the crowd.

The mages then left the conversation as well, forming a circle, lifting their staffs high into the air.

Jarius started to chant in another language. Kolvar didn't know what he was saying. The chanting continued for about a minute when finally, a beam of light shot high into the air, and a cloud of mist built up around them like a wall.

Jarius made his way back over to Kolvar. "Give the spell a little time. Soon, we will be able to see out, and no one will be able to see in."

Kolvar gave his thanks and then dismissed everyone to go and help their people where they could. He went inside the hall and sat down, putting his head in his hands and then laying back. He sat alone in silence for a while until Vigrod joined him and sat down.

"What are we to do Vigrod," Kolvar said.

The elf lord was tired, out of ideas, and yearning for guidance. "I really don't know, Kolvar. I think our best option is to go back to Ravenhall and try to hold out. We cannot run from them much longer," Vigrod replied.

Aegis and Godwin left immediately, finding a little bit of food and water from those who were willing to give them anything before they departed. The two stepped out of the mist and into the open, the sun was going down, and they needed to get going. Their king was in peril.

The first day of the journey went by quickly. Traveling through the night and under the stars got them on a good pace. They rested throughout the day briefly but truly wasted no time. As the days rolled by, they finally made it back to the Elder Branch. They were passing through Lokfur's wall after their arduous two-week journey.

"We will wait until nightfall, so get comfortable," Aegis said.

The two masters of stealth had become great friends ever since Godwin was indoctrinated into the Shrouded. Aegis took the young man under his wing, training him to be his successor, while Arthur Riverglade was given command over the scouts, no longer in the shadow of Aegis.

Hours rolled by, Godwin decided to close his eyes and rest while Aegis sat in silence, focusing on the task at hand. Night finally fell, and they were ready to undertake the Elder Branch.

They approached the walls, not daring to venture near the gates. Both grabbed climbing spikes from their packs. They began their ascent. They moved as quietly as mice. Reaching the ramparts, Aegis began to talk using only hand signals, saying there were three guards patrolling.

Aegis made his first move, hopping over the rampart and quietly behind the guards that were unaware of his presence. He took out his dagger and slit all three guards' throats with ease. The commander of the night was in his element. Aegis then signaled for Godwin to come up. Looking down at the city from the walls gave the two stresses, for they had no idea where to look.

"The tree itself would probably be our best bet. That king would keep someone like Nathan close and tightly guarded," Aegis whispered.

Godwin gave him a nod, and they started their journey to the tree by leaping off the walls and onto a nearby rooftop. Their footsteps were as silent as the grave. Even running on rooftops in the night, they could not be heard. The stars shone brightly in the night sky, and the light emitting from the Elder Branch made their trip easy.

The Elder Branch loomed over them. The two hid in the darkness scouting out the scene and taking note of where the guards were posted. Aegis communicated with his hand signals, telling Godwin that they would work from the bottom to the top. They moved in, making quick work of the two guards outside the throne room and moving down into the roots.

Slowly, they crept down the stairs to where all the Elven prisoners were held, and it was completely unguarded. Aegis stood up, scanning the room. He was very on edge. It was odd that the Elf prison was empty, save those inside the cells.

"Be on your guard. We will go front to back and investigate every cell," Aegis said.

The two went from cell to cell, looking for Nathan, but he could not be found.

They reached the back of the prison and saw a man chained to the wall, not in a cell, not guarded by anyone, just left to rot, alone and in pain. Aegis approached the man, telling Godwin to watch their backs. The man had his head down. Aegis lifted his head to see that his face was covered with dirt and blood, his beard was patchy, and his jet-black hair was extremely messy. It was Nathan.

Aegis shook Nathan to wake him up. Nathan then awoke with the most fearful look on his face. He was terrified at the prospect of being awake while he was here because it meant that Dominus was visiting him.

"High King, it is alright. It is I, Aegis," he said softly.

"No, no, you must leave this place now. You do not understand what he will do to us if he sees us," Nathan replied slowly.

Aegis did not heed Nathan's warning, and he used his dagger to pick the locks on Nathan's chains. Aegis had to catch the High King when he was unbound, then bring him up to his feet.

"Quickly, Commander," Godwin said.

The three hurried to the staircase where they came in. Nathan was so weak that Aegis had to carry him up the stairs. They were welcomed to the quiet night sky, the stars beaming down upon them.

Godwin led them throughout the city, sneaking through the city streets. It was going surprisingly well. But it did not stay that way for long. They made their way through the streets when they were caught. Dozens of armored soldiers surrounded them, then out walked King Dominus.

"Well, Nathan, I was starting to trust that you would stay put," Dominus said.

They were caught in the middle of the street, and Aegis only had one idea. Quickly, he took a smoke bomb from his belt and threw it to the ground. The bomb exploded on impact and enveloped them in smoke. Aegis grabbed his two companions and led them behind a house so they could try to escape the gray humans.

Yells could be heard from their enemies; the loud stomps and the clanking sounds of the armor could be heard as they searched for them. They avoided the gray humans long enough that they made it back to the wall, but they were still searching for them.

When they reached the wall Aegis then slung Nathan onto his back and used all his strength to scale the wall as fast as he could. Aegis was about half-way up, and Godwin was a little behind them. The gray humans found them, though. The guards on top of the wall alerted reinforcements to their presence.

Dominus and his men ran to the wall, Aegis and Godwin were almost up, but suddenly, an arrow being shot could be heard from multiple yards away. The arrow hit a target. Godwin was shot in his calf. He let out a yell and he tried to pull the arrow out of his leg.

The gray humans approached the wall, but Aegis and Nathan had reached the top while Godwin was still lagging. Guards from the ramparts started to make their way toward them. Aegis had to fight them off while Nathan cowered in fear. Dominus had reached the wall when Godwin had finally reached the top. The guards from below were ready to release a barrage of arrows upon them. Aegis only saw one way they could escape. He quickly hurled himself from the wall, landing on top of multiple gray humans, knocking them down.

Aegis was on his own, surrounded by multiple guards his tricks would not get him out of the situation in front of him. The gray humans attacked the commander, and one by one, they fell to his dagger, but there were too many. Aegis fought with all the energy he had in him, stabbing and leaping and kicking, but it was not enough. The commander threw his dagger right into the helmet of one of his enemies. He fought for minutes on end, hoping that it was enough time for Godwin and Nathan to escape.

He couldn't hold out any longer, dozens fell to Aegis and his mighty dagger, but the gray humans were overwhelming. Finally, Aegis fell to his knees, accepting defeat. The guards then ceased their assault, and Dominus then approached him, sword in hand.

"How brave"—he paused for a moment—"but ultimately hopeless."

Dominus then swung and took Aegis's head clean off, letting it roll away and watching his lifeless body hit the ground.

Godwin and Nathan had made it over the wall, getting safely onto the ground. They tried to get as much distance as possible before Godwin heard the swing of a sword, then he heard nothing. He knew what it meant, but he knew that Aegis had bought them enough time to escape.

He had suppressed any feelings of sadness for the meantime and hobbled away with the high king into the dark night.

THE PRODIGAL SON

Two weeks passed, and Nathan and Godwin had reached the hall, stepping into the now completely clear mist, and upon entering, hundreds of thousands of people, humans, elves, and Vikings alike all looked at them. People created a path for the two. Godwin and Nathan were holding each other up as they walked through the parted sea of people.

Reaching the end of the path, Kolvar, Vigrod, Aedric, and Jarius stood, waiting for them. Aedric ran to them and grabbed Nathan, who still looked like a mess and was on the verge of passing out. Godwin then fell to his knees in front of Kolvar and Vigrod, waiting for them to say something, surrounded by everyone in the camp.

"Thank you for what you have done. What happened to Aegis?" Kolvar said.

"He sacrificed himself for the two of us."

Godwin then stood up after regaining his energy. "Where are my brothers?" he said.

Out of the crowd, the Shrouded came, all with concerned and sad looks on their faces.

Godwin could hardly stomach telling them, but there was no point in hiding it from them. "The commander is dead. He sacrificed himself for the High King and me."

They all said nothing. Every member of the Shrouded placed a hand upon Godwin's shoulders, connecting with each other and sharing a bond as brothers.

"What are we to do without him? Who will lead us now?" Godwin asked.

His brothers then took their hands off him. "We must anoint a new leader," Arthur Riverglade said.

Godwin turned to face him. "You were always closest to him. Even before I got here, it should be you."

"He made me first scout to take you under his wing. You were the prodigal son," he replied.

Arthur made a brief pause. "All in favor of Godwin, say I."

Many responses could be heard from the assassins in black. Arthur was right. Godwin had spent the past year learning under Aegis. He was a prodigal son indeed.

"Kneel, friend, and say the oath," Arthur said.

Godwin got on one knee and started to say the Shrouded oath.

> Through light, we find peace. Through dark, we find chaos. Through days and nights, we come closer to the goals of our gods. For they are the creators, the architects, the craftsmen of this world. And I am their servant.

"Now rise, Commander Godwin."

Godwin stood and took in the moment. He was now the leader of the greatest organization of assassins in the world.

Some time had passed. The sun was setting, and the three lords sat inside the Hall of the Lords. Nathan had regained some of his strength. He was now able to walk on his own, and some of his cuts from Dominus were starting to scar.

"What is the plan?" Nathan said, who was now in finer clothes and more cleaned up.

"We leave for Ravenhall tomorrow morning. We plan to make our final stand there," Vigrod replied.

"Vigrod, I don't know if there will be a final stand. They hold so much power over us. We should flee Yrfel," Nathan said.

"Nathan, what did they do to you?" Kolvar asked.

Nathan stood up and lifted his shirt, revealing dozens upon dozens of scars. His body was ravaged by Dominus. Kolvar's eyes widened.

"I am sorry. I didn't—"

"This is what they did to me in just a few days! You don't know them like I do. We all need to flee," Nathan interrupted.

After that, their conversation ended. They tried to enjoy each other's presence for a while longer, but it did not last long. The day was ending, and the three lords decided to go to sleep.

The next day arrived. Jarius and his mages had lifted the spell of concealment, and now the company was ready to go. They moved slowly, but they were organized and on the road. Their journey was not very thrilling. They went along Rose Road and camped occasionally.

Finally, after weeks of traveling, they reach Ravenhall. All the citizens of Yrfel were held up there, but soon, they might have to fight in this war whether they liked it or not.

"It feels good to be back here," Vigrod said.

After he sailed home from Drangar, he didn't spend much time in his second home. Vigrod and his army stayed with the Elves at the Elder Branch. The first thing he did was go visit his father's crypt. He also had not spent much time in the crypt the past year either.

Walking around the back, he then entered the crypt, the candles were not lit, and there was no torch to light them, so the pale northern sun gave the crypt some light. Vigrod walked up to the altar and knelt, praying to his father and Thalmur, asking for guidance and for calm. War had made Vigrod angry. War had brought so much pain and death, and Vigrod was growing tired of it. He began to wonder why he fought. Maybe it was because of his name or pride or something else. He asked himself, Why should he care? Just about all the loved ones he watched die.

Vigrod stayed there a little while longer, trying to calm himself, but nothing worked, but a part of him liked to be angry and spiteful. He thought this rage would help him in the eventual battle to come.

RISING FROM THE ASHES

Dominus sat on the throne of the Elder
Branch, waiting for his generals to come
into the throne room.

"My friends, I have grown bored of this place.
It is time to enact our plan. We march for High Yrfel
today," he said. "Chelmere, keep a company here.
I would not have our enemies snaking us while we
move east."

Dominus stood up and walked toward them.
"The throne is yours," he said, giving a bow jokingly.

Dominus, Gruk, and Sirius made their way
outside to their troops, gathering them up and then
starting to make their way east. The journey was
underway. Dominus led his horde of soldiers from
the front with Sirius and Gruk. They passed by the
forest of Ashbeard, which was now a ruin, burned to
a crisp. It was a husk of its former self. A while later

exited Lokfur's wall and passed out into the open Greenlands, and although the mountains were in sight, they were still weeks away.

As the days passed, the gray humans grew closer to the mountains. They passed into the stark eastern side of Yrfel. Dominus saw a pack of wolves running out of the corner of his eye. He saw it as a good omen and decided that they should keep going for a while longer instead of camping. The moon rose into the sky when Dominus decided that they should stop for the night.

He sat in his tent, which was at the center of the camp and the largest out of all the tents in the camp. Inside his exquisite tent was a bed fit for a king, tables and chairs, maps and compasses, and a stand for his armor if he wanted.

Sirius and Gruk entered Dominus's tent, and the two sat down.

"We will be at High Yrfel in a few days, my King. Assuming it is empty, how shall we proceed?" Sirius said.

"If it is occupied, we will take it the hard way, and if there is anyone important inside, we take their head and send it to Nathan. If it is empty, Gruk and a company of soldiers will occupy it, and we will move onto Ravenhall," Dominus replied.

Gruk looked confused. "You would not take me to Ravenhall, my king?" Dominus sighed.

"Do not take this personally. I am entrusting you to rule from there and install a dynasty when the fighting is done."

Dominus knew Gruk had no interest in the political aspect of war like Sirius and himself did. But Dominus wanted his heir to be at his side for the final act. Gruk was visibly mad. He stood up and stormed out of the tent. Dominus thought to himself that if he had to, killing one of his generals to save his reign was necessary.

The journey to High Yrfel had concluded, and just as Dominus expected, the place was completely empty. He decided that since they were in no rush, they would stay at High Yrfel a while, give the men a break, and let Gruk get used to his new castle. Soon, the march to Ravenhall would begin. Dominus could hardly wait. His triumph was at hand, and he could hardly believe how easy it came to him, for all his life, everything he had was earned.

*****

The forest of Ashbeard was in ruin. For years, this was a place of protection and safety. But now it was falling apart, and Lokfur Keawynn could hardly believe his eyes. Emerging from the cave he had lived in for the three years that was hidden by the magic of Ashbeard, who had become very good friends with Lokfur.

Lokfur the Curious had wandered into this forest a few years ago, falling to the ground in prayer, asking for Ashbeard and Greenleaf to protect him. To his surprise, his god and his son had answered him. Ashbeard appeared to Lokfur, taking him in.

He stood in the clearing alone, in awe of what he was looking at, the ground started to rumble, and Ashbeard rose out of the ground like a tree being uprooted. Ashbeard was not like his Ashwalker sons, Ashbeard was a much bigger Ent with a very angry face, and being a titan son of Greenleaf, he was much stronger. Ashbeard looked around at his ruined forest and became very enraged, stomping the ground and roaring at the sky.

"My old friend, I am so sorry," Lokfur said.

"I must convene with Greenleaf. I can no longer be of use to you. Begin north and reunite with those who thought you gone," Ashbeard said.

He spoke in an extremely deep and scratchy voice, but he did not speak as long-winded as his sons did. He then sunk back into the ground, leaving no trace that he was there.

Lokfur gave a little laugh and a shrug and then began his walk north.

NO FEAR IN DEATH

Vigrod lay in his bed. It was very late in the night, and he could not sleep. He stared into the darkness that enveloped his quarters, trying to fall asleep. Vigrod closed his eyes, and he could start to feel himself drifting off to sleep.

He awoke again in Thalmur's halls. At this point, Vigrod was getting used to waking up in this dream. Some time passed, and no one came out to greet him. He then started to walk toward the halls in the distance. Every time he had been here, Thalmur's hall of celebration and feasting had loomed in the distance, but he had never been able to enter.

Walking closer to the hall, someone finally approached him.

"Who goes there?" the voice said. "Vigrod Frostbane, son of Rhagnar Frostbane."

The voice took shape, and it was a tall man, shorter than Vigrod but still tall. He wore leather armor and a fur cloak; his hair was tied up in a bun at the back of his head. He had a large nose and a nicely kept beard, with brown eyes.

"Another Frostbane? Your family has been packing the halls lately," the man said.

"We have a habit of dying in battle. Who are you?" Vigrod asked.

"I am Olvir, the gatekeeper," he replied.

"It is strange you are here, so close to the hall when you have not yet died. Your life must be slipping away from you."

Vigrod scoffed. "Truly it is."

"Can I enter the hall?" he added.

"You are not dead yet, Vigrod," Olvir said. "But you are so young. Thalmur has not yet sent for you."

Eventually, he felt his eyes start to grow heavy. Vigrod said his goodbyes to Olvir and opened his eyes to the world. It was now morning, and he walked out of his quarters to Ravenhall bustling. They were preparing for the battle that was to come. Vigrod went down the stairs to find Nathan, who was still in his fine clothes, not wearing armor like he usually would.

"No armor?" Vigrod asked, putting a hand on his friend's shoulder.

Although they weren't the greatest friends, Vigrod knew that Nathan had been through a traumatic ordeal, so he put the past behind him for good.

"I am lacking a set of armor. Dominus took it and had it melted, along with my swords. Besides, I don't know if I will be half the fighter I was anymore," Nathan said.

"Please, I will have my blacksmith forge you a new set, along with your swords," Vigrod replied.

"You do not have to—"

Vigrod did not let Nathan get his words out. "Just shut up and come with me," he interrupted.

They made their way to the blacksmith, who was named Egmund. The smithy was hidden away in the corner of Ravenhall, but the sound of Egmund's hammer could be heard all throughout the stronghold.

"Egmund," Vigrod said.

"Highlord, how can I help you?" the blacksmith replied.

"The high king here needs a new set of armor and two new swords, put this project above forging weapons for the army if you please," Vigrod said.

"I can do that. Come here," Egmund said, pointing at Nathan. He took a step toward the blacksmith, and Egmund proceeded to get his measurements, going from top to bottom.

"I can get this done in the next few hours. Come see me then," he said.

The two lords then walked away and took a trip outside the gates of Ravenhall.

The people were preparing for the war to come. They were building trebuchets and putting up pointed wooden barricades. Aedric was training the common people in the art of the sword. Everyone was now required to fight, whether they liked it or not.

Vigrod went and found Eirik, deciding that today he would finally break the news to him about his future in Drangar. He found the boy alone, waving his sword through the air elegantly, but when he saw Vigrod coming, he instantly stopped everything he was doing.

The Highlord gave a slight laugh. "Please, don't let me stop you." Eirik gave up a little smile. "There is something I need to speak to you about," Vigrod said seriously.

Eirik stood, looking at him attentively. "Since I have no wife or no heirs, I have decided that you, Eirik, will be heir to Frosthaven and all of Drangar. I ask that you would forget your past name and become Eirik Frostbane, heir to the north."

Eirik then knelt in front of Vigrod. "Highlord, I am not worthy of your name and lands."

Vigrod scoffed in reply. "You are, and you will be. Now do you accept my offer?" he asked.

Eirik then stood. "I would, Highlord. If this is what you are asking of me, then it shall be done." Vigrod put his hands together. "Good. Now I shall give you an order instead of an offer. There is a ship on the harbor waiting to take you back to Frosthaven. I will hear no rebuttal. The crew is trustworthy, now go," Vigrod said.

Eirik sheathed his sword and then jumped into Vigrod giving him a hug.

"Thank you, Highlord," Eirik said.

After a moment, he let go of Vigrod and left to go find his ship.

Nathan went to go talk to Aedric. "How is the training going?" he asked.

Aedric sighed. "Slow, but they are learning. We might not have enough time to get them up to snuff," Aedric said.

"I don't know if it will matter. We will need everyone," Nathan replied grimly.

The high king was very nervous. He had no idea when the enemy would be here, and he had no idea how they would survive.

Later, the sun was setting when Nathan went back inside. He went back over to the blacksmith to find Egmund. Although he was afraid of the fight to come, and he was worried about not being the same fighter anymore. Nathan couldn't help but be excited for a new set of armor.

"How is the armor going, Egmund?" Nathan asked nicely.

"You are just in time. It is now finished. I got a tip from your commander, and I think you will be quite pleased," he replied.

Egmund walked over to an armor stand and brought it into the light.

Nathan looked upon his new armor. Instead of the usual gray steel, this armor was colored black. It had fancy bracers with a sword on one and a hammer on the other. In the center of in chest plate, the sigil of House Eastmoore was embroidered. Egmund then grabbed two swords, the blades were beautifully forged, and the hilts were colored blue for House Eastmoore.

"This is wonderful, thank you," Nathan said.

"There is one more piece," Egmund replied. He then grabbed a blue cape and put it around Nathan's armor. "It is now yours, High King," Egmund said.

Nathan looked at his armor. Then he realized why Egmund said he got a tip from Aedric. This armor was identical to his father's.

He was in awe but also a little afraid, in love with the idea that he could wear armor identical to James Eastmoore, the legendary warrior and king. But the expectation that Nathan was setting in his mind made him wary of the armor. Nathan thanked the blacksmith and had his armor taken to the quarters that Vigrod was letting him stay in. When he was back in his quarters, he looked at his armor and put it on, getting a feel for it. Unsheathing his two magnificent new swords, which he decided he might eventually name.

Nathan swung one of his swords, feeling the power of the sword, remembering who he was. He was Nathan Eastmoore. He would no longer allow himself to be afraid forever. He had to be strong; otherwise, they were surely doomed.

7

A CURIOUS JOURNEY

I t had been roughly two days since Lokfur began his journey north. He didn't really know what he was looking for. The only hint he was given was "reunite with those who thought him gone." He assumed that this just meant his son and his father, but he told his father of his plan. Obviously, Aerimir must have kept his word.

Lokfur enjoyed going through his wall, and he couldn't help but inspect the wall, letting all the memories of building it and its completion flood his mind. He passed through the wall and into the Greenlands, looking at all the plants and insects closely, taking notes of what they looked like in his small journal. Lokfur had always been a curious person. From the time he was a boy to now, he always enjoyed nature and the larger world around him. He kept traveling until he came across a small river. The sun was going down, so he figured this would be a good place to camp.

He didn't have many supplies left. Before he left the Elder Branch, he took enough for months on end, but eventually, he had to rely on fishing and hunting. Setting his pack down against a tree, he put his hood up, then got comfortable on the hard ground and fell soundly asleep.

On the fourth day, he continued his way north. Lokfur hadn't been to the Frostlands or Ravenhall in many years. Last time he was there, things were much different. There were not many things he was afraid of, except for the Shrouded. Lokfur didn't know if Deathshade was still alive. For all he knew, they could be watching him now.

A few bluebirds flew overhead of Lokfur. He took that as a good sign and wondered if there would be rain soon. To him, birds usually meant certain things were about to happen. The day Rhagnar and James were killed. He saw two blackbirds. Ever since, he has thought birds to be signs of what's to come. Maybe they were messages sent from his god. Lokfur couldn't tell.

After more weeks of travel, Lokfur got to the Hall of the Lords. He knew that no one was expecting him any time soon so he would take his time. He pushed the large double doors open and walked inside; the large statues all seemed to stare at him. Lokfur walked in front of the statue of him. He hadn't looked at it in quite a while.

"Hmm, I suppose I should get someone to add my beard," Lokfur said aloud to himself.

Lokfur looked very similar to his son, but he didn't have flowing blond hair. His was much shorter.

Lokfur continued his journey. He did not stay at the hall too long. He was growing hungry and decided to go to a nearby river to catch a few fish. The curious elf built a fire and put his fish over the fire, cooking it to his preference. The sun was setting, and Lokfur then put out his fire and went to sleep.

Weeks blew by, and Lokfur was on the cusp of reaching Ravenhall. Lokfur walked through a village, and it was completely empty. He found no Vikings in it, which he thought was quite odd. Ravenhall grew closer, and Lokfur saw what appeared to be a sea of people. His sharp elf eyes could discern that it was Vikings, elves, and humans alike.

He arrived in the camp, and every elf in the area came to see him. Lokfur Keawynn was loved by all. His people could hardly believe his return, but he was here, greeting all those who came to see him. Lokfur made his way inside the stronghold, and there up on the walkway, he saw his son, his flowing blond hair standing out in the crowd. Lokfur was a bit nervous about how he would react, but admittedly, he was very curious.

CHAPTER

8

FAMILY REUNITED

Kolvar looked down in the courtyard, and he
saw dozens of Elves pouring in, and he had
no idea why. He made his way down the steps
to see what was going on.

"What is happening?" Kolvar asked.

"My lord, your father has returned," one of his
soldiers replied.

Kolvar's jaw dropped. He thought he was dreaming. Did this Elf just say his father has returned?

"What? Take me to him now, please," Kolvar
said excitedly.

He followed the crowd, nudging his way
through the sea of elves. When he reached the end of
the crowd, he saw what the fuss was about. There he
was, Lokfur Keawynn, alive and well.

"Father!" Kolvar yelled.

Lokfur turned around. "My son!"

The two embraced with a long hug, tears streaming down Kolvar's face. He could not believe his father was alive.

"I can't believe it. Where did you go?" Kolvar said.

"I stayed with our friend Ashbeard for some time, but now I have made it back to the waking world," Lokfur replied.

"Where is my father? Someone, bring Aerimir to me at once," he added.

"At once, my lord," one of the Elf soldiers said.

The respect that the soldiers had for Lokfur was equal to the respect they had for Kolvar. Lokfur was their leader for many years before Kolvar made his way onto the throne, but still, he was loved by every elf.

"My son! At long last, you have returned!" Aerimir yelled from a distance, making his way through the crowd.

The father and son shared a long hug with the return of Lord Lokfur Keawynn, the mood in Ravenhall had risen drastically.

A few minutes later, the Keawynns and their elven company made their way inside the great hall to dine. Kolvar requested that they share a meal in honor of his father's return.

"So tell me what has been going on. It has been many a year since I have seen elves, humans, and Vikings all gathered peacefully," Lokfur said.

"The gray humans have returned, Father. We assembled the largest force of all three races in recent history, but still, that was not enough. We have lost the Elder Branch and have reports saying they have moved into High Yrfel," Kolvar replied.

Lokfur looked up from his plate of food. "How much time do we have till they get here?" Lokfur said.

"We do not know. As far as we know, they are still in High Yrfel," Aerimir said.

Lokfur folded his hands together. "Do we have a plan?" he asked.

"No, but if you saw, we have defense mechanisms in place, but that is the extent of our so-called plan," Kolvar replied.

Lokfur messed around with his hands a little more, then took a bite of his piece of bread.

"Tomorrow, I want to meet with your fellow lords and all their accomplices. We need to prepare for this threat thoroughly and thoughtfully," he said.

In the meantime, the Keawynns enjoyed their reunion. Music was played, and many stories were told by Lokfur, but soon, they would have to endure a long dark night.

SUNDOWN

The next day came, and as soon as the sun rose, Lokfur was already getting acclimated to the war room and starting to draft his plans. Kolvar was the first to come in, and Aerimir followed shortly after him. Rion came in a few minutes after that. The elven commander had not yet got to see Lokfur.

"Old friend, it is good to have you back," Rion said.

Lokfur stood up and greeted his old commander and friend with a hug. Rion was still commanding the elf army when Lokfur had first came to rule in Yrfel, so the two were very good friends.

"Have you come up with anything?" Kolvar asked. "Not just yet, but there is plenty of time ahead of us. The day is still quite young," Lokfur replied.

A good amount of time passed before any-one else walked into the war room. Vigrod, Dane, Magthar, and Hilgar were the next few to come in.

"Lord Lokfur, my father talked about you a lot when I was younger," Vigrod said.

"You must be Vigrod. Rhagnar always talked of you very highly and very often," Lokfur replied.

Vigrod gave a small nod, and then he sat down in his usual spot at the head of the table, and his company stood around him.

The last group to come in was Nathan, Aedric, Jarius, and Godwin, finding a spot to stand next to Vigrod and his company.

"Is this everyone?" Lokfur asked.

"Yes, Father. This is everyone," Kolvar replied, scanning around the room.

"Very good. Now that you all are here, I want to devise a proper plan to defeat the enemy ahead of us. All of you have now fought the gray humans, so all of you should have good input," Lokfur said.

"We may have an advantage this time, not being so crowded, and they will not be able to use ships," Nathan said.

"You are right, but this time, we are without Ashwalkers. They have returned home," Kolvar inter-jected. "Vigrod, how many of the giants are left?" Kolvar asked.

"There are only ten giants left in Yrfel," the Highlord replied.

369

Lokfur gave Vigrod a nod of acknowledgment. "Young Raven, we need to defend this stronghold with everything we have. I suggest we line the ramparts with archers and use our barricades and trebuchets until they have breached us. But ultimately, command of Ravenhall is yours," Lokfur said, looking to Vigrod.

"I agree with you, Lord Lokfur. Archers will be lining my ramparts, and yes, we will have to hold behind our defenses until they no longer can provide any use to us," he said.

Godwin then took a step forward to make himself known. "We will try to cause chaos in the night if they camp near the Old Forest, but it might not be possible to get to Dominus."

"A fine idea, Godwin. I suggest that you leave soon. We do not know when they will march," Nathan said.

"I received a message from my scout in High Yrfel. They will begin their march soon," Godwin added.

Nathan gave a sigh. "The beginning of the end then."

"If we need, do we have an escape plan?" Lokfur asked.

Vigrod scratched his head. "Gunir probably knows of a place if we need to leave Yrfel, but I don't know how we could get out of the battle." Kolvar then leaned back in his chair. "I don't think we can get out of this battle."

*****

Back in High Yrfel, Dominus sat on the throne, with Sirius and Gruk sitting in chairs on both sides of the throne. The throne room had been completely redesigned, the blue carpet leading to the foot of the throne had been changed to red, the blue drapes had been removed and changed to red, and lastly, all the Eastmoore banners were taken down.

The plan was made; they would take the three-week journey to Ravenhall, and then the last step of the conquest would be complete. Dominus had no plan for when the battle was won. He did not know what kind of world he intended to build. To him, there were so many options. Would he conquer the rest of the world? Would he stop with Yrfel? He did not know.

It was about midday, and Dominus then stood up and declared that it was time to march to Ravenhall. Gruk then sat on the throne, then Dominus and Sirius left the room to gather the men for the journey.

On a mountain high up above sat Victor, a scout of the Shrouded, tasked with monitoring the gray humans while the main army was still in High Yrfel. He sat down on his mountain high above the rest when he heard something. Victor then looked down to see the gray human army marching out the gates, starting north toward Ravenhall.

He then grabbed his ink and quill and wrote two words on the parchment; he rolled it up and tied it to his messenger, then released it into the sky.

*****

A few days after the meeting took place, Kolvar, Nathan, and Vigrod sat in the great hall, enjoying a drink as friends. They did not know when the gray humans would arrive, so they would make the most of the time they had. One of Vigrod's elders walked into the great hall and approached the three of them. He then handed Vigrod a letter and left the great hall.

Vigrod then opened the letter and read it. After a moment, a look of fear took over Vigrod's face.

"What news?" Kolvar asked.

Vigrod looked from the letter. "They're coming."

NIGHTFALL

G odwin and his Shrouded stayed in an empty village for a few weeks, always watching for the gray humans to pass them by. As another day was upon them, Godwin was up in a tree, watching his surroundings, waiting to catch something in his eyes.

A few hours passed, the Shrouded enjoyed their meals, and there was still no sign of the gray humans. Godwin went back up to watch out of a tree so he could get a perfect view of the land. The sun was going down when Godwin finally caught wind of anything. Lo and behold, the gray humans were approaching the forest. Godwin whistled down to his brothers, signaling for them to conceal themselves. They would continue with the plan that Godwin presented nearly three weeks ago cause chaos in the gray human camp but not sacrifice themselves.

Night fell, Godwin silently climbed down, and when he reached the ground, he raised his hood and drew his dagger. Their camp seemed to go on for miles. Had they kept going, Dominus probably would've stayed in the inn by himself.

He crept through the camp. It was the dead of night, and he knew no one could hear him or see him. Collectively the Shrouded spent an hour slitting throats, killing the gray humans quietly while they slept. Godwin came up to Dominus's tent. He knew it was his due to its abnormal size.

Godwin heard Dominus's voice from outside the tent. He was talking to someone. He resulted in the potion of handheld fire on his belt. Godwin took a few steps back and released the bottle at the tent. On impact, fire started to engulf the tent, then Godwin and his men silently made their way to the forest, completely out of sight.

*****

Vigrod, Nathan, and Kolvar sat by the fire. They knew death was almost at their door, so they decided to spend a few moments together. The fire roared as the three of them stared into it, sharing stories and times when things were better.

Ulfir then entered the great hall. "My lords, all of you have been requested on the ramparts."

The four of them made their way up to the ramparts, where Jarius and Aedric had been waiting for them. They had to nudge some of the archers out of the way so they could see what was going on. The army had been gathered and organized. Archers lined the ramparts. The infantry sat behind their defenses down below, and a few soldiers operated the four trebuchets that they had built some time ago.

"High King, they are almost here. Godwin and his men spotted them," Aedric said.

Time seemed to slow down. Everyone was silent, and all that could be heard was the shrill noise of the wind blowing.

Kolvar spotted something a fair distance away. "There they are. Each one of them is carrying a torch."

"Archers, ready!" he yelled out.

Vigrod then demanded for the gate to be opened. He wanted to get down to the ground to join his people. Nathan accompanied him also, finding his army.

The loud blow of a horn could be heard in the distance, and Kolvar could see that all those little flames were starting to speed up.

"Archers, fire at will!" Kolvar yelled out.

He watched as all the elven bowmen were in perfect synchronization with each other as they released their arrows.

Commands on the ground could be heard, the massive trebuchets were loaded, and the mechanisms were twisting and turning. Then suddenly, four large boulders were thrown out into the dark.

Fear, that was the only emotion Nathan felt. He tried to tell himself for weeks that he would not be afraid. But when he saw the enemy charging toward them, fear took over his mind. A voice in his mind told him to run and cower, but another told him to stand and fight. Nathan did not know who to listen to.

The gray humans had reached the barricades. A few of them were impaled on the large wooden spikes. The barricades could not withstand the wrath of the gray humans for long. It only took them a few minutes to break through the line, and now they were too close to hit them with the trebuchets, and now the war of Yrfel would culminate here.

Nathan unsheathed his sword and pointed it at the gray humans. He said nothing, then charged into the fray, and his army followed behind him. Nathan decided that if he would die, he would die a brave man, not someone who cowered in fear.

The two forces met in the field, crashing into each other with powerful force, and when their swords met, blood was spilled all over the snow. The battle looked like a swirl of black, gray, blue, and gold.

Vigrod was on the front lines with his cousin Dane. The Highlord enjoyed the moment cutting down one by one, sustaining a few cuts but nothing that would slow him down. He turned his mind off, letting go of all the pain that the war had caused him,

Vigrod would fight until the battle was done or he was killed.

Nathan carved through his enemies. He knew that Dominus would eventually reveal himself to him, and he had to be ready.

"There you are!" Nathan turned, and there was Dominus. It looked like he had a severe burn on his face. Nathan walked toward Dominus, this was the physical embodiment of his fear, and Nathan knew it would take everything to overcome his fear.

"You dare approach me, boy," Dominus said. "This time, I will not be merciful. I will enjoy killing you. Here ends your pitiful reign."

Nathan stood stoically, waiting for Dominus to make the first move.

Dominus made his move going for Nathan's chest. The high king parried the strike easily. Nathan analyzed his opponent; Dominus would be aggressive, going for a killing blow with every attack, unlike last time, where he let Nathan play right into his hands. Nathan was strictly playing defense, just like his father had taught him. He had to feel the flow of his swords, letting his metal and eyes do the work.

Dominus took a step back; Nathan could see that rage was swelling within Dominus. The southerner let out a scream and leaped toward Nathan, sword high in the sky, bringing it down toward his head. Nathan blocked his attack, flipped Dominus onto the ground, and put a sword to his neck. He was shocked. He had got the better of his foe, the manifestation of his fears fallen at his feet.

"Yield!" Nathan yelled.

"Don't be a fool. Kill me and be done with it," Dominus retorted.

The battle raged on around them as Nathan held the life of the most valuable being in the world in the palm of his hand.

"You will tell your people to retreat, or I will kill you where you sit," Nathan said.

"My life is meaningless, you kill me, and my heir will take my place," Dominus replied.

While he lay there in the snow, Dominus South did not know what he would do, he was disarmed, and his life was in Nathan's hands. Dominus really had no interest in dying, but he knew that Sirius would continue the rebellion, and he would continue it faithfully. He hoped that something would get him out of this scenario. He was so certain that they would be victorious and was not ready to lose.

Nathan approached him, raising his sword in the air, and when he brought it down, the divine intervention of a sword saved Dominus. The southern king looked to who held the sword, and it was Sirius. His heir had saved him. The two of them then were locked into combat. Dominus grabbed his sword and stood up, watching Sirius try to deal with Nathan.

The high king had let his enemy slip away, and he could not be angrier with himself. The man who was attacking him was half the fighter that Nathan was. Nathan waited for an opening. Sirius was far too aggressive, and he moved his feet too much, and for a good swordsman like Nathan, it could be easily exposed. Sirius went for Nathan's neck. Nathan then used his left sword to parry the strike, then taking a step forward, he plunged his sword deep into Sirius's heart. Nathan had no time to relax before Dominus came charging toward him.

Dominus was enraged that his heir had just been killed so handily he craved vengeance. Letting his rage fuel his hands, he went at Nathan with all his energy, but Nathan was not moved by Dominus's quick-paced assault. The battle seemed to revolve around the two of them. The world was at their mercy.

The momentum of the battle shifted from one side to the other. They fought within the confinements of the barricades that were once there. The giants did a vast majority of the work for the three banners. The lack of cannons for the gray humans kept them alive for much longer than the previous battle.

Hours passed, and the sun started to peak over the mountains in the east. The fighting still raged on, with hundreds of thousands of soldiers going at each other's throats.

They could not retreat into Ravenhall. Opening the gates was far too risky. Kolvar still stood on the ramparts with his archers, letting arrows fly toward his enemies. He let arrows fly so fast his arm started to get tired. There were so many gray humans, and even with the reinforcement of the citizens of Yrfel, they were still starting to lose momentum.

Vigrod and Dane fought side by side, backed up by their clans but still surrounded by their enemy. The pressure was unrelenting. Dane was starting to struggle, and the two were being separated. Vigrod looked over to his cousin. He could no longer allow his family to be killed. In the heat of the moment, Vigrod jumped from a pile of corpses and into the fray to save his cousin, taking all the pressure from Dane's attackers.

Vigrod Frostbane knew that this sacrifice needed to be made. He valued family more than everything, and he would no longer let his blood fill Thalmur's halls. He yelled for Dane to retreat, holding the gray humans back, but soon, they began to surround Vigrod, and they went after him three and four at a time.

He knew that this was the end of the line. Soon, he would see his family, Thalmer, Brodir, Freja, Rhagnar, and all the rest of them. The Frostbanes were the most powerful dying clan in the world. Vigrod was hounded by the gray humans, and he could only fight them off for so long. He may have sacrificed his own life, but it was for someone else. A pile of them jumped onto Vigrod, and he could feel his life start to slip away. His vision started to blurry, his strength started to fade, and then Vigrod was released from the pile of gray humans, and he fell to the ground. As he lay in the snow dying, he realized that rage and his losses had consumed him, and now he had just paid the Viking toll.

The sky was so beautiful, he thought. Vigrod then took his last breath, and his eyes saw no more.

SUNRISE

Vigrod woke up to a calm snowfall, the dark clouds above him, and Thalmur's hall staring at him from a distance. This time, he could enter the hall. He wondered what everyone would say to him. They would probably be confused as to why he was there at such a young age.

He approached the gatekeeper. Olvir said nothing; instead, he stretched out his arm, guiding him to the hall, and he moved out the way, letting Vigrod through. The doors opened for him, and he entered to find a throng—Vikings dancing, drinking, feasting, and singing. Vigrod searched around to find his family. As he was walking through, many Vikings came up to him and greeted him with pats on the shoulder and loud hellos.

The crowd seemed to dissipate when he reached the back. When he reached the end of the sea of

Vikings, he found a large table that was seating more than twenty Vikings.

But there was one empty seat at the very end of the table, next to a boy, Vigrod finally realized that this was his family, and he found it surprising that there was only one chair left. It was as if they were waiting for him. He started to make his way over to his seat, and then someone noticed him.

"Vigrod! You finally made it. All be it too soon." Vigrod recognized the voice instantly. It was Rhagnar, his father, that was brutally taken from him not so long ago. When Rhagnar made his son's presence known, the whole table stood to greet Vigrod.

"Father! It is great to see you, all of you," he said.

Rhagnar then went to get his son to introduce him to every member of his family, save Freja and Thalmer, whom he already knew. Once he was done greeting his family, he then sat down at the end of the table next to Thalmer and his mother.

"So are you the last of us, son?" Rhagnar asked.

"We still have a last hope. I legitimized Thalmer's brother, Eirik. The only thing he needs to do is return to Drangar and claim our name and land," Vigrod replied.

Rhagnar smiled. He had a proud fatherly look on his face. "I knew you would have something planned. If it works, then hopefully, we will not have to add any chairs to this table for a long time."

*****

Nathan woke up slowly, letting his vision return to him. He woke up to the sight of Aedric and Jarius sitting by his bed, and his bedroom looked like it was inside a ship.

"Where am I?" Nathan asked.

Aedric then sat up in his chair. "On a ship, High King, sailing south."

Nathan rubbed his eyes; his head had a throbbing pain, and he couldn't remember how he got to the ship.

"How did we escape?" Nathan said.

"You called for a retreat. Some tried to get back to Ravenhall. Some ran to the ships. Gunir came and grabbed you and delivered you to us. Now we are on the course that he set for us," Aedric replied.

Nathan then slumped back over in his bed.

"We lost," he said in a somber tone.

"Yes, High King," Aedric replied.

"I have so many questions. Where is Kolvar? And Vigrod? How many died?" Nathan said,

"Come, Gunir can tell you everything?" Jarius said.

Nathan gathered himself then made his way out to the deck. He exited his quarters, and he was greeted by the blinding bright sun. Their ship was massive. It was Gunir's own personal ship, built spe-cifically to be able to hold him.

"Gunir, tell me what happened," Nathan said.

"Ah, High King, well, where to start? Vigrod was killed in the battle. You called for a retreat, and many ran to the ships, I had to get you and get you to this ship, so you had the best chance of survival," Gunir replied.

Nathan was taken aback. Vigrod was dead. The last Frostbane had been killed in battle.

"What of Kolvar?" he asked.

"Lord Kolvar stayed and held Ravenhall with his remaining forces. I do not know what transpired after we boarded the ship. All we can hope is that they survived," Gunir answered.

Nathan made an angry scream. "I had him, in the palm of my hand, and he slipped away. What are we to do? They were probably taken as slaves and now the rest of the world is at their mercy," he said.

"You speak the truth, but listen, you are the sole survivor of what is now possibly the greatest house in the known world. If we are to try to overthrow our enemy, the people will need someone to rally behind, you must be the savior, High King," Gunir said.

Nathan had to stop and think. He knew that Gunir was right. If the world was to be saved, then he had to be the face of their rebellion, but it was unfortunate that his friends that he had fought with and against were not by his side.

"Where are we going?" Nathan said.

"The Deep South. There is a whole world that is unknown to the rest, and it will be a haven until we can rebuild and eventually rebel," Gunir replied.

Nathan nodded solemnly in reply.

Deep down, Nathan was worried. He was far away from home, and he had no idea what would happen in Yrfel, in the Steel Isle, or anywhere else in the world. He had abandoned everything in hopes that one day he would return, and he had hoped that his return would be with an army behind his back.

SUBMISSION

The battle was lost. Kolvar had to hold up with his men inside Ravenhall while all those outside either surrendered or were killed. He could not believe that they had lost a second time, and now their forces were scattered, Nathan was gone, and Vigrod was nowhere to be seen.

They fired arrows out from the ramparts for as long as they could, but eventually, their supply ran low. The gray humans had no siege weapons, so the elves would have to hold out for as long as they could. The gates were holding. If they did not get in, they could hold out, but Kolvar knew that no help was coming. As the fighting progressed, more and more surrendered, laying down their arms and submitting. The sun was high in the sky, and the gray humans were trying to break down the gate.

"Lord Keawynn! Surrender now, and I will spare you and your kin," a voice said from down below. Kolvar located the speaker, and it appeared to be Dominus.

"How can I trust that I and mine will be spared?" Kolvar called back.

"Make this easy for yourself, my lord. Come treat with me," Dominus said.

Kolvar knew that going to talk to Dominus was the worst idea, but he had a sense of honor about him. He had won the battle. The only reason he would kill Kolvar was for pride.

"Very well! Tell your men to sheathe their blades. I am coming down," Kolvar said.

He slowly walked the ramparts, and he then meandered down the stairs going to face the gate. The gate started to rumble, and when they opened, the sun showed brightly in his eyes. Kolvar put his bow on the ground, raised his hands in the air, and began to walk out onto the field.

Dominus walked toward Kolvar with his arms stretched out as if he was going to give him a hug. The two stared deeply into each other's souls, the most powerful players left on both sides.

"Name your terms and name them quickly," Kolvar said.

Dominus then gave a quick laugh. "Do not try to turn this into a bargain. You have no power now. You all will be my prisoners now, and your people, along with all your allies, will serve. I will allow you to be a prisoner in your own home, and you all shall witness as a dynasty is put in place. Then I will conquer the rest of your world."

Kolvar said nothing. Their army was shattered. It would make no sense to let everyone inside Ravenhall, along with himself, die as martyrs. He had accepted that they had lost, and they would live out their lives as prisoners of war. Kolvar remained quiet. Dominus eventually called for a few of his guards to detain Kolvar. They stripped him of all his weaponry. The gray humans then sacked Ravenhall, killing the elves who would not submit and then finding torches and setting Ravenhall to the flame.

Dominus watched as smoke started to fill the sky. Yrfel had been won, his conquest had begun, and he could not be happier.

THE ARRIVAL

After months at sea, Nathan and his crew were becoming restless. Only Gunir knew where they were going and how long it would take them to get there.

"Gunir, it has been nearly two months. My crew will be at my throat soon if we don't arrive soon," Nathan said.

"We should be approaching soon, High King, I promise you," Gunir replied.

"Look over there!" he yelled, pointing out to the port side of the ship.

Out in the distance was a large lagoon, and Gunir had been speaking of the leviathan's lagoon for quite some time.

The crew then made their way over to the port side of the ship, staring out toward the lagoon, watching and waiting for the gargantuan-sized leviathan. The waves began to grow, and the ship slowly began to sway back and forth. Suddenly out of the water, the leviathan emerged, catching a sea snake in its mouth and swallowing it whole. The crew gasped; the leviathan was as tall as a mountain, and only half of its body was out of the water. It had what appeared to be like the wings of a bird, with its pointy scales and rows of razor-sharp teeth.

It was easily noticeable that the morale of the crew rose significantly. The leviathan was one of the wonders of the world. Then when they were done enjoying their fish watching, their destination was close.

"Here we are! The port of Oceantown, the largest fishing port in the unknown world, and home to the House Vulcari," Gunir said.

They had finally arrived. Nathan was nervous about exploring this unknown world. His name and his titles would mean nothing here. The natives of the island probably didn't even know that the Steel Isle existed. Their ship had made its way into port. They flew no flag, so there was no questioning when they made landfall. Nathan stepped onto the dock, stretching his arms and legs, glad to finally be off the boat.

The crew gathered and made their way into the port. It was the grandest thing Nathan had ever seen. So many colors and things that he was not used to backing in his homeland, people trading and talking, and not one person lacked a smile or something to give.

"Are you known here, Gunir?" Nathan asked. "I am. There aren't many giants on the island of Verium. I am quite a sight for the people."

Nathan did not know where to start, he was in a foreign land, and a rebellion was on his mind.

"House Vulcari rules here, you mentioned. Will they offer any support?" Nathan asked. Gunir shook his head. "I doubt it, High King. War is not a game that is often played here. Politics is their game of choice. It is a very dangerous game, and we need to play our cards correctly."

Politics was not a game that Nathan was used to in his experience as a leader, not in Yrfel or the Steel Isle, and he was not well versed in trying to get people to join in a rebellion.

"Our first course of action should be to find a place to stay, and somewhere we can formulate a plan," Nathan said.

"I can look around for a tavern, High King," Aedric chimed in.

"Very well. I am sure we can find information there, along with some much-needed refreshment," Nathan replied.

Aedric then walked off to explore the port, and the rest of the crew went to do the same, enjoying the wonderous Oceantown.

"What kind of system does this place have, Gunir?" Nathan asked.

"The people of Verium all answer to one king, who resides in the Stormfalls in the southern reaches of the island," Gunir answered.

"That is why they play the game of politics, lots of powerful figures with ambitions, and only one way to assume power," Jarius intruded.

Eventually, they approached one of the shops. It was a clothing shop with tons of fine-looking linens and silks all in a line. Nathan felt them, and they felt better than the fanciest clothes that he had been supplied by his clothiers in the isle.

"Something catching your eye, my friend?" the merchant asked.

The women had an accent, but she spoke fluently and quickly, as opposed to the traditional blunt and slow tones that Nathan was used to hearing.

"No, ma'am, but I appreciate the offer," he said.

"Suit yourself, but if you need fine threads, you come back to me," she quickly retorted.

For a little while, they strolled throughout the market, walking, talking, and enjoying what Oceantown had to offer. But Aedric then found them as the sun was starting to fall.

"High King, I have located a tavern on the other side of town," he said.

"Very well, Gunir, will you be able to join us?" Nathan asked, turning to face his large tour guide.

"If I remember correctly, this tavern can hold one of my sizes, but we shall see," Gunir said.

The group then made their way to the tavern as the sun went down. Nathan was amazed that the music and vibrance continued throughout the entire day. When they arrived at the tavern, the building stood over. It was one of the largest buildings they had seen all day, with dozens of flags flying the black-fish of House Vulcari. They entered the tavern, and the noise that came from inside was almost deafening. There were hundreds of people yelling at the top of their lungs, and everyone had a mug in their hand.

All inside the inn looked up at Gunir, and they all bid him welcome as if he was a long-lost relative. Nathan and his crew had to shove through the crowd to get to the bar, but Gunir stayed behind to say hello to all who greeted him.

"How can I serve you, gentlemen?" the innkeeper said loudly.

He shared the same foreign accent as everyone else, but Nathan was still not yet used to their beautiful accents. He found them so elegant.

"We need a guide. Is there anyone you can point us to?" Nathan replied, and the innkeeper looked around his establishment. "Somewhere throughout the tavern, there is a hooded man. I have heard he can give good directions and information if you pay the right price."

Nathan nodded and walked off, telling the rest of his crew that they could stay to eat and drink their fill.

He looked around for the hooded man. It took Nathan a while to find him, but eventually, he came across the hooded figure who appeared to be brooding in a corner all by his lonesome.

"I was told that you can give me directions and information," Nathan said.

The hooded man veered up to look at Nathan. "I can. What do you need to know, and where do you need to go?"

The hooded man wore leather armor like his Shrouded did, and he shared the same accent as Nathan, not the one that the Verians had. His first instinct was to question him immediately about where he was from.

"Where are you from, sir?" Nathan said respectfully. "I could ask the same of you. You are clearly not from here," the hooded man replied.

Nathan then sat down and got close to the hooded man. "I am Nathan Eastmoore, High King of High Yrfel and the Steel Isle," he whispered.

Nathan could feel the surprise that the hooded man was feeling. "High King? I am honored by your presence. My name is of no importance, but I come from the Isle, and I have great admiration for your family. Anything you require of me, you need only ask," he said.

Nathan thought carefully about the next thing he would say. He didn't know who had eyes where and if those eyes would be friendly.

"Listen closely, the gray humans have returned, and they have taken the whole of Yrfel. That is why we have fled here, in hopes of gathering an army for a chance of rebellion," Nathan said.

"You will need to win over King Tristari if you want to have a true army. The royal army is nearly two hundred thousand strong. Some of the minor houses are always good for a fight, but I don't know if it is of that magnitude. Other than that, I do not think you will find much support anywhere, High King," the hooded man said.

"How long will it take us to get to King Tristari?" Nathan asked.

"Stormfalls is on the southern side of the island, High King. It will take a few months on foot, perhaps a few days less on horseback," he replied.

Nathan then paused, this man was at his behest, and he had to think more about what would help him at this moment.

"I would ask that you come with us. In truth, we are short on money, and Gunir doesn't know his way around the entire island."

"I am honored, High King. Meet me outside the tavern in the morning. Do not tell anyone of our mission outside those you brought. Even if you are a king somewhere far away, no one will hesitate to capture you," the hooded man said.

He then stood from the table and then blended in with the throng, disappearing from Nathan's sight.

14

ALWAYS TRUST THE HOODED MAN

Nathan woke up the next morning in a comfortable feather bed. He had not the slightest clue as to how he got there. Some of his crew had made it back to their room. When Nathan made it back to the main part of the tavern, he found the rest of his crew, along with Gunir, there. The crew had gathered themselves, and all were served breakfast. They were given a plate stacked high with bacon, ham, and a half loaf of bread, along with a mug of beer.

When they had finished their breakfast, Nathan led them all outside, and the hooded man was already there waiting for them.

"High King, it is good to see you this fine morning," he said. "Follow me to the stables. We will need a couple of horses."

The hooded man directed them through the port, which, even early in the morning, was still very lively. When they had reached the stables, Nathan was surprised at how large the stables were. It was more of an inn than a stable, with dozens of horses trotting around minding their own business.

"Ulmere, my friend, we need a few horses for myself and my friends here," the hooded man said.

"Tsk…tsk, my friend requiring so many of my fine steeds is going to cost you," the stablemaster Ulmere replied in his fine accent.

"How much?" Nathan said, not counting himself, the hooded man, Jarius, Aedric, and Gunir. The crew had around thirty members.

"At least a hundred gold," Ulmere said.

Nathan developed a sort of grimace. They did not have that much gold. He turned to his crew.

"Some of you will have to stay behind, watch after the ship, and I will return whenever I can."

The crew gave them nods and farewells, then walked off into the crowd to enjoy themselves in Oceantown. It was now down to Nathan, Aedric, Jarius, the hooded man, and Gunir (who obviously did not need a horse).

"Now we can make a more reasonable transaction," Ulmere said, rubbing his hands together.

The hooded man emptied his pockets, and Nathan and the rest of his group emptied theirs, combining to have enough gold to get them all horses. Once they handed over the gold, Ulmere went back into his stables and grabbed a horse for those who needed one.

The journey began. The sun was high in the sky, and they found the road that would eventually lead them to King Tristari.

"Tell me more of this place, friend," Nathan said to the hooded man, not knowing what to call him. He wouldn't reveal a name or anything to him. "This place is mysterious. It is very unlike the one we know, cults, prophecies, griffins, vampires, and goblins."

Nathan just had to nod. He had no idea what any of those creatures were, but he pretended like he did.

"Loads of major and minor houses, all with different ambitions, the world of Verium only needs you to unravel its mystery," he continued.

Nathan did not know how to take this statement; he did not know how different this unknown world was from the one he grew up in.

For hours more, the horses carried them along the road. Nathan often found himself watching many birds and beasts pass them that he had never seen before.

As the sun started to set, Nathan grew a bit worried. He did not know if any of these creatures the hooded man mentioned would attack them during the night.

"Shall we make camp soon?" he asked.

"Yes, High King. I have a feeling that with our large friend here, no one shall try to get the better of us while we sleep," the hooded man replied.

Eventually, when the sun set, the group found a formation of rocks that would provide them with a comfortable enough place to sleep.

Nathan gave his horse a bite of an apple, then ate the rest for himself, then he found somewhere to shut his eyes and get some sleep. That night, Nathan would dream of home, then realize he missed the isle and Yrfel very much. He missed the peaceful days of his youth, but all he missed was very far away.

THE CONQUEROR
OF YRFEL

Dominus now had Yrfel in the palm of his hand. He traveled back to the Elder Branch with the elves as his prisoners, planning to make them all servants to tend to the armies and his every single need. Since he had put Ravenhall to the flame and all traces of the Frostbane clan that he knew of had been erased, perhaps he would put his prisoners to work on building a new palace.

The only thing he was upset with was that he had not been able to exact his revenge on his old captive. Dominus knew that if Nathan was still lingering, then hope of overthrowing him would linger as well.

He entered the throne room to find Chelmere keeping the wooden throne warm. The general then got up to approach Dominus, kneeling in front of him.

"Your Grace, we awaited your return, hoping for good news," Chelmere said.

Dominus motioned for his general to stand. "Yrfel is now ours, but Ravenhall is now a husk of its former self, I must admit," he replied.

Chelmere stood, and he had a confused look on his face. "Sirius is not with you either, Your Grace." Dominus gave a sigh. "Sirius did not survive the battle, and it would appear that I am in need of an heir."

Chelmere gave a humble bow. Dominus knew what his subordinate wanted to hear, and he figured he might as well say it.

"Kneel." Chelmere knelt and stared down at the floor. Dominus then slowly unsheathed his sword and held it on Chelmere's shoulder. "Chelmere, you may rise again but now as my heir." Dominus then removed his sword from its resting point and sheathed it carefully.

Chelmere then stood up. "I am not worthy, but I am ever thankful, Your Grace," Dominus just gave a slight smile. "You are more worthy than Gruk, to say the least."

Later in the evening, Dominus wanted Chelmere to meet him in the war room so they could discuss their plans moving forward.

He sat comfortably at the head of the table, waiting for his heir to enter. When Chelmere arrived, he gave his usual bow, and then he sat down. The day was November 1, of the seventh summer, and Dominus was ready to plan his domination of the world outside Yrfel.

"Are we still in complete control of our prisoners?" Dominus asked.

"Yes, Your Grace. Their morale is extremely low. Not even the Keawynns inspire any hope," Chelmere replied.

Dominus rubbed his hands together excitedly. "Good. We still must be wary of them. We did not win this war by not being fearful of our enemy." He paused briefly. "We still have all the Keawynns, yes?" he asked.

Chelmere looked up to the ceiling. "Yes, the youngest, Kolvar, his father Lokfur, and the eldest Aerimir." Dominus nodded in reply. "Now what is our plan for the rest of the world? The Bloodweaver has taken his army back to Drangar so that will be taken care of"—Chelmere sat up—"what if we stayed in Yrfel for now? The rest of the world is not going anywhere. Perhaps we erect a fortress, one worthy of one such as yourself, that will break the spirits of our prisoners even more."

Dominus smiled, another grand citadel for him to sit in and be admired. He loved the idea his heir presented. It would be a throne to unite Yrfel.

"Wonderful idea. I shall leave the planning in your hands Chelmere. That fortress shall be yours someday after all," Dominus said slyly.

Chelmere stood and took his leave. He was excited for another throne to sit on, but he was a little worried about how long it would take the outside world to respond.

INTO THE GRIFFIN'S DEN

The journey throughout Verium continued. Nathan's hooded friend had led them to the gates of Castle Felmar on the eastern coast, home to the strong House Felmar, the sigil of House Felmar was a sword engulfed in a green flame on a black field.

Nathan was in awe of the sheer size of the castle. The walls were intimidating, archers could be seen lining the ramparts, the turrets were massive, and it was all a very dark stone color. The gates into the outer city were open. Nathan did not know why they were there, but he assumed it was because House Felmar could help them somehow.

The hooded man looked at Nathan from his horse.

"We shall go to the stables first, then we can speak with Lord Felmar. I know him personally, and he can offer us some sort of help."

"How can I trust him?" Nathan asked.

The hooded man stopped his horse, and the company stopped with him. "Do not worry, High King. I have fought alongside Dathmir many times. He may be the one person in power that we can trust."

Nathan nodded in reply. He had been with this man long enough to at the very least trust his words.

He noticed that the city of the Felmar was emptier than the port of Oceantown nor as colorful. It was very stark in comparison. They took their horses to the stable and began their walk toward the main castle of House Felmar. The street led them straight there. The large houses seemed to cover the sky, and Nathan felt sort of trapped in although he could see the open gate from where they were standing. They soon approached the large Castle Felmar. It was both beautiful and monstrous. The castle was very traditional, with four turrets in every corner, and huge walls, and the keep itself was very square and boring. The gates to the castle were open. The guards did not question them walking inside, which Nathan found very odd.

They entered the castle; the interior was more like a cathedral than anything else. The Felmar sigil could be seen everywhere. Green linens made the room more colorful, and in the very back was a large stained-glass window of the flaming sword.

The hooded man walked toward the throne, kneeling once he was close enough in proximity.

"Lord Dathmir Felmar, I have come to ask for your aid."

Lord Dathmir Felmar stood up from his throne. He was a tall, muscular man. Nathan glanced at him and was almost instantly reminded of Vigrod. Dathmir was just a bit shorter. Dathmir had flowing black hair with peculiar, fiery green eyes and a beautiful face, but it wrinkled due to his age.

"The Angel! Welcome back to Castle Felmar!" Dathmir yelled out, walking down to see the hooded man, picking him up and hugging him.

Nathan had to take a moment to process what was being said, "Angel? That is your name?" Nathan asked. The Angel turned to face him. "No, High King. It is more of an alias, but I suppose I will reveal more of my true self now that you know this one's name."

Dathmir gave a laugh as though he knew what was happening. "So tell me, what is it you need from me?"

Nathan then took a step forward. "My friend here assures me you can be trusted."

He took a breath. "I come from a land far away from here, and the gray humans, beings of pure cruelty and hatred, have stolen my home and enslaved my people. I have come here in hopes of building an army strong enough to rebel and win back what was stolen."

The smile started to fade from Dathmir's face. "Gray humans, I know what they are. I am one of the few people in this country who dare to venture outside Verium. Who are you? What power have you to ask the help of the Verians?" he said.

"I...," Nathan started.

If he said his name, he did not know who would hear it and if it would put him in danger but taking this chance was necessary.

"I am High King Nathan Eastmoore of the Steel Isle."

"A high king? I have not been so far as this Steel Isle, but I presume your family is the prominent one?" Dathmir asked.

Nathan nodded back. He had no idea how or why Dathmir would give him any support, so he was curious as to what he would say.

"My family respects strength. If you can prove yourself in battle, then you have my allegiance," Dathmir said, raising his hands as if to say Nathan had no chance.

He was baffled. Battle was what Nathan was best at. He was more than confident he could take on any swordsman from this strange land.

"Who will I be fighting?" Nathan asked confidently, as if there was no challenge that could be presented to him.

"You will be fighting a griffin," Dathmir replied.

408

Nathan had no idea what that was, and he didn't know how to respond, but he looked over to the angel and had a terrified look on his face. Then a little worry started to creep into his mind.

"Very well. When will I fight?" Nathan said, trying to sound as confident as he did before. "Tomorrow, tonight we sup," Dathmir said kindly, lifting his arm, motioning for the group to follow him, but Gunir had to stay behind, then insisting that he would find some sort of food and drink.

Lord Dathmir led the company throughout the castle to where all the feasts at Castle Felmar were held. The room was lit with candles and torches and decorated with beautiful paintings and banners. The group all sat down. Dathmir called to one of his servants, asking for a meal for his guests and something for Gunir to eat.

"Dathmir," said a feminine voice.

They all turned to see a woman dressed in a green dress with pale skin and brown hair, walking toward them. Dathmir stood up. "My love, what brings you here?" he said. "Allow me to introduce my wife, Evelynn Felmar," Dathmir said to Nathan and his company, then gave his wife a kiss on her cheek.

"I just came looking for you. I couldn't find you in the throne room." Lady Felmar paused and looked at Nathan.

"Who are our guests?" she asked.

Nathan then approached the two.

"I am Nathan Eastmoore. It is good to meet you, my lady."

Jarius and Aedric introduced themselves, then the Angel and Lady Felmar greeted each other as if they had been friends for years. After the pleasantries were exchanged, they sat down, and their dinner was brought to them.

Nathan was ecstatic with the food that was brought to him, elk and potatoes, with asparagus, along with a mug of ale.

"Tell me more of Verium, Lord Felmar," Nathan said.

"What would you like to know?" Dathmir replied.

Nathan took a second to think about what he would say, but he decided he would take a political approach to his answer.

"Who can I trust that will help me in my rebellion? Aside from you, if I win tomorrow," he asked.

Dathmir took a deep breath in. "House Gilveri, they are bound to us by blood, House Leonin, they're always good for a fight, and I trust them well enough. But aside from those two, I do not think there will be anyone else unless you convince King Tristari to help you, which, if I am being honest, is unlikely," Dathmir replied.

The group exchanged stories for a while longer, finishing their meals and drinks, but eventually, Nathan desired to go to sleep, being escorted to his chamber. His escort left him in his nicely decorated and dimly lit quarters. Nathan then took his armor off and crashed into his bed, falling into the most comfortable sleep he had taken in a long time.

CHAPTER

17

THE TRIAL OF NATHAN

The sun rose on a new day. It was November second of the seventh summer, the eve of Nathan's day of birth. He was awoken by two Felmar guards, who, upon waking him up, told him to put on his armor and head to the dining hall to meet with Dathmir.

Nathan did as he was bid and made his way through the mazelike castle back down to where he had spent his previous night.

When he got there, Dathmir sat waiting for him. "Nathan, good morning, my friend. I hope you are ready," he said.

Nathan replied with a nod and a smile. The two sat and talked for a little before long breakfast was brought to them, two eggs and a few slices of bacon, with a cup of fine Verian wine. Nathan ate his meal slowly in hopes that it would not come back to him when he was in the arena.

"So when will the trial happen?" Nathan asked.

"In a few hours' time, we will let the arena fill up. If you win with the eyes of the people on you, you will win more respect," Dathmir replied.

With every word that came out of Dathmir's mouth, Nathan found more respect for him. He was very smart and honorable, and Nathan admired him.

The time rolled on, and eventually, Dathmir raised his hand for a few guards to escort him to the arena.

The arena was daunting. Nathan could hear the cheers and screams of the people from outside. They walked to the portcullis of the arena. It slowly opened, and the guards guided Nathan to a room off to the side where he could relax before he would come out.

The guards left, and Nathan was now by his lonesome, sitting on a bench, surrounded by tons of weapons and armor. He was looking straight forward at another portcullis that led out into the arena. Nathan's heart started to race. He had no idea what he was facing. Trying to calm his nerves, he stood up and bounced around.

Suddenly, the portcullis made a loud thud, and it started to creep upward. Nathan slowly made his approach out to the arena. When he left the room, the sun hit him in the face like a slap, and the wave of noise from the crowd showered over him.

He looked around and saw Dathmir and his wife, along with his company, on a fancy platform covered by a gazebo to give them shade. Gunir even got to sit in the crowd.

Nathan could hear a loud screeching noise from the other side of the arena, and he could only imagine who or what was making this noise. Out of a dark room emerged a few men, all holding ropes, trying to pull something which seemed extremely heavy. The screeching became louder and louder, then suddenly, out came this beast. It took the form of an eagle but much larger, and its wings and tail were twice the size of its body.

Nathan was horrified. The twenty men dragged it out into the arena could barely hold it, so how would he be able to kill it? The griffin grew angrier as it started to toss some of its holders around. Suddenly, the men let it go and sprinted back into the dark.

The griffin let out another screech as it let the men run. It then turned its head toward Nathan and started to glide toward him. He unsheathed his swords quickly, trying to think of what he would do. But he had virtually no time. Before he had any chance to form a thought, the griffin rammed its large head into Nathan's chest, sending him flying yards back.

When he hit the ground, the wind was completely knocked out of him. He took a few seconds to get up. The griffin looked at him as if he was studying his prey. Again, the griffin started to glide toward Nathan, picking up speed as it got closer.

Quickly, Nathan rolled out of the way and slashed the griffin on the neck, causing minor damage but enough to stun it momentarily. The griffin went to bite Nathan. He had to move quickly out of the way and try to get attacks in when he could.

After a few moments of dancing around, it was clear the griffin had enough of Nathan. It then swept Nathan off his feet and onto his stomach. Then picking him up in its large beak and bringing him up into the air. Nathan's eyes widened as he could feel the ground become further and further away from him. The griffin carried him far above the arena, and Nathan felt its grip on him start to loosen. Nathan then started to hack and slash at the griffin, trying to grab at its neck.

Using all the momentum he could, Nathan grabbed on to the griffin's head, then pulled himself up and ended up on its back, clutching on tightly to its feathers. The griffin then reacted by diving down, and Nathan held on for his dear life.

Down they went. Nathan just had his head buried in the thick feathers of the large griffin. He peeked his head up to see them hurtling toward the ground. They landed down hard. Nathan still clinched to the back of the griffin. It screeched and cried, trying to get him off. Nathan then rolled off the griffin onto the ground facing the sky, dropping his swords. He could hear in the background as the crowd gasped and went completely silenced.

The griffin then turned to look down at Nathan. All he could do was wait for it to kill him. He already had no idea how he was still alive. It then veered its head down, rubbing its head against his. Nathan was so confused; this thing had just spent the last few minutes trying to kill him, and now it wanted to befriend him?

He did not really care; Nathan ran his hand through its feathers. Eventually standing up, he began walking with the griffin over to the gazebo where Dathmir was sitting.

"Do I still win?" Nathan asked.

Dathmir responded with a laugh, "Out of everything that could've happened today. That was one I did not see coming."

Dathmir then began clapping, and the whole crowd followed suit.

"Nathan Eastmoore, you have proven yourself against this fearsome beast, and as promised, my army, along with House Gilveri's, are yours," Dathmir said.

Nathan then replied with a smile as he continued to pet his new friend.

18

A KINDLE OF HOPE

Kolvar walked in line with the rest of his captive kin. On his way to continue the labor they had been doing day after day. First, the day started with farming, hours on end planting, tilling, and so forth, without break.

The sun beat down hard on Kolvar. He often would have to wipe sweat from his brow. The gray humans overworked them so much that his pretty blond hair was beginning to turn brown. After a few hours, Kolvar could feel himself start to crumble. His legs started to lose feeling, and his stomach began to churn.

One of the guards came around and tossed a piece of bread in Kolvar's direction. Instantly, he dropped everything he was doing, and he began to devour the bread. The sun was now high in the sky, and the guards started to gather all the prisoners up to bring them outside the city to continue building a gargantuan-sized statue of Dominus.

Kolvar carried out his usual duties until the sun set, carrying up stone and wood for the builders. He had no opportunity to speak to anyone. The guards kept everyone silent. The build site was silent as the grave, save for the sounds of hammers.

When the night had rolled on for a while longer, the guards again gathered the prisoners and led them back to the roots. Kolvar stood at the door, waiting for the guard to shove him into his cell. The shove felt like a shock of lighting sent up his spine, and he fell into the ground getting dirt in his mouth.

The guards left the cell to go stand by the entrance to the roots, and Kolvar watched to make sure he would be able to speak.

"Listen carefully. I have a plan for some of us to escape," Kolvar whispered. "Tomorrow at the statue, I will pretend to collapse. All of you must call the guards over." Kolvar briefly paused to look back to make sure he wasn't heard speaking.

"Once we have them gathered, we will strike. We must steal what we can off them, and we shall escape into the night," he finished.

"What then?" one of his cellmates asked.

"I shall think of something. For now, sleep, gather your energy," Kolvar replied, then lay down and closed his eyes.

Kolvar was woken up by the sound of swords banging against shields and the guards yelling, "Up!"

The day would drag on as all the previous ones had, out on the large wheat field that the elves had for half the day. Kolvar was more than fed up with living the same day repeatedly, but now he hoped that would all be changing.

The time dragged on, and the sun got lower. Kolvar's mood raised drastically, but he did not show it to anyone around him. He wanted the guards to buy into his miserable look.

Kolvar looked around for his cellmates. As he walked by and saw some of them, he gave a little nod to signify it was time. Carrying his piece of stone to where he was told, he then dropped it down and walked away to go grab another.

He looked around for one of his cellmates, and once he spotted one, Kolvar began to stumble around, then fell on his face, laying there lifelessly.

"Guards! Someone! Help!" the elf yelled aloud.

Instantly, a crowd swarmed around Kolvar. Once the guards arrived, they backed off the crowd and came over to Kolvar. He was still facing the ground, but he could hear the metal boots of the guards and instantly tell there were three of them.

One of the guards turned Kolvar over.

"Elf, wake up. Can you hear me?" the guard said.

Kolvar slowly began to open his eyes. "I am sorry, sir…now!" Kolvar yelled, jolting up Kolvar, then quickly grabbed the guard's sword from its sheathe and buried it in the guard's neck.

The other cellmates began to attack the two other guards, trying to pry their swords from their hands. Kolvar then came over and assisted them. Kolvar knew that they only had so much time before more gray humans arrived.

"Quick, grab their swords and shields. Take what armor you can!" Kolvar yelled. They gathered up and began running off. "Do not worry, my people. I will come back for you!" he yelled as they ran off into the deep, dark night.

*****

Chelmere entered the throne room to speak with Dominus. He regretted with every fiber of his being that he was going to say something, but he knew Dominus would eventually find out.

He approached the throne and knelt. "Your Grace, some of the men have just informed me that we have lost some of our prisoners," he said.

Dominus had a dumb look on his face. "Lost? Have they misplaced them?" Dominus replied.

"They escaped, Your Grace," Chelmere said.

Dominus sat back on the throne. "There's the word, but you know I would care not for any common escapee. Who have we lost?" Dominus asked.

Chelmere put his head down. "It was, Lord Kolvar, Your Grace, accompanied by a few others."

Dominus clenched his fist tightly. It was so loud Chelmere could hear it without seeing it.

"How!" Dominus took a breath in and out. "Did they possibly escape?"

"I was told that Lord Kolvar feinted, and when our men went to attend to him, Kolvar and his accomplices killed three of our men, stole their weapons and armor, and ran off into the night," Chelmere said.

"How could my men, our men, be so stupid!" Dominus said.

Chelmere then looked up to his king.

"Go! Have our soldiers search for him! As long as he is running throughout this continent, hope survives."

WALKING IN THE
SHADOWS

Since the battle, the Shrouded have been invisible to the outside world, only sending out one or two scouts every few days and leaving the base to hunt when they had to.

It had taken some time to gather the whole of the Shrouded's forces, but Godwin was certain that whoever was left would make their way to the mountain, and no one new had entered the base in quite a long time. He had taken a head count just a few days ago. Before the battle, there were a few hundred Shrouded. Now there was just eighty.

Godwin sat comfortably in the commander's chair that Aegis sat in before him when Arthur entered his office.

"Commander, we have word from our eyes in the Elder Branch. A few Elves have escaped captivity and are on the run," Godwin sat up.

"Very interesting. Call our eyes back, and bring the elves. I would not allow them to be run down by the gray humans," he replied.

Arthur left the office, and Godwin followed him out, going to talk to his friend Darwyn in the alchemy room. He entered, and all the steam seemed to gravitate toward him. Darwyn turned to look at him, and his extravagant black cloak seemed to dance as he moved.

"Commander, to what do I owe the pleasure?" Darwyn asked.

"Just came to see how everything was going," Godwin replied.

Darwyn seemed to jump at the prospect of Godwin coming to check on his work. He proceeded to walk Godwin through every little detail of what he had discovered, new mixtures he had come up with. Although he truly had no interest in potions, he was glad his friend could be in a good mood during their dark times.

Hours passed, and Godwin's scout from High Yrfel had returned. Godwin was back in his office when his scout came to see him.

"Any sign of Nathan? Or any of his council?" Godwin asked before his scout even had a chance to speak.

"No, Commander, I have searched as thoroughly as I can without being seen. I am sorry," the scout replied.

"Nothing to be sorry for, my friend. Go, rest now. You deserve it," Godwin said.

His scout gave him a nod and left his office. The commander was slumped in his chair, worried about his king that his leader had bonded them too. Godwin refused to give up hope, and he knew somehow Nathan would be alive.

Godwin waited patiently for four more days when his other scout, and the elves arrived. He went out in the courtyard to meet them, and Godwin was surprised by who he was greeted.

"Lord Kolvar, it is good to see you're alive," Godwin said.

"Thank you, Commander. Godwin, is it?" Kolvar replied.

Godwin gave a quick nod back. "Come, let my men get your crew fed and properly clothed."

The Shrouded's lead cook, Jackson, guided Kolvar and his company to the mess hall. Godwin accompanied them, anxious to ask Lord Kolvar questions about his escape. The cooks brought the Elves bread, stew, elk, and a tankard of water. As they ate, Godwin could tell how starved they had been.

"If you don't mind me asking, Lord Kolvar, how did you escape?" Godwin asked.

"It's no problem. It was baffling truly, I feinted and waited for the guards to attend to me, and when the time was right, My crew and I crew struck, stealing the armor and weapons we have now," Kolvar replied.

Godwin replied with a noise of approval. He was surprised the guards could be so stupid.

Arthur then entered the mess hall with Shrouded garbs for Kolvar and his crew.

"These are for you, Lord Kolvar," Arthur said, setting down the clothing on the table in front of them.

"Well, Lord Kolvar, with the armor you brought, we may be able to walk in the shadows of our enemy," Godwin said.

"What do you have in mind, Commander?" Kolvar asked.

"If you brought us three sets of armor, we can infiltrate the Elder Branch and free more of your people," Godwin answered.

Kolvar took a deep breath in and out. "It could work. Is there any way we could take down a statue?"

Godwin didn't say anything. He just looked at Kolvar and let out a little smile.

20

TOWARD KING TRISTARI

Nathan awoke from his comfortable bed chambers in Castle Felmar. It had been several days since his "duel" with the griffin, and he had never been feeling better. The day was November tenth of the seventh summer, and Nathan Eastmoore was ready to make his journey to meet King Tristari.

He made his way down to the throne room, where Dathmir and his wife were sitting comfortably.

"Nathan, good morning!" Dathmir yelled out.

Nathan was still half asleep, and Dathmir's yelling wasn't exactly what he was looking for so early in the morning.

"Lord and Lady Felmar, good morning," Nathan said, fixing his hair to try to make himself presentable.

Dathmir stood and approached Nathan. "So today, you're departing, yes?" he said, putting a hand on Nathan's shoulder.

"Yes, will you be joining us?" Nathan said in a persuasive tone.

Dathmir sighed. "I…am not so sure, my friend. The journey is long and arduous. I do not know if I can be absent for so long," he said hesitantly.

"Come now, Lord Felmar. We could use a powerful friend in your capital," Nathan retorted.

Dathmir looked back to his wife. Nathan could see Lady Felmar roll her eyes and follow that up with a smirk.

"On second thought, I will be joining you. I will meet you at the stables in an hour. To be safe, I shall bring a few of my own guard along with us," Dathmir said. Nathan gave Dathmir a pat on the back and left to go find his company.

It did not take Nathan long to gather up all his things. He put his armor on, threw whatever he had into a satchel, and went out to go find Jarius, Aedric, and the Angel. Nathan wandered around the castle a little before he eventually came into a courtyard, where his archmage and commander were waiting for him, while the Angel stood patiently in the background. The four left the large Castle Felmar and found Gunir sitting outside, waiting patiently.

"Gunir, it is time we made our way to the capital," Nathan said.

"Wonderful. I shall wait for you all outside the city gates," Gunir replied, standing up slowly.

They walked to the front of the city back to the stables, exchanging a conversation with the stable master until Dathmir and his guards arrived.

"Gentlemen, ready to go?" Dathmir said from top of his beautiful steed.

"Quite the horse, my lord," Nathan replied.

"Thank you. Her name is Lightheart. She's been in my family since I was a child," Dathmir said. "Truly, Lightheart was quite the horse, pale white hair with an astonishing blond mane."

The long and arduous journey had begun. Everyone was saddled and ready to go—the Stormfalls in the southern reaches of Verium, home of the new royalty, House Tristari. Nathan wanted to gain all the information he could about King Tristari, so hopefully, when the time came, he would know how to best persuade him to help his cause.

"Dathmir, tell me about your king. I would like to know as much as I can," Nathan said.

"Quite an interesting man, very young, younger than you, I would think, only sixteen. I have heard he is a formidable combatant, cunning for his age, and a good leader," Dathmir replied.

Nathan jolted with surprise. "Only sixteen? How long has he been king?" he asked.

"Only for three years. It is a strange tale how he became king, but you will meet him in a few months' time," Dathmir answered.

As the time rolled on, Nathan noticed that Gunir was starting to lag back a little bit, so he told everyone to stop and insisted that they would continue soon. He climbed off his horse and tied it up to a nearby tree with the rest of the company's horses.

Nathan walked over to see Gunir, who was sitting alone, staring at the sunset. He was surprised the giant wasn't telling their new traveling partners about all the interesting stories he had. He sat down next to his giant friend and patted his tree trunk-like leg to try to comfort him.

"You seem troubled, Gunir. What has been bothering you?" Nathan said softly.

"Probably the same as what has been troubling you, High King, thoughts of home. My people on Yrfel are most likely all dead. I have not been to Drangar in such a long time that I can hardly remember what it looks like," Gunir replied solemnly.

"There are no Frostbanes left in this world. Our homes beyond Yrfel will soon be taken by our enemy, I am sure. It seems this conflict has become quite taxing, my boy," Gunir said with a slight laugh, but Nathan could tell there was no true joy in his laugh.

"When we return home, Gunir, I will bring you Dominus's head, and we will give Vigrod the greatest funeral pyre the world has ever seen, I promise you," Nathan said.

Gunir again let out a slight laugh. "Thank you, High King, but you may keep Dominus's head. I am afraid I won't have much use for it."

STORMFALLS

After a long three-month trek across the country of Verium, Nathan and his company had finally reached the Stormfalls, home of House Tristari. The day was February eleventh of the first fall of the year three hundred three.

The rain was beating down on them from the time they had been five miles from the city until they reached the gates. The city of Stormfalls got its namesake from its uncanny ability to attract rain.

Nathan and his company passed through the gates. He noticed the guards in their light gray armor with white tabards, showing a red crown, which was the Tristari house sigil.

"Where shall we go! We need to get away from the rain!" Nathan said, trying to speak over the loud rain.

"There is an inn nearby, but we need to tend to our horses first," Dathmir replied in the same loud tone.

They trotted along for a little longer before Nathan eventually asked one of the citizens where the stable was.

"Gunir! Where will you go?" Nathan asked.

"I will find somewhere to stay dry. I will meet you at the gates of the king's keep," Gunir replied, walking away, trying not to step on anyone.

Once the horses were safely leashed and inside the stable, the rain began to let up a little more. The company continued, being led by Dathmir and the Angel, who seemed to have the most knowledge of the city out of everyone present. The streets of Stormfalls were wide and crowded, and often Nathan could feel mud being kicked onto him from those behind and in front of him. Architecture in Stormfalls was very different from that of the Fell City, with much lighter stone and what looked like a brick tile on the roofs.

"Here we are, an inn I am all too familiar with, the Stately Storm," Dathmir said. He pushed the door open, and the crowd that was inside seemed to form a wall at the door. "Excuse me, my friends. If you wouldn't mind moving out of the way for me and mine here," Dathmir said charmingly. His voice parted the way. The people made just enough room for all of them to sneak through.

Most of the inn's customers were gravitated toward the bar, so the company was able to find a table in the corner of the inn. They sat down while the guards stood idly watching their surroundings.

"What is our plan? We have come this far, and now we need to finish the job," Nathan said.

The table was silent, and it had every right to be. The task in front of them couldn't be done easily.

"Come now. You are my council, council me," Nathan continued.

"I am not sure, High King. There is nothing we have that can convince him to join us, save Lord Felmar, but what do we have that will make this young king risk his people's lives for ours," Jarius replied.

"I am sure that this is a conflict we are not able to fight our way out of. You might have to pester the boy, we are eager to return home, but we cannot do it without his help," Aedric added.

"The best I can get you, my friend, is the opportunity to talk to him, but you will have to convince him or, at very least plant, the seeds in his mind to help you. At the very least, you still have my army and House Gilveri's. I know you are a capable warrior, and you have a good heart, so even if you fail with Tristari, we are still with you," Dathmir said.

Nathan felt tears in his eyes, but he held them back. These men truly cared for him. They didn't follow him just because his name was Eastmoore.

"If all else fails, Houses Felmar and Gilveri will be enough. Get me in a room with him, Lord Felmar.

For now, we shall enjoy ourselves. We are in an inn, after all," Nathan said.

The company got their drinks and enjoyed themselves. Nathan and Dathmir conversed with everyone in sight. For the first time in a long time, Nathan could feel genuine joy within himself.

Nathan was on his way back to his table when he bumped into someone on accident. "I am so sorry," Nathan said, turning around to see whom he ran into.

The lady who he bumped let out a light laugh. "You're alright. I haven't seen you around here before. Who might you be?" she said.

Nathan was so enthralled by her accent it took him a second to remember what his name was. "Nathan," he said nervously.

Again, the lady laughed. "It is nice to meet you, Nathan. I am Rose," she replied, extending her hand.

Rose had flowing brown hair and the common brown eyes, but there was a certain beauty in them. They had Nathan entranced, after all. She was a shorter woman, not even being up to Nathan's chin.

"Come, Nathan. I'd like you to come to my table and share a drink," she said.

Nathan just nodded in reply and followed her lead. Nathan was introduced to everyone at Rose's table. They all welcomed him in with open arms, and Nathan couldn't be happier.

The time started to drag on, and Nathan began to worry about Gunir, so he thanked everyone at

Rose's table and then went back to gather up his party. Nathan went to the bar and threw the innkeeper a few gold coins, and then he left the Stately Storm.

They continued following Dathmir and the Angel around, making their way toward the castle. Nathan kept his eyes open for Gunir, getting more worried with every passing second. He didn't see his giant friend. Dathmir led them toward Stormfalls' large pavilion, named the Storm Cover. The cover was as long as a river and as tall as a castle. The company walked under the pavilion in hopes that they would find Gunir.

As they walked on, Nathan noticed out of the corner of his eye a large crowd gathering around some large figure. His brain did not take long to register that it was Brodir. The people were gathered around.

"There he is, come on this way," Nathan said, walking hurriedly toward the giant. When he reached the large crowd, he nudged himself in between everyone, gently pushing to get toward Gunir.

"Gunir! There you are. I am sorry we took so long," Nathan said.

"It is alright, my boy. These people here were very interested in all the stories I had for them," Gunir replied, then turning toward the crowd that was amassed around him, "until next time, my friends."

Once they left the Storm Cover, Stormfall Castle was in sight. Nathan was a bit anxious to meet King Tristari, hoping that somehow. He could convince him to help their rebellion.

CHAPTER

22

ROYAL MEETINGS

Three days after they had arrived in Stormfalls, King Tristari was finally ready to meet with Nathan. As promised, Dathmir got Nathan the meeting with the young king. The company stood outside the castle as they did when they arrived, and Nathan was ready to walk in, but his people wanted to give him luck.

Nathan began his walk into the castle. He had not even been inside yet. Dathmir and his guards were the only ones to go inside. Once Nathan reached the gate of the outer wall that surrounded the castle itself, two guards stepped toward him.

"What is your business?" the guard asked.

"I am Nathan. I have a meeting with King Tristari," Nathan replied.

The guards gave no reply. They moved out of the way, letting Nathan pass.

The castle itself was very robust, with plenty of towers sprouting out from different parts of the castle. Nathan liked the different look of Stormfall castle compared to all the ones he had seen in his life; it had a peculiar white stone instead of a classic gray. The castle took no true shape. It was very erratic. Nathan thought it fit perfectly in this place.

The yard outside the castle and between the gate was small. The large keep loomed over him like a storm cloud. The doors into the throne room were opened. He walked into what was like a guard of honor, two lines of guards parallel to each other, making a path for him to walk to the throne. The throne room was also quite beautiful. Nathan looked around as he walked down the aisle. Lots of red and white linens hanging around, along with the banner flying the red crown.

Nathan reached the end of the aisle, and there was the grand throne which was being sat on by King Tristari himself. Next to him stood an older man wearing a set of fine black and gold clothes.

"Nathan of House Eastmoore, you have the honor to be in the presence of King Leon Tristari," the speaker said proudly.

"High King, Dathmir spoke very highly of you. On behalf of myself and Stormfalls, we bid you most welcome," King Tristari said.

Nathan gave a bow. "Thank you, great King. I am pleased to finally be able to meet you."

"As am I although Lord Felmar did not speak much of your purpose, so if I may ask, why are you here?" Leon replied.

Nathan took a deep breath in. He had to be perfect with the next words he said, "I come from a land far away from here, where my people lived peacefully with Elves and Vikings. But an old enemy of ours rose from the shadows, the gray humans. They sailed into our home and drove us out, slaughtering thousands and taking those who survived as prisoners. I fled here in hopes…that I could build an army strong enough to sail back to my home and take it back, saving my people and sending the gray humans back to the dark from once they came."

Leon leaned back on his throne; Nathan could tell the young man was, at the very least, moved by his speech. All he could do was hope that Leon's next words would be what he wanted to hear. Leon leaned over to his speaker; the old man whispered in Leon's ear, and Nathan had to watch and wait, the anxiety building.

"What you are doing is truly honorable from what I understood from Dathmir, your home is half a year away from where we stand now. I understand the cost of war, and what it feels like to lose something you love, your home was taken from you, and you and your people have suffered for it. My consciousness will not allow me to sit idly by as those around me are in pain, regardless of where they are from"—Leon paused and stood up—"we will help you. The full strength of Verium is with you."

APPENDIX

lan Frostbane. Long ago on Drangar, the Vikings fought each other for control of Drangar. But not long after this fighting started, a great blizzard came in. Many died in this storm. In their hour of greatest need, a man called the giant led his people to peace and helped them to live through the frost. Henceforth, they were named Clan Frostbane and have been lords of Drangar ever since.

> "The Giant"—BAV lived for 101 years
> Eirik Frostbane I—BAV lived for 99 years, named Wolfslayer
> Thalmer Frostbane I—BAV lived for 100 years named Godbearer
> Eirik Frostbane II—BAV lived for 103 years
> Rolf Frostbane I—BAV, 30 AV named Greyslayer, Ranger

Rolf Frostbane II—20 AV–110
AV named the Younger
Rhagnar Frostbane I—80
AV–181 AV
Thalmer Frostbane II—126
AV–207 AV
Tyrson Frostbane I—160 AV–20
AV
Helvir Frostbane I—180 AV–265
AV
Eirik Frostbane III—210
AV–295 AV
Rhagnar Frostbane II—250
AV–299 AV, island lord
Vigrod Frostbane I—280 AV,
island lord

House Keawynn. Born in the west, house
Keawynn was started by Lokfur. House Keawynn
started to rule the west when they took over because
they were simply the richest. House Keawynn started
to build, and when they did, the other families
seemed to have liked the way they ruled. The west
has forever prospered, and they have one of the most
powerful armies in the world. They are very smart
and live longer than most.

Lokfur Keawynn I—BAV lived
for 512 years

Eldrin Keawynn I—BAV lived
for 427 years
Kolvar Keawynn I—BAV lived
for 500 years
Lokfur Keawynn II—BAV lived
for 467 years
Eldrin Keawynn II—BAV lived
for 454 years
Aerimir Keawynn I—BAV lived
for 520 years
Virion Keawynn I– BAV, 31 AV
named Greyslayer
Virion Keawynn II—BAV, 250
AV
Aerimir Keawynn II—0 AV
Lokfur Keawynn III—240
AV–299 AV, the curious,
island lord
Kolvar Keawynn II—275 AV,
island lord

House Eastmoore: In the east long ago, the
first humans were born. The first Eastmoore was
King Brandon, but when he was named king, the
gray humans rose in rebellion. And Brandon led the
humans to victory and made blacksmithing a trade
that all men must know how to do. The Eastmoores'
are one of the most praised families in the world.

Everyone loves how useful they are, especially in battle.

> Brandon Eastmoore I—BAV
> lived for eighty-six years
> Aedric Eastmoore I—BAV lived
> for ninety years, firstborn
> Aedric Eastmoore II—BAV lived
> for ninety-three years
> Robert Eastmoore I—BAV lived
> for ninety-seven years
> James Eastmoore I—BAV lived
> for eighty-one years
> Richard Eastmoore I—BAV lived
> for eighty-nine years
> Brandon Eastmoore II—BAV,
> 110 AV Greyslayer
> Robert Eastmoore – II—90
> AV–200 AV
> Richard Eastmoore – II—120
> AV–218 AV
> Brandon Eastmoore III—143
> AV–226 AV
> James Eastmoore – II—180
> AV–280 AV
> Brandon Eastmoore I—220 AV
> James Eastmoore III—257–299
> AV, island lord
> Nathan Eastmoore I—282 AV,
> island lord

Yrfel is home to many birds and beasts, but as of late, the three great races of the world, the humans of the east, the elves of the west, and the Vikings of the north. For years, they have been fighting over this island, for the wars have been ongoing for around sixteen years.

Highlord Vigrod Frostbane, lord of Ravenhall and Drangar, is a man of his word. He is willing to negotiate but isn't afraid to use his axe. Vigrod is a tall young warrior at the age of twenty. He takes on the tall and muscular shape of his forefathers, making him a force to be reckoned with.

High King Nathan Eastmoore, king of High Yrfel and of the Steel Isle is the youngest among the three island lords is only eighteen years of age and is doubted by his opponents. He has no true experience in battle and has never actually killed anyone, but has spent his eighteen years of living training to do so.

Lord Kolvar Keawynn, lord of the Elder Branch and the Ancestral Grove, is the oldest of the three lords, at twenty-five years of age, but Kolvar is undoubtedly the smartest of the three lords. He leads the strongest militia in the entire world. Gifted to him by his father, who mysteriously wandered off into the forest of Ashbeard.